OFF THE RESERVATION

LEE GULL

DEDICATION

For all indigenous people

Chapter 1

SOUTH OF KAYENTA

FROM HIS VANTAGE POINT UNDER THE TRUCK, MICHAEL watched the determined steps of his Auntie Jean's tiny red cowboy boots. He knew the boots belonged to his aunt because she'd stitched "Jean" across the instep, unequivocally marking them as hers. He didn't hold this aberration against her, although others talked about it. He sighed and kept wiring the bean can to his rusted exhaust pipe. His hope that Jean would walk past and go to the hogán were dashed when the tiny boots stopped about two feet from his head.

Michael added caulking around the can edges and lined up some hose clamps. He scraped his knuckle tightening a clamp and cursed, under his breath. By the time he finished, dripping sweat had made mud under his shoulders. He shook the exhaust assembly. It remained solid. The whole process took a bit of time, but Jean was determined. She waited silently, as courtesy demanded. With nothing more to do, Michael took a breath.

"Yes, Auntie?" he asked without sliding from under the truck.

"I need you to go find Jon. He went to the pow-wow in Phoenix. He's gone too long now. You go get him home." She squatted to peer at him. "Thomas will watch your cows. I made you food."

She had all his objections covered. Michael couldn't cry poor. Everyone within two hundred miles knew to the penny how much he'd won at bingo last night. There went his new muffler. He shimmied out from under the truck and wiped his dirty hands on a rag, wasting a few seconds while he tried to think of a way out of this chore. He leaned back against his truck and contemplated the ground. Muddy sweat dried on his shirt and scaled off in dusty chunks. His boots were considerably more scuffed than his aunt's. He took a deep breath and looked up without moving his head.

"OK, I'll go look for him."

Michael watched Jean's eagle eyes read his reluctance. She knew the reason. Jean knew her son.

"You're a good boy. I know you'll find him. I think whiskey stole my boy's mind, otherwise, he'd be home by now." Barely five feet tall, Jean had the presence of someone twice that height. Even wearing a heavy skirt and red plaid shirt, she carried herself as though she commanded an army, rather than one dusty nephew.

Michael couldn't imagine why, even for a minute, he thought he could refuse her. She handed him a paper sack dark with grease stains. "You'll eat good on your trip. I made my special cakes."

He smiled. His Auntie Jean might have some quirks, but she did make great fry bread. Situating his billed cap with the Tractor Store logo on his head, he watched Jean, skirt swaying with her rolling gait, trundle toward her little pinto horse. Jean rode four miles to get here. She'd want to stay to visit.

"I'll put him in the pen, auntie." Michael pitched her food in his truck and hurried over to take the reins of the horse. He mentally kicked himself for hesitating to go to look for Jon. His aunt would do anything for her family, including him. Who was he to say no to a simple a request?

Michael knew the real reason Jean came to him with the job of finding his cousin...it wasn't only because he had gas money. It was because he was the whitest looking guy in the clan. He had curly blond hair and a white man's tan, so the family always asked him to help take care of problems outside the Navajo Lands. As a kid, people borrowed him when they went to Flagstaff or Gallup. It was as if he were a good luck charm, a talisman against the chaos of the world outside the Navajo Nation. Beyond their lands was a world most of the older folks didn't care to understand.

Their confidence in his white skin never made sense to Michael. He had no special understanding of Belagáana culture, just because his father's skin wasn't brown. He'd spent most of his life on the Navajo lands, the Diné Beklah, the same as about everybody else he knew. When he thought about it, Michael realized he hadn't said more than fifty words in a row to a white person in the two years since he'd finished high school.

The last time he saw his cousin, Jon invited him to go to the pow-wow. Michael told him he was busy. The guys Jon hung out with were all into drinking and carousing. That wasn't Michael's style. He never liked going to the noisy, smelly city. People there always seemed so unhappy.

Michael pulled the saddle from Jean's little horse and hung it on the fence rail. The clearing where he was raised surrounded him. His bay mare trotted up, whickering to the pinto. Aunt Lila's hogán glowed warmly in the sunshine. A big cottonwood tree guarded the spring. Wind sighed through the junipers on the hillside, bringing their fresh scent on the breeze and making the cottonwood's leaves wave to their friends on the hill. The harsh squawk of a jay was a counterpoint to the faint bleats of goats. Given a choice, he didn't believe he would care to be anywhere else in the world.

Michael put a halter on the pinto and turned him into the pen. Jean was already sitting under the arbor next to the hogán fanning herself. She'd be fine while Michael gathered up things for his trip. A glance at the rusty tin thermometer hanging on the cottonwood tree showed over a hundred degrees, and it wasn't even noon.

Inside the hogán's thick walls, the temperature was twenty degrees cooler. The only light came from the open door, but his eyes adjusted quickly. He couldn't find the old duffel bag his uncle Elias brought back from the Vietnam War, so he stuffed some clothes in a burlap sack that used to hold beans. He stretched his back and contemplated what else would be needed in case the trip took more than a couple days. He hefted a gallon plastic jug with water on top of the clothes. The interlaced beams of the roof yielded a strip of mutton jerky and a blanket to complete his bundle.

Aunt Lila entered carrying a pail of water. She was the eldest sister of three Yazzie women. Taller and more slender than Jean, she wore khaki pants and a blue collared shirt. In contrast to her modern clothes, her hair was tied in a traditional tail-like bun wrapped with blue yarn for summer.

If you asked any of the people who knew her, they'd say, Lila had hozoh, she walked in beauty, totally in balance with the world around her. Michael couldn't remember her ever saying a bad thing about anyone. She'd raised him as though he were her own child.

Lila's eyes met Michael's and looked down at the sack of clothes. "I was on the hill with the goats and saw Jean ride in," she said.

"She asked me to go look for Jon in Phoenix."

"You boys have different dreams."

No kidding, Michael thought. He had plans for building a ranch, while Jon was happy to amble through life taking what ever came along. Different lifestyles aside, the cousins might as well have been brothers.

"Do you want me to go along?"

This was the first time he'd gone to Phoenix without any family as backup. Usually, his uncles took him to bail out drunken relatives. Michael figured he'd find Jon in a bar. He didn't want to embarrass his cousin by letting Lila see him drunk.

"I think I know where to find him. He probably didn't have gas money and is too proud to call for help."

"Maybe so. Who is looking after the cattle?"

Michael explained Jean's arrangements. Thomas, at fourteen, was a responsible boy. Lila nodded in approval, so Michael moved back into the heat of the day. She went out to sit with her sister and enjoy what little breeze the day could spare. Before he got in his truck, he rubbed the dust off the neat sign on the door, which said "Michael Yazzie Cattle Company." He glanced at his aunts. They were talking. He was a little miffed that Aunt Jean didn't comment on the sign. It had taken him the better part of a day to get the letters perfect. He'd embellished the black printing with the decal of a long-horned steer. Unless you got up close, the sign looked as good as a professional job. He looked at his aunts one last time before climbing onto the wide bench seat. He slammed the door a little harder than it needed.

The old truck started with a wheezy roar. The muffler didn't sound too bad. Michael waved to his aunts and the truck rattled down the trail that passed for the road to the camp. A particularly deep rut bounced his head off the top of the cab. Not for the first time, he thought it was a lot more comfortable to ride a horse to the main road. A rooster tail of dust followed the truck for six miles until it turned onto the asphalt road headed west.

A few hours later Michael turned south toward Phoenix and left the Navajo Nation. The Diné radio station, KTNN out of Window Rock, had a talk show going. An elderly woman was carrying on about the loss of family values among younger men. She didn't think they were paying enough attention to their sisters' children. Her voice faded as Michael rolled out of range.

Michael turned the radio off, but the old woman's comments lingered in the truck cab like a skunk's scent. It made him wonder about his own family. His aunts and uncles raised him after his mother died. He couldn't complain for a minute. But the radio show got his mind drifting to the mystery of the unknown man who gave him his yellow hair.

He recalled the day his father left him. Aunt Lila told him at age four he was too young to remember, but the images remained fixed in his mind.

THE BRIGHT SUN BEAT DOWN AS THE MAN CROUCHED AND waited for Michael to climb out of the car. He touched the man's pale-pink face and hair so blond it looked white, like a ghost man. The father's eyes were a peculiar light blue. His father smelled of tangy fruit and spices.

Michael flexed his fingers from the memory of the man's hand, smooth in his as they walked away from the car. Auntie Lila's hand was rough when the man put Michael's hand in hers. She knelt next to him and they watched the green car disappear into the red dust.

———

IT WASN'T MUCH OF A MEMORY, BUT IT WAS ALL MICHAEL HAD.

He didn't remember his mother at all. Lila had a faded photo of her, but she didn't seem real. Michael wanted to think his mother took after her oldest sister, Lila. But in her heart, she couldn't have been like Lila, who knew where she belonged in the world. His mother left their people, married a white man, and moved away from the family. She died among strangers.

As a child, he cried for her, but he didn't much anymore.

Chapter 2

INDIAN SCHOOL ROAD

Jon's sodden brain only worked at about half power. Something wasn't right, but he didn't care enough to open his eyes. His stomach hurt, and his mouth tasted like pocket lint. One hand absently groped for his bottle. He found it, held it to his mouth, nothing came out. Shaking yielded no blissful drops.

Eyes still closed, he shifted his shoulders to a more comfortable position in the trash. The bags, next to the Bodega's dumpster, were soft. They smelled rank, but so did he. *What was that sound?* A dawn bird whistled a plaintive note. Jon frowned. The bird wasn't what drew his attention, but it wasn't worth the effort to figure it out. His arm fell outward. The bottle dropped from his lax fingers and clinked, a tiny ringing sound on the cement of the loading dock where his trash pile lay. His world faded. The noise didn't matter.

Voices startled him. He turned his face to the sound. His eyes opened wide and light seared his brain. He squinted, his muddled mind trying to make sense of what he saw. A couple of guys stood silhouetted by the spotlight over the

Bodega's loading dock door. They spoke in harsh whispers. Jon couldn't focus enough to translate English yet. Maybe they weren't arguing. Maybe they were planning to have sex? Who really knew what white people were doing?

His stomach wrenched, bringing up a mouthful of vomit. He rolled over to retch and noticed the men lean closer to each other. *They must be in love.* His vomit-filled snort of amusement caused him to choke. Jon leaned farther over to cough his lungs clear. He didn't see the knife slide under the ribcage of the shorter man or hear his final gasp.

"Son of a bitch," a gruff voice growled as the taller man slipped on Jon's empty bottle. He fell and Jon heard a loud crack as the man's arm hit the edge of the dumpster. Backlit by the light over the Bodega's door, the face looming over him was a black hole. Jon felt the tug of his shirt as he was lifted to a sitting position.

"What?" Jon mumbled. In his condition, he couldn't frame a full sentence in English. He flailed at the arm holding him. The man hissed an indrawn breath as Jon's scrabbling fingers scratched him.

The shadow man grabbed Jon's hand and slapped a wet knife into it. The movement caused a painful heaving breath from the big man. With one smooth motion, he hit Jon at the base of his skull, dropping him back into oblivion.

Chapter 3

EASY COLLAR

DESPITE THE GROWING HEAT OF THE MORNING, DETECTIVE Rudy Garcia's clothes were tidy and crisp. His wife was adamant he not shame her by leaving the house looking rumpled.

He met the uniformed officers behind the Soledad Bodega. They were not impressed by his wife's fastidiousness. Rudy gave a surreptitious glance at the patrolman's badge.

"What do we have so far, McCafferty?"

The officer pulled out his notepad. "Sanchez and I responded to a liquor store robbery at the end of this block of shops, when we got the call about a body. That was at..." McCafferty looked down at his book. "...6:50 A.M. We left the robbery and came here. While we were securing the scene, we found the drunk Indian." He waved his hand toward the cruiser. Inside a man with stringy black hair leaned against the closed window of the car. McCafferty continued. "He was over there, lying in the trash bags with the knife in his hand." He tilted his head toward the bags piled at the base of the dumpster.

"Don't you think you ought to crack a window for him?" Rudy asked.

"Nah, maybe a hot car will soften him up a bit. The son-of-a-bitch is pretending he doesn't speak English."

Rudy gestured to the corpse at their feet. "He wasn't much to look at, was he? You got a name?" The body leaned against the wall next to the door on the loading dock. His head tilted back, mouth open in a silent scream with teeth protruding from receding gums, a good indication of extended meth usage. Blood spattered the concrete. The rank smell of what had spilled out of the man's entrails was ignored by the forensic tech taking measurements and making notes on a diagram. It would only get worse as the sun warmed the loading dock.

"His street name was Twitchy. I think his real name was Ortega or Orteese. He's a frequent flyer. I'm sure there's paper on him." McCafferty wiped the sweat off his neck with a dingy white handkerchief.

Chet, the Medical Examiner, stood up, pulling off his latex gloves. "You can get his wallet. Where's your partner?"

"Ray broke his arm yesterday."

Chet tilted his head inquisitively. "What happened?"

"He tripped over his dog." Rudy gingerly pulled the wallet from the emaciated corpse's pocket. "We're shorthanded, so I'm on my own." Flipping the thin worn leather open, he evaluated the license inside. "Simon Ortega, rest in peace. It doesn't look as though you had much peace in life." He rifled through the sparse contents and dropped the wallet into an evidence bag. Rudy looked at Chet. "You got any insights?"

"He was cut deep. It looks like they got his abdominal aorta. That's why there was so much blood spray. We'll know more when we open him up." Chet waved the techs over with their body bag. "I'm releasing the body. I've got another call over in Sun City."

"Must be a busy morning," Rudy said.

Chet shrugged and continued to make notes on his clipboard.

Officer Sanchez walked up. "I did a sweep. There's nothing but the body and the drunken Indian. He's got blood on him. It's probably a drug deal gone bad."

"You don't mind if I take a look around?" Rudy smiled to soften his comment.

Both uniformed officers stared at their feet. Sanchez said, "We took pictures before we got the Indian up and put him in the car."

"You had to get him up?"

"He was drunk, not cooperating. We Mirandized him," McCafferty added, nodding at the man in the car.

"I'll need to talk with him." Garcia walked over to the white vehicle, one of the newer squad cars. Blood smeared the window where the man's head leaned against it. He started to fall out when Rudy opened the door. "Awww, shit." The detective caught the falling man with his hands, dropping his notebook in the process. "Help me, you guys."

The uniformed cops hustled over and helped lay the unconscious man on the concrete. They held their breath to avoid the smell of urine and alcohol wafting from him.

"Aw, damn, he got blood on my pants." Rudy crouched next to the prone body and rolled an eyelid back. "We're going to need an ambulance for this guy." He stood up. "Anybody got some water? These pants are going to be ruined." He took out his handkerchief and swiped at the filth on his leg.

The ambulance pulled away as Garcia came out of the Bodega shaking his wet pant leg. McCafferty walked up.

"The EMT says the guy might have a concussion and needs some stitches. They're taking him to County."

"Did Sanchez ride with him?"

"No, he's cleaning out our unit." McCafferty gestured toward the car, still parked next to the loading dock entrance. The back end of Sanchez protruded from the door as he swiped at the rear seat, grumbling curses.

"Why didn't one of you ride with him? He's a suspect." Rudy bounced on his toes.

"Ah...we still have to process the robbery. We didn't have any orders beyond securing this scene."

Rudy took a deep breath. "Do a canvas that includes both the murder and the robbery. Copy me on the reports." When he got nods from the officers, Rudy headed toward his car. The forensics tech stopped him to sign for the evidence bags he'd collected. "I'm going over to Sun City now. You'll need to log all this stuff."

Rudy took another breath and scribbled his name on the clipboard. Grabbing the sack with the evidence, he raced to his car. He dropped the sack in his trunk and jumped in. Working without his partner was a pain in the ass.

His wheels spun a little as he took off. He needed to oversee the forensics collection at the hospital. The chain-of-custody requirements were a part of the job he hated. Damn drunken Indian.

Within a couple of miles, he saw the ambulance ahead. His hands unclenched from the steering wheel, and he started whistling the theme from the "Thomas the Train" cartoon his kids were favoring this month. At least, he finally had a murder that solved itself. A drunken Indian with the knife in his hand was a gift from God. He deserved an easy win. A dozen cases filled his desk. With his partner out, he was pulling double duty. Maybe he could convince the Lieutenant to let Ray come back just for the paperwork.

Weaving in and out of traffic, Garcia kept track of the flashing lights. As he started through the intersection, the ambulance was only a few hundred yards ahead of him. A rusty red Ford truck ran the light, ramming into his back quarter panel. The airbag slammed his sunglasses into the bridge of his nose. The trunk flew open. The unmarked car spun three times, strewing evidence bags in a fan shape onto the street. The car behind him careened around the accident, skidding on the evidence, and throwing the bags even further.

"Oh, shit." The airbag deflated and Rudy scrambled for his radio. He keyed the mic and got nothing. He pounded the steering wheel with both hands. His nose started swelling.

The truck's driver came over. "You ran the light, you asshole."

Garcia held up his badge with one hand and pinched the bridge of his nose with the other. So much for his good day.

Still holding his bloody nose with one hand, he reached in his pocket for his phone with the other. Despite his effort, his voice cracked when he called dispatch. "I need you to send a unit to County Hospital to take custody of a suspect? I don't have a name on the guy, but he came in from the murder scene at Indian School and 17th."

"I'll send someone over as soon as I can," the operator assured him.

An hour later, Garcia convinced the traffic officer to wait for the damaged cars to get towed. The Detective drove the man's patrol car to the hospital. He rushed through the emergency entrance and arrived just as the stocky male nurse finished wiping off the Indian's hands. A tube ran from the unconscious man's arm to a bag full of yellow fluid.

Garcia's jaw clenched. *What the hell is wrong with dispatch?* "Didn't they send anyone to tell you this was a murder suspect? You needed to wait until an officer was present?"

"No, the Doc just told me to clean him up and hang a banana bag." The nurse shrugged. He peered at the detective with professional concern. "Do you need some help? You're starting a couple of nice shiners there." He nodded toward the bed. "This guy do that to you? He's so drunk he doesn't seem as if he'd be able."

"I had an accident. Maybe you could get me an ice pack?" No sense in getting upset, the nurse was just following orders. Garcia gestured at the bed. "Where are his clothes?"

"In the sack under the bed," the nurse said. "I'll get you an ice pack. You sure you don't want to see a doctor?"

Garcia shook his head.

The nurse pulled a chair over for the detective. "Sorry about cleaning him up. Without anyone here, we didn't know you needed forensics."

This time Garcia shrugged. "It's done. At least I got his clothes and the crime scene pictures." He decided to wait for the doctor's report. Enough evidence was lost today. Besides, he wanted to extend the time until he had to explain his accident to the Lieutenant.

Chapter 4

THE LUCKY BUCK

Rolling along in the old truck, wind blowing through his hair, Michael listened to mechanical songs about a world where he didn't care to live. He chewed his lip and worried about Jon. His cousin had been making a lot of bad decisions lately. Michael had his cattle business. It wasn't much yet, but if he was patient and lucky, it could make him a good life. Jon was still tending his mom's sheep and wandered from odd job to odd job. He spent his money as soon as he got it. Not to say Jon wasn't a great guy. He was the first one there when anybody needed help. Michael'd just seen too many aimless guys lose hope and end up as drunks living on the government handouts. It would be too sad if his cousin ended up on that path.

Michael watched a family in a big motorhome bus as they drove beside him. A red-haired woman brought a cup to the man driving. Twin boys threw a ball back and forth across the rolling room. *Where were they going in their house on wheels?*

On the radio, a raspy-voiced man sang about the heart of rock and roll. Michael noticed the pastures along the road looked overgrazed. He should know who cared for this land. Navajo don't technically own property. The Clan elders assigned grazing rights to people who had livestock. It's a solemn obligation. The people in this area weren't protecting the land. It bothered him.

The tortured rocks, mesquite, and ocotillo the Navajo and Hopi call home gave way to the tall pines of Walnut Creek Canyon. Old Route 89 to Red Butte only led Michael a little out of his way through Sedona. The red rock buttes and mesas surrounding the town were beautiful. He always enjoyed seeing them. No one would begrudge him an hour of natural beauty, considering he was going to a city.

He pulled off at the slide rock, where the creek flowed over smooth stone. He needed to add water to his radiator. He'd have to wait until the truck cooled before he could fill it. People were playing in the water, hurtling down the stream on their bottoms. Michael leaned against the side of his truck and watched their antics out of the corner of his eye. Some of the girls in their skimpy bathing suits were cute. Few of the women he knew showed that much skin unless they ran out when their house was on fire.

With his radiator topped off, Michael continued his journey. This far south, the fast food world began. Soon, he was in the sanitized, politically correct version of the Old West housing the art mills of Sedona. The counterpoint of the city to the beauty of the surrounding hills always struck him as terribly sad.

Tears dripped from the eyes in the paintings of 'Genuine Indians' in the store windows, but the paint didn't run. Those painted eyes saw Michael and his battered truck, which was so out of place among Sedona's sedans and polo shirts. The painted Indians' hearts recognized the worry Michael had for his cousin. However, as many of Michael's people do among strangers, they stared straight ahead and pretended not to feel, not to be there, no matter how prominently they were displayed.

The orange glow of desert dusk surrounded Michael as he left the red rocks behind. He drove on, chasing stars now. After a while he turned the radio off and whistled the comforting rhythm of his auntie's corn grinding song and followed the sky glow toward Phoenix.

Eventually, the city brightness blotted out the stars who'd been his friends throughout his life. The highway was called Black Canyon Freeway in the city. The land was flat. He wondered if the people here thought the buildings make it a canyon. Neon snakes climbed the walls of the unnatural chasm.

The part of the city where Indians went was made of cement, dust, and sorrow. The roads were lined with clubs and bars, each one shabbier than the next. After sunset, the city made a light of its own. Faded ghosts and drunken Indians flickered in and out of focus as they walked the streets. Michael searched their faces for the shade of his cousin. He drove quietly so those faded souls wouldn't recognize him.

When recruited to deal with the outside world, Michael liked to think about his father as the ghost man who gave him special power when he left the Navajo Nation. In a way, Michael was right. His father did give him the blond hair that helped him blend in. He wasn't afraid to be in the city, but just in case, he tried to think white man's thoughts like an actor rehearsing lines.

MICHAEL PULLED IN TO THE LUCKY BUCK BAR AND GRILL, A

place where he and his uncles had found relatives before. He left the truck facing the road next to a car with no wheels that had fallen halfway off its blocks. Three guys leaned against a wall under the single bare bulb which illuminated the sagging door. The men's long greasy black hair hung loosely to their shoulders. Dressed in jeans and filthy tee-shirts, they stared out into the glittering city night. There was a large stain on the wall near where they were standing.

Approaching the men, Michael started to raise his hand in a traditional greeting when he realized the men were in various stages of inebriation and in no shape for courtesy. His hand dropped. He passed them without a look. The stain on the wall was urine.

Entering, Michael was assaulted with the mingled odor of old sweat, cigarette smoke, and sheep. No one in the bar looked like him. Most of his life he'd walked in as the only blond, pale-skinned person, so it didn't bother him. Looking so different didn't matter as much as it did when he was a child.

"You lost, boy?" the bartender said as he wiped the counter with a rag only slightly cleaner than the floor.

"I'm looking for my cousin Jon. He's Navajo. He's been in town since the pow-wow last week."

"You law?" the man grunted.

"I'm just looking for my cousin. He comes here when he's in town. He's about my size, hair to his shoulders, with a scar down his jaw," Michael said, running his hand down his own jaw.

"I don't remember him." The bartender shrugged.

A familiar voice emerged from a dark booth. "I know you, buy me a drink." It was Sam Tsosie, who had gone to school with Michael. Michael liked his sister Salina and spent time with her at the dances. They weren't officially a couple, but people were starting to talk about them.

"Ya'at eeh." Michael greeted Sam. "You seen my cousin Jon?"

"I heard they busted him," Sam slurred. "You going to get that drink?

"I'll buy you some coffee and give you a ride home, if you want." He knew Sam's traditional family would be worried about him.

"Fuck you and the horse you rode in on!" Sam shouted.

Michael sighed as he went out the door. At least he tried to save Sam the embarrassment of having his family come looking for him.

Sam called after Michael, "Don't think you're better than me, you yellow-haired fake fuck. Stay away from my sister."

Michael put his head down and shoved past some men in the doorway. Nothing a drunk said meant anything. He'd make a call to let Sam's family know where to find him. The Tsosie's had their own telephone, but Michael decided to call the clan chapter house. Let Sam be embarrassed, maybe next time he'd think before he went on a bender.

Leaving the not-so-Lucky Buck, Michael headed to the jail in the city center. He'd been there before with his uncles. They usually came to bail out drunken family members. Michael'd been in more police stations than he cared to count. Even when he was a little kid, the family always took him along as if he and his blond hair were a charm against the systems of a people they didn't understand.

The police station smelled worse than the Lucky Buck. Michael waited with his back to the wall and breathed shallowly through his mouth. He didn't meet the policeman's eye when called to the desk. Shoulders hunched against the tension in the room, he asked about his cousin.

"Jon Pete's your cousin, you say?" The man's swollen fingers squirmed like pink slugs as he flipped through the papers on his clipboard. His dark blue uniform collar made a crease in his neck. "You'd best sit down and wait to see the detective."

"Why can't I just bail him out?" Michael asked, briefly meeting the Sergeant's eye. A chill crept down his back, his knees wobbled. Unconsciously, he stepped back into a defensive stance, one foot behind the other knees slightly bent.

"You just sit and wait, boy. The detective will tell you what you need to know."

"Any chance I can see Jon?"

"Fill this out and wait till you get called."

He slid a piece of paper across the desk. Michael wrote down details defining his life for the bureaucracy. Then he sat on a bench thick with scars of boredom. The room's yellow lights made everything look unreal. This was an angry place. He could tell people died here. Michael couldn't see them, but the weight of their souls pressed on him as they wandered the rooms weaving between the desks, muttering their anger into uncomprehending ears. *Maybe I have too much imagination,* Michael thought. He stared at nothing, letting his mind return to the summer pasture where calves were gaining weight in the lush grass.

"Michael Yazzie!" A loud voice interrupted his reverie. The Hispanic detective wore a rumpled tan suit. He had blue-black hair and was sporting two bruised eyes. People with brown skin usually didn't make Michael uncomfortable, but the detective's tense shoulders put him on edge. The man held a brown paper file folder.

"I'm Detective Garcia." He waved the file in a gesture for Michael to follow him and they traversed a maze of corridors between glass-walled offices. The detective walked stiffly, with his shoulders hunched. Michael didn't know much about non-Navajo people's body language, but if this guy were a horse, he'd say the man was foundered and wasn't going to make it.

"You're lucky I was still here working late." Garcia gestured again, ushering Michael into a small windowless room with glaring lights. The only furnishings were a table, two chairs, and a camera mounted high in the corner of the room. He knew from TV that police used places like this for intimidation.

It was working.

They moved to opposite sides of the table. Michael's chair was next to a large ring bolted to the floor. He pulled it out to sit and waited politely for Garcia to start the conversation.

"You say you're Jon Pete's cousin?"

"Yes, I am. His mother asked me to bring him home," Michael replied. When the detective raised his eyebrows, Michael added, "I'm half white."

"I see," Garcia said. He watched Michael as he opened a file folder.

Michael saw a picture of a dead white man lying awkwardly against a block wall. He had been gutted like a deer.

"Do you know this man?"

Garcia shoved the picture in front of Michael. He looked at it for a few seconds, considering what the detective asked.

He swallowed, trying not to puke. "No, I've never seen him before." Michael'd never seen anyone killed before. He didn't even care for violent movies.

"Any idea why your cousin killed him last night?"

"Jon, killed?" Michael stammered. His mind raced like a ground bird...He and Jon, riding ponies...Jon, caring for a sick lamb...Jon, holding his niece, singing about baby rabbits. "Jon wouldn't kill anybody."

"When did you last see your cousin?" the detective asked.

"A week ago. He came south for a pow-wow."

"When did you get to Phoenix?"

"I just drove in. I got here just after dark. They told me at the Lucky Buck, Jon had been picked up, so I came here." Michael's hands clutched the seat of his chair.

"Does Jon drink a lot?" The detective scribbled a note on his pad.

"What do you mean by a lot?" he asked. "I've never seen him drink at home, and I've never had to come get him before."

"Does he do drugs?" The detective wrote some more.

"Jon doesn't do drugs."

The detective looked Michael straight in the eye, as though he didn't believe him. Maybe it was a Belagáana thing, trying to be direct. Michael caught himself before he squirmed in his chair. The air in the room became hard to breathe. The walls started to get closer together.

"I thought you Navajos do peyote and other stuff to get right with the Great Spirit or something." The detective never took his eyes off Michael.

Michael looked at Garcia's receding hairline, wanting to answer politely. He didn't want to antagonize this man. "It's the people in the American Indian Church who do that. It's not really part of the Navajo way." Michael couldn't believe he was explaining this. "Jon raises sheep. He wouldn't even have enough money to buy drugs." The detective still stared at him, right in the eyes. The man didn't believe him.

Michael's gut ached. He didn't know how to get this man to believe him, to let Jon go free. There was no way his gentle cousin would ever hurt anyone. He decided to act White and ask some of his own questions. "Who was the guy who got killed? Why do you think Jon killed him?" He stammered, trying to get enough air in his lungs.

"You'd better get your cousin a good lawyer," Garcia said. He gathered his folder and abruptly stalked out.

"When can I see Jon?" Michael asked Garcia's retreating back. He guessed trying to act White wasn't the right approach.

"Fill out the forms with the desk sergeant," Garcia replied, without looking back.

Michael found his way to the front desk and asked again to see Jon.

The officer's fat fingers flipped through some papers on a clipboard. "He isn't here. He's at County Hospital."

"What happened? Is he all right?" Alarmed, Michael put his hands on the desk. His heart rate increased.

"Back off, kid. I don't know what is wrong with him." The sergeant's voice softened when he saw Michael's stricken face. "It can't be too bad. He's scheduled to be here tomorrow for his arraignment."

"Can you give me directions to get to the hospital? Jon's Navajo, he's going to be scared. We don't do well in hospitals."

"They won't let you see him. He's in custody and you're not his lawyer. You can see him when they bring him here tomorrow. Fill out these papers and bring them in the morning." The sergeant pushed forms across the desk.

Michael took the papers and went to sit on the scarred bench.

"You going to wait here all night?" the sergeant asked.

He shrugged. "I've got no place else to go."

"Well, you can't sleep here. There's an all-night diner a couple of blocks east. Their parking lot is pretty safe and the food's good."

Chapter 5

DETECTIVE GARCIA

Garcia watched the blond kid leave. He didn't know what to make of him. He was white, but dressed like a cheap day laborer from some ranch. There was no way the murdering drunk from behind the Bodega was that kid's family. For the life of him, he couldn't think of what kind of game the kid was playing. He hoped Michael Yazzie wouldn't cause any complication to his easy case. Garcia straightened his desk to leave. When he looked up, a worn, angular face below a gray, flat-top haircut leaned around the door to his office.

"Hey, Garcia." Tom Norris wasn't the tallest cop on the force, but he was close. The rest of his rangy body filled the door. "How's the murder from the loading dock going? I hear it's a slam dunk." Norris wore his grey suit as though it were tailored for him. His arm was in a sling.

"This one is about as close to a swish as I hope to see. The arrest gods are smiling on me." Rudy's comeback was automatic. He didn't remember ever talking to the senior detective this casually before. "What happened to you?"

"Tennis elbow, nothing serious. The sling is just a

precaution." He raised his arm. "I heard about your wreck, tough luck. You know you look like a raccoon, don't you?"

"The airbag got me." Rudy grinned. "I was following the ambulance, thinking how I needed an easy case with Ray out, when some jerk ran a light and knocked my unmarked into next week." Rudy stacked some papers and set them in his to-do tray. "You're working late, Tom. I thought I was the only over-achiever on duty today."

"I had to finish up some paperwork, saw you here, so I figured I'd stop in and see if you needed any help. It's a bitch working solo. When's that gold-bricking partner of yours coming back?"

"Seems like the department's week for injuries. Ray's going to be off another month, at least. Can you believe it, fifteen years on the job, and he breaks his arm tripping over his dog?" Rudy shook his head.

"I'd have shot the damn dog." Norris wiped a hand over his hair and massaged his forearm in the sling. "Ray's had a lot of bad luck in the past couple years."

Rudy slid another set of papers into his out tray. "I've heard some of it, but he doesn't talk about personal stuff much."

"Losing his son was hard enough on him..."

Rudy gave a little shudder. He couldn't imagine how he would survive the death of one of his children.

"...then his partner goes only a year later. It's got to be tough losing your partner the way he did."

"Ray never talked about him, but I heard some things. You must have known his old partner, Gelender." Rudy said with eyebrows raised in inquiry.

Norris rubbed his arm, again. "Yeah, he was an old-time cop. Anything you heard is probably true. Gelender was a rubber hose kind of guy. Ray had to work hard to keep him out of trouble. I thought he handled losing him pretty well, though." Norris grinned. "Who knows, he might have been relieved to get a young guy like you to raise. You weren't around to see Ray when his son died. He took it hard. You know his wife left him right before Gelender died?"

"I never knew the timeline," Rudy said. "I knew he divorced. I didn't want to bring up bad memories. Do you know how Ray's son died?"

"Overdose."

"Damn."

The two men stood silently for a minute.

Norris looked at the clock high on the wall. "You on your way out? Want to go get a beer?" He massaged his arm, yet again, as though it had a deep ache.

"Nah, as much as I could use a beer, I have to get home to my wife before she trades me in on a newer model."

"Yeah, you better go explain to her why you look like a freaking cartoon animal. Next time then, we over-achievers need to stick together." Norris slapped Rudy on the shoulder as Garcia slouched past.

On the way home, as his smoking Chevy chugged at a stoplight, Garcia thought, *I should have taken Norris up on his offer.* The guy had never seemed friendly before. He always thought it was because Norris didn't want to work with Chicanos. He'd met enough passive-aggressive bigots so he didn't even try to deal with Norris or his partner Phil Davis. He'd written those guys off and looked elsewhere for support when he needed it. He kicked himself now. As one of the newer detectives, he couldn't afford to tick off one of the old guard like Norris. The man had closed a lot of big cases. He also had some clout with the Lieutenant, which wasn't something to be taken lightly. Next chance he got, he should do a little creative sucking up.

"HOLA, ME CORAZON," GARCIA SAID AS HE SHUT THE DOOR of his stuccoed bungalow.

"Don't even try to sweet talk me, Rudolfo," wife said from the kitchen.

He could hear the clink of dishes and the splash of water.

"This is the third night this week you missed..." Antonia appeared in the kitchen doorway wiping her hands. "The kid's—oh, Rudy, what happened?" She dropped the dishcloth and gently cradled his face.

"Some nut-bag ran a stop sign and T-boned me."

"Why didn't you call?"

"It isn't as bad as it looks. Most of this is from the airbag."

"You're going to be sore tomorrow. You're sure it wasn't part of the job?"

"No, baby, I was just driving along. The same thing could've happened going to the store."

She held him at arm's length and gave him a searching look. She must have believed him.

"Let me get you some supper," she whispered and kissed him gently on the cheek.

He grabbed her in a hug. "You're the best."

"Don't you ever forget it."

Chapter 6

HOW DRUNK?

THE NEXT DAY MICHAEL WAS AT THE POLICE STATION BY SEVEN. It took three hours to get in to see Jon. He walked to the jail's visiting room through dreary halls painted a pinkish tan color. Dirt created a line along the base of the walls with scuffs and smudges decorating the sides at arm level. Fuzzy grey dust rimmed the fins on the air vents spaced every twenty feet or so along the ceiling.

His muscles, stiffened from a night sleeping in the front seat of the truck, loosened up during the trek. The air was stale with despair and the odor of fear. A brown man wearing a khaki uniform ushered him into a little room painted an unappetizing pus green. Four glass-fronted cubicles lined the wall. Sleeping in the truck seemed fine compared to a night in this place.

Jon was waiting behind the glass, like an exhibit in the zoo. He looked terrible. There was a bloody bandage on the side of his head and his right hand. Grime rimmed his fingernails. His eyes reminded Michael of a little, speckled heifer calf he'd found once. Trapped in barbed wire, she was pitifully glad to see him. She never struggled as he cut the wire away. Looking at Jon, what worried Michael was the calf never got up once it was free. She just laid there and died.

The glass between them was hard for Michael to bear. He wanted to touch his cousin's shaking hands. To reassure him things would be all right. "Why didn't you call someone?" Michael asked gently, as though he were talking to a nervous colt.

"I didn't want Mother to know." Jon's reply was sheepish.

"This is serious. They think you murdered a guy".

"Wha... I was drunk, but I didn't murder anybody."

"Why do they think you did? They didn't just lock you up for nothing." Michael slapped his hands on the counter. They only had fifteen minutes.

Jon wrinkled his brow and bit his lip. "I had a knife in my hand," He said without looking up. It sounded as if he was going to leave it at that.

"Was there a fight?" Michael prompted.

"No, I was drunk behind a store. There were two white guys, and then the cops were there, and I had the knife," he said all in a rush. "I got no clue, Mike. I was really drunk — sleeping it off. I can't remember." His eyes closed. Sweat dripped from his face. "I'm scared." He put his hands on his forehead. The gunk under his nails was blood; his hair was greasy and stuck out at odd angles because of the bandage.

"Are you sure you didn't fight? You have blood on your hands."

"No, I swear. I just have a knot on my head." Noticing his cousin's alarmed look, Jon added, "I'll be OK."

His eyes were open so wide Michael could see white all the way around the dark brown iris. Michael was scared too, but didn't want Jon to panic. "We'll work this out. Don't you worry, I'll get you a lawyer and..."

"I already got a lawyer. A guy gave me his card. I called him from the hospital. He's supposed to be real good. He defends a lot of Indians in Phoenix." Although Jon's shoulders were still hunched, his eyes didn't look as wild.

Despite Jon's assertion, there were too many Indians in jail around here for Michael to think a Phoenix lawyer was going to be of any use. "Is he white?"

"He's got a white name."

"You haven't seen him yet?"

"He's coming this morning. He said he'd be here for the rain or something."

"I think that's the arraignment. It's when you first see the judge. How are we going to pay the lawyer?"

"He said he'd get the court to pay for me. Something about right to council," Jon countered.

The guard was coming to get Jon. He was huge, the kind of guy you call when cattle get loose on the freeway. There was an irritated set to his shoulders.

"You better get going. Tell the lawyer to talk to me after you see him. I'll wait out front, on the bench by the statue of the blind lady in the lobby." Michael got up, hoping Jon would move quickly enough not to irritate the big guard.

Jon started back to the jail with a bit more energy, but the look he gave over his shoulder, just before he passed through the door, reminded Michael of that speckled calf.

Chapter 7
GHOSTS OF FAMILY PAST

A PAY PHONE IS DIFFICULT TO FIND IN MOST PLACES THESE days, but the county jail always had one available. Michael's fingers rubbed the wall next to the phone feeling the scratches under the multiple coats of paint. He dialed the only number he knew by heart.

Little Mary Begay answered the phone at the clan's chapter house. "Michael Yazzie, are you ever going to marry Salina Tsosie and settle down?" Mary wasn't raised traditionally, so Michael didn't mind how she used his name when talking to him. He was sure she didn't realize it was rude.

"I'm waiting for you to get old enough to dance with before I make any decision," he said. After asking about her family and hearing the details of her brother's broken leg, Michael got down to business. "I'm in Phoenix. Can you get a message to my Auntie Jean?" Mary had to get a pen for a note. "Tell her she needs to find someone to help bring her sheep in, and remind Thomas to keep an eye on my yellow cow with the scar on her neck. She gets stuck in the mud by the stock tank."

Mary giggled when she repeated what she was writing, "For Auntie Jean Pete." Mary giggled a lot. Michael guessed it was kind of funny that he called Jean and her sister, Lila, auntie in English, rather than little mother in the Navajo language, like a good boy would. He didn't remember why he started thinking of them as aunties in English. The words for aunt or uncle, in Navajo, were used for people your parent's age who were not of your clan. It wasn't that he didn't have the Diné ingrained respect for family. He guessed it was just his quirk.

Once Mary was finished taking the message, Michael asked her to find the number of the tribal legal services. Mary's enthusiastic chatter stopped. He didn't have to go into any detail about the situation in Phoenix, She knew something bad must've happened. Anything involving the law outside of the Nation had to be serious.

"Tell Auntie Jean I'll call again." Michael made a quick calculation as to how long it would take to find Jean, for her to make arrangements, and find a way to get to the chapter house's phone. "I'll call tomorrow about three. I should have some details by then." Of course, everyone within a hundred miles was going to know all the details as soon as he told Aunt Jean. They should have a sign at the border of the Navajo Nation that said, 'The Land of No Secrets.' After Mary took a message about where Sam Tsosie's family could find him, Michael hung up and made the call to the tribal legal service. It wasn't very useful. They just told him to have the Phoenix lawyer contact them after he talked to Jon.

There was a big room between the jail and the old courthouse. Michael found a bench. Now, all there was to do was to wait. He was good at waiting. It seemed most of his life had been spent waiting for something. He waited for school to end to build his herd of a few cows into a profitable herd. He was waiting for his ranch to be profitable to get serious about Salina Tsosie. A rancher knows every creature has to wait for the conditions to be right for life to start.

His wandering mind was going to get him in trouble. It ambled back to his parents. What conditions ended their wait and allowed them to begin a life together? Their wait ended with him on a dusty, red road watching a car drive off into the billowing dust.

The family told him his mother died somewhere in Phoenix. He didn't know if his father still lived here, or even if he was still alive. Michael thought he'd seen him once in Tuba City, the "ghost man." Michael was just a child. He closed his eyes and mouth, covered his ears, afraid the ghost would get inside and push his soul out. When he became brave enough to look again, the ghost had disappeared.

Aunt Lila said his father was a wise man, and probably wasn't a ghost. He left Michael because he knew his heart would die if he didn't live as a Diné. Michael wasn't sure she was right. She also told him to be careful if he ever saw his father again. Not because he was a ghost, but because it's just a good idea to be careful around white people. They had strange ideas.

Michael couldn't get past feeling uneasy about his 'ghost father.' At school, the teachers told them ghosts didn't exist and the superstitions of our ancestors weren't important. They said the Diné lived in a modern world. The old stories were designed to keep illiterate people safe from potential harm.

He understood what the teachers meant, but the old ways somehow felt right to him. It's hard to throw those ideas out, no matter how modern the world became. When he went through the ceremony giving him his place as a man of the Diné, Michael saw and felt some things he couldn't explain with the science he'd learned in school. The modern ways versus the old ways dilemma always gave him things to think about, especially when he left the Navajo lands.

Michael thought it was too bad the school didn't give kids advice about dealing with people off the Reservation. They watched TV and were fed information about the world outside, but the teachers didn't tell them why those people in the larger world do all the unusual things they do.

To get his mind away from the mysteries of his family, Michael looked at the statue of the blindfolded lady holding a scale. She'd locked her elbow. He wondered if her shoulder was as sore as his. After sleeping in the truck last night, his whole left arm throbbed along with the beat of his heart.

Michael watched each person as they came out of the jail door, trying to guess which one was going to help Jon. He figured the lawyers would be carrying a little suitcase for their papers, but couldn't remember the special name they had for those suitcases. It was something simple. He should know the word. It started to bother him, papercase, lawyercase, lawcase. *How was he going to help Jon when he couldn't remember a simple word?*

Between one breath and another, he was there. Michael's hand instinctively covered his mouth. It was the ghost man, his long-lost father walking toward him. The pink face and light blue eyes were just as Michael remembered. The fine pale hair was slicked down with some oil and combed across the bald spot on the man's head.

Michael found himself on his feet, his muscles surprising him with the motion. Fight or flight? He was too confused to know. Adrenalin coursed through his body. He prepared to run, and forced his muscles to stop, not knowing which direction to take.

The ghost man's suit was the color of his eyes. Uncle Elias had a wall-eyed horse with eyes that color. The man had on a white shirt and a dark blue tie. He walked with a heavy tread as though his feet hurt, or he wasn't used to walking far. His shoulders were slumped. He didn't look dangerous, but you could never be sure. Michael stood his ground as wary as a wild colt.

When he noticed Michael, the ghost man stopped abruptly, eyes widening. He reached out his hand as if he was going to touch the younger man then brought it to his mouth.

"Michael?" he said, searching his son's eyes. "I didn't expect... I'm David Lawson, your... Michael, do you remember me?" His pink hand dropped. He took a step closer. He smelled of perfume.

"Don't," Michael said, holding up a hand, palm out, imitating a cigar store Indian. "I remember you." He kept his face expressionless. "Are you the one helping Jon Pete? He's my cousin."

Lawson looked away. "Jon's Jean's son? I didn't realize." He shook his head as if he'd taken a chill and looked at Michael. "Yes, he called and the court appointed me his lawyer." The ghost man tentatively held out his hand.

Michael looked at it, glanced quickly at the older man's face, his pale hair and eyes, then at the case in his other hand. "What's your little case called?" *What a great way to greet your father after twenty years,* he thought as soon as he'd spoken.

Lawson looked startled and confused. "It's called a briefcase." He cleared his throat and dropped his outstretched hand. "I know this is awkward. I don't really know what to say, I always thought I'd come visit you when..." He trailed off looking at his son intently.

Michael wasn't breathing. All he could think was briefcase, briefcase, of course briefcase. He took a gulp of air and swallowed. It would be dangerous for Jon if he antagonized this man. Despite his reservations about Lawson's character, right now the lawyer might be all his cousin had. "Are you going to help Jon?" Michael spoke in an almost normal voice.

"Uhm." Lawson looked down and shifted his feet like a child. Looking up, he said, "Yes, of course, I understand." He took a deep breath. "Let's help your cousin. Then we can catch up." He gestured to the bench Michael recently vacated.

Michael was glad the lawyer understood, because Michael was still trying to breathe regularly. He hoped this wasn't some sleep-deprived delusion. Maybe he was dreaming this whole thing. His shoulder ached as he sat down. It wasn't a dream. Could this man be trusted with Jon's life? The lawyer sat, careful not to touch his son.

Michael wished his uncles were here. Uncle Leon was the one who taught his nephew to be a man. He gave Michael tools to find balance in his life. As Uncle once told Michael, a lack of options makes life simpler. Since he'd definitely lost his balance, Michael decided to go for the only choice he had right now and deal with this man... his father. He shivered at the thought.

Michael snuck a sideways glance at the lawyer as he

shuffled a handful of papers. The man looked old and tired. He didn't seem as powerful as Michael remembered. Maybe it would be safe to be around him as long as Michael was careful.

"Do you have a plan?" Michael asked.

"I need to look at all the evidence first, but I think we could plead this case down to manslaughter and he should be out in no more than seven years," Lawson replied.

"But Jon didn't do anything. You have to get him free," Despite the air conditioning, sweat trickled down Michael's back. He gripped the edge of the bench and his knuckles crackled.

"I have to be honest with you. Looking at the evidence the police have right now, the prosecutor has a strong case. I'm not sure anyone can get Jon off." He put his hand on Michael's shoulder.

The younger man tried not to flinch.

Lawson took his hand away. He looked down and flushed bright red, even the top of his head where his hair didn't quite brush over the bare patch. "I mean, to get him free."

Michael slid back a bit, not sure why the man was embarrassed. Was he was more afraid for Jon, or afraid of David Lawson? He didn't owe this person anything, but he needed him.

"I'll try my best," Lawson said. "I know telling you not to worry is useless, but this is a long process. We start with the arraignment today at two o'clock in courtroom seven upstairs." When Michael didn't respond he continued. "The arraignment is where they make the charges and set bail."

Michael nodded slightly.

Lawson continued, "I'll try to get a low bail, so we can get Jon out, but with the seriousness of the charges, I doubt bail will be reasonable. Do you have any money or anything you could use for a bail bondsman?"

Michael swallowed a lump in his throat. "I have a hundred-fifty dollars, my truck, nineteen calves, twenty cows and a good cutting horse I could sell." The information the lawyer said was still registering, and Michael thought of all the courts he'd seen on TV. Jon was in bad shape. The White court would only see a filthy Indian. He knew in his heart they would just put Jon away and forget him. His cousin would die in jail.

"Can you at least get Jon a cell where he can get clean? He's still half groggy from his concussion." Michael asked, sitting up straighter.

"I saw his head injury. He didn't tell me it was a concussion. Did he get it in jail?"

The Lawyer — *He wouldn't call him his father* — had a funny look on his face. Michael couldn't read the expression. "I don't know where he got hurt," he said. "They had him at the hospital overnight."

Lawson stood up abruptly. "I need to check something out." He gathered his papers.

"What about the bail?"

"Let's worry after the arraignment," he said. "I'll see you upstairs at two."

Chapter 8

SPEAKING LEGAL

THE TALL ROOM WHERE THEY HELD THE ARRAIGNMENT WAS AN alien place. Nothing seemed natural. The ceiling was the highest Michael had seen, except for the gym at the High School in Shiprock. But there were no beams holding the roof up. Sound didn't echo in this room. Noise was muffled, like in winter when you wrapped scarves around your head to keep your ears from freezing. The windows were small and high on the walls and the lights left no shadows. There were no smells. Even the wood of the benches was an odd greenish tan color. Michael sat as close to the front as he could, hoping he would be near Jon when they brought him in. The Lawyer was not there. Michael tried to imagine what to do if he had run away and left Jon. The thought that The Lawyer wanted to get away from his problematic son again crossed Michael's mind.

For nearly an hour Michael sat listening to random cases. He couldn't make sense of most of what they were saying. Lawyers talked Legal. Michael grew up speaking the Navajo language, Diné Bezaad. A teacher told him it was one of the hardest languages. It was so different, they used it for keeping secrets during World War II. Michael spoke English pretty well, even if he forgot words sometimes, but Legal was a language he would never understand.

Finally, Jon's lawyer came in. He smiled at Michael as he pulled some papers from his briefcase. His pale eyes made a little shiver of cold go up his son's back. Michael nodded at him, but kept his face still.

A short fat Hispanic guard, with a huge gun on his hip, and inch-long hair that stood up around his head like a porcupine, brought Jon into the cavernous room. Jon seemed shrunken in on himself. Michael's cousin was wearing an orange coverall which made him a cross between an auto mechanic and a clown. The bandage on his head still had a tinge of pink blood. Jon's feet and hands were shackled with chains, so he was especially clumsy. He shuffled over and sat beside The Lawyer without even looking at Michael. A sad auto mechanic clown, he looked even more scared than he had in the jail. At least he was clean.

A man at a desk next to the judge recited some Legal. The Lawyer and Jon stood up and Jon mumbled, "Not guilty." He didn't raise his head.

The other lawyer spoke some Legal and said Jon was likely to flee back to the Navajo Nation, and out of local jurisdiction. Michael made out a few other words, something about the right to a speedy trial.

The Lawyer stood next to Jon, but never asked for bail. He mentioned Jon didn't have a record, and that he was no flight risk.

Michael was trying to figure out why the lawyers didn't speak plain English, when the judge responded, "Bail set at one million dollars." Michael didn't need a translator to understand that. The air rushed out of his lungs. Jon flinched as though someone hit him. The judge banged his gavel, and the little fat guard led Jon away. His head was hanging so low, his hair covered his face.

Michael didn't even fool himself into thinking he could find a million dollars. On his way out of the courtroom, he bumped into a big man with his arm in a sling who was also leaving. Michael slumped in a chair in the hallway. Blood pounded at his temples.

The Lawyer came out and greeted the big man who'd bumped Michael. "Hi Ray. Sorry to hear about your arm." He nodded at the cast.

"Thanks, Dave, it was a stupid accident. I'll be off the street a while, but I was here talking to the prosecutor and thought I'd stop in and see what my bowling buddy was up to."

The Lawyer looked down at Michael with his head in his hands and said, "Ray, I'd love to talk, but my son just got some bad news."

As discouraged as Michael was, a jolt still went through him when The Lawyer introduced him as his son. *He doesn't have a right to call me his son*, he thought.

The big man raised an eyebrow. Looking at Michael curiously, he patted The Lawyer on the shoulder. "I understand. I'll see you later." He lumbered off.

The Lawyer sat next to Michael. "Sorry, Ray's an old friend. I know you're upset. The bail was high. Native Americans are always considered a flight risk, because if they go back to the reservation they're hard to extradite." He laid his briefcase on the chair beside him. "Do you think the family can get hundred thousand dollars for the bond?" He could see Michael was confused, and explained how a bail bondsman would put up most of the money, if the family could come up with ten percent.

Michael shook his head. "If the whole family sold every animal on our range, we couldn't come up with a hundred thousand dollars." He tried to imagine how long Jon could live in a jail cell. "What was the part about a speedy trial?"

"The prosecutors don't have as good a case as I thought at first. We don't want to wait and see if new evidence can be found. I don't want to get your hopes up, but the detectives won't be able to use all the forensics from the murder scene. It may work in our favor, but it's too soon to tell." Michael's wrinkled forehead caused him to explain. "Jon got cleaned up at the hospital without the police being present. That causes the chain of custody to be broken. They can't use information from his body as evidence. Also, there was a car accident and a lot of the evidence from the scene was ruined."

Seeing his son's raised eyebrows, he continued, "It was the best thing that could have happened. I can argue the evidence they have is not conclusive, because of the error. I looked at the doctor's report. Jon's head injury was definitely not from a fall. Someone hit him."

At Michael's alarmed look The Lawyer reached to pat his son's hand, but pulled it back. Lawson continued as though he'd not made the gesture. "Jon has a minor concussion. He'll be fine with rest. The best thing is, he remembers scratching a tall guy. That and his head injury may be enough to convince a jury of reasonable doubt." He looked at Michael expectantly.

Michael didn't shift gears quickly at the best of times, and this definitely was not the best of times. He waited, thinking about what The Lawyer had said. "Wouldn't DNA make them let him go free?" It always did in movies.

"The DNA from under his fingernails could be used for the investigation, but not in court. If it turns out it's the victim's DNA, that's in our favor." Lawson smiled at Michael as if the young man should understand the situation. When he saw his son's blank look he said, "If it is incriminating evidence, they can't use it against him, because they didn't handle the samples correctly. The DNA can only help our case by supporting Jon's story of another man being there, although the prosecutor could argue he could have scratched anybody anytime that day. All it really does is exclude Jon having contact with the victim. If I present it right it adds reasonable doubt."

The Lawyer started to put his hand on Michael's shoulder. He caught himself and changed the gesture to scratch his balding head instead. "I know it's foolish to tell you not to worry, but try the best you can. I'll try to make arrangements for Jon to be in the medical ward, where he'll be more comfortable. I'll give you a call and let you know how he is doing. Where are you staying?"

"I'll be over by the Star Diner. It's a couple of blocks up the street. I think there's a phone in the parking lot. I could get the number, so you can call me," Michael said.

"That won't be a problem. I eat there a lot. I'll swing by as soon as I can," Lawson said as he hurried away. His airy, "Don't give up hope," barely registered over the ringing of a hundred thousand dollars in Michael's head.

From behind her blindfold, the statue lady watched the young man leave.

Chapter 9

DAMN LAWYERS

Garcia slammed into his office door. It flew open with a bang, deepening the dent already gracing the wall.

Tom Norris followed and shut the door behind him. He held his right arm to his chest. "What's up? We can hear you clear down the hall." He gripped his raised arm and massaged it with his long fingers.

"The damn lawyer had to get smart and notice the Indian in the loading dock murder had evidence on him that was lost at the hospital. He even went to the DA and filed papers to have my handling of the suspect examined by IA. I'm not the one who put the injured guy in a hot car. I called for the ambulance, for Christ's sake."

Rudy flopped into his chair. "I got my balls busted about not getting a subpoena for blood work on the Indian. They're always talking about saving money by not doing unnecessary tests. The case was a slam-dunk." He slapped his hand on the table. "The son-of-a-bitch had the knife in his hand. What more was forensics going to tell us?"

Norris nodded in agreement. "You're right. I wouldn't have worried about the lab either. Not for the murder of a junkie crack dealer. Even if your partner were here, Ray wouldn't have done anything different. Hell, you were lucky not to get hurt more than you did in the wreck. It's just tough luck the lawyer decided to get ambitious. Who's the lawyer, anyway?"

"Lawson." Ray Chamberlin said, hulking through the door.

"Speak of the devil, Ray. We didn't think we'd see you for a couple weeks." Norris said.

"I was over at the courthouse tying up some loose ends, and ran into Lawson after the Indian's arraignment." Ray flopped into the plastic chair next to Rudy's desk. "Jeez, Rudy, you look awful. I heard about the wreck. You OK?"

"I'll live."

"What's going on?"

"Lawson's being a problem about the forensics for the murder on Indian School Road," Rudy said. "The one that happened the night you broke your arm."

Ray shrugged. "Lawson's not usually so motivated."

"Who's heard of a court-appointed lawyer getting delusions of grandeur?" Norris leaned against the door post and massaged his forearm, digging his fingers in and wincing.

The other men watched his action.

Ray nodded toward Norris. "Sympathy pain?"

Norris stopped rubbing. "What? I used it too much and got bursitis. I don't think either of us are going bowling any time soon." He shrugged. "Back on point, what do you think got Lawson going so hard?"

"He's got his son with him now. Maybe he's trying to impress the kid," Ray said.

Garcia fussed with some papers on his desk. "Some kid

came in the night before arraignment. Said he was the Indian's cousin. I bet he lit a fire under Lawson."

"Blond kid, dark tan, dressed like a day laborer?" Ray asked.

"Yeah, that's him." Rudy scratched his head. "No wonder Lawson's motivated. The Indian must be related by marriage. Shit!"

Norris, shaking his head, stood to leave. "Let me know if you need any help, Rudy." The tall man left the door open behind him.

Garcia shuffled the papers some more. He took a deep breath to calm himself. "Hey, Ray, you want to come over for dinner tonight? I need to pick your brain about this last case."

Chapter 10

THE STAR DINER

THE STAR DINER WAS ONLY A COUPLE BLOCKS FROM THE police station. It was a square space with a curved counter in front of the kitchen grills. Booths surrounded the exterior walls. Each booth had a big window looking out on the parking lot or the road out front. Tables filled the open area between the counter and the booths. The table tops and counter were covered in a gray plastic that was supposed to imitate polished stone. Michael knew there was a name for that type of surface, but didn't have the energy to think of what it was. He could watch his truck from his chosen booth.

Around five o'clock, he switched from coffee to tea. At six, he ordered a burger. By eight, Michael was contemplating a piece of lemon pie, but wasn't sure how well it would set on top of the apple pie he'd devoured after his burger.

If her badge didn't lie, the weary-looking waitress was named Jenny. She was the prettiest girl Michael had seen in Phoenix. He tried to compare this delicate blond woman wearing a fine gold chain around her neck, to the sturdy

49

Salina Tsosie at the Squaw dances wearing ten pounds of her family's silver.

Phoenix Jenny was like a spirit. The word ethereal came to Michael's mind. He marveled at how he could think of a word like ethereal and forget briefcase. The mind is a weird thing. Jenny was about his age. She smiled each time she gave him a refill. He was pretty sure her kindness was because she didn't know he was an Indian.

While he waited, Michael didn't want to make himself crazy worrying about Jon, so he tried to imagine what life would be like if he married this sweet woman and lived here in town. His mother married a Belagáana. The aunties told him she was happy. *Could he do the same, and live away from his people?*

Michael's imaginings about life with Jenny weren't dirty thoughts, although a couple images flitted by causing him to duck his head and blush. He tried to picture how simple day-to-day things in a life with this gentle woman would be so different from the life he knew.

He'd have a job in an office where his clothes would never get dirty. At the diner, after work, he would surprise Jenny with flowers. While he ate apple pie, she would tell him of the customers she had seen during the day. They would drive a new car with soft seats home to their apartment, which was never too warm, nor too cold. Auntie Lila would be looking after their baby daughter, who would have her mother's silky hair and Lila's wise eyes. The two of them would sit on a plush sofa and watch television while the baby played.

On weekends, they would shop at the supermarket and buy food in plastic packages. As vacations, they would take trips to the ocean. He would ride on a boat, and catch giant jumping fish. Michael chided himself for such silly ideas about a life that would never be, but kept imagining, none-the-less.

The busboy was cleaning up the dinner plates around nine when The Lawyer's entrance broke Michael's reverie. The real world came swirling back. Lawson walked right over to the booth, smiling the whole time. Michael got up, not wanting to be trapped. An involuntary shiver ran up his back.

The Lawyer slid into the seat across from Michael, setting his briefcase on the floor.

"Is Jon all right?" Michael asked, wondering if he could trust what the man said.

"His injury is minor, but I'm worried about his mental state," Lawson replied. "I'm building a reasonable doubt defense. I tried to explain to him what was going on, but he's too scared to think straight. Maybe you could come with me to see him tomorrow, and explain the situation to him."

Michael relaxed a bit and eased a little further into the booth. He tried to keep his legs from touching The Lawyer.

Lawson watched his son intently. "This is good news, you know," he said.

Michael nodded.

Jenny came over, smiling brightly at Michael and handing the lawyer a menu. "Can I get you anything?"

"Just coffee," Lawson said.

"It isn't hard to tell you two are related," she said conversationally. Her smile faltered when neither of the men replied. "I'll be right back." She hurried off.

The Lawyer looked down at the table. Michael looked at their reflection in the window, and was startled to see she was right. Both had the same cowlick above their ear, the same set to their chin. The Lawyer met his son's eyes in the reflection. Michael rubbed the side of his nose and pretended to see something in the parking lot. Not wanting to resemble The Lawyer wasn't going to change the fact that he did. He'd just have to get used to it.

"Michael, how are you?" Lawson started. "I know I don't have any right to expect anything from you. I just want you to know I have thought about you often through the years. My life was crazy after your mother died. I thought you would be ..." he trailed off when Michael wouldn't look at him. The younger man's stillness was instinctive, a rabbit hiding from a hawk. Michael didn't take a breath until The Lawyer stopped.

"Just save Jon," Michael said quietly, still not looking at the ghost man. Michael got up. "What time are you going to see my cousin tomorrow?"

"I should see him early. I have court in the afternoon," Lawson replied quietly. "Where are you staying tonight? Do you have a motel room?" He got up and threw some money on the table.

"No, I'll be in my truck in the parking lot," Michael looked down at his scuffed boots next to The Lawyer's shiny black shoes. He got out his wallet and picked up the check.

"You don't have to do that," Lawson said. Michael started to explain how the people in the diner didn't mind, when The Lawyer said, "Why don't you come and stay at my place. I have a spare room. Actually, it's your room. The one you had when you were a little boy." His voice cracked slightly because he gulped when he said it. He had an odd look in his eyes. "You could stay there again."

Michael's gut tensed up. He didn't know what to do. Instinct told him not to trust this man, but Jon needed him. *Would The Lawyer run out on Jon, too?*

"I understand you probably don't trust me. Let me do this for you," Lawson started.

Michael's involuntary jerk stopped him.

"I mean, let me do it for me. I'd feel awful thinking of you sleeping in your truck." He looked at his son, his eyes searching for any hint of acceptance.

Michael nodded. He didn't want to owe the man anything, but if he stayed at his house, it would be harder for The Lawyer to abandon Jon. Michael knew he would have to be very careful.

Chapter 11

MY MOTHER'S HOUSE

THE LAWYER'S HOUSE WAS A LOW RECTANGULAR BUILDING with a roof overhanging the walls by about two feet. The paint was faded and chipped. The Lawyer parked under a metal ramada stretching over the driveway. Michael parked on the street. A door on the side of the house led into the kitchen. There was a coffee pot with stains of long forgotten brew on its glass. A stack of newspapers and magazines were piled on the metal-legged kitchen table. The open trash can was filled with fast food bags and pizza boxes. A couple of dishes sat in the wire drainer next to the sink.

"I eat out a lot." The Lawyer set his briefcase on the table and moved the pile of newspapers. He indicated Michael should sit. "You had dinner?" He sputtered around the room without waiting for his son to respond, pouring out the old coffee and getting rid of the grounds. "I know this is hard for you. I want you to know, leaving you was the hardest thing I'd ever done."

Michael stood near the doorway, watching him. *If it was so hard, why did you leave?* He decided The Lawyer wasn't going to get the chance to crawl into his brain, so he said nothing.

Lawson put a new filter in the machine and scooped coffee from a can on the counter. "I knew you'd be happier with Lila. She was better able to take care of you."

What kind of a man abandons his child and doesn't come to see him for eighteen years? Michael took a few steps across the room to sit at the table. He didn't look at The Lawyer. Lila had told Michael his father left him because he thought his son would be a better man if he were raised by the Diné. Michael trusted Lila. She'd never let him down. But The Lawyer could have at least come to visit and not let his son think he was a ghost.

Lawson gazed at his folded hands. "After your mother... died, I was no good for anything. I was...you needed more than I had left."

The comforting smell of coffee began to fill the room, but Michael wasn't soothed. *What a convenient way to look at things. If I hadn't come across him by accident, I probably never would have met him. It wouldn't have hurt me.* Michael sat very straight and still, with both hands on the table top. He wasn't going to ask why The Lawyer never came back to see him. Michael had his pride.

"Do you understand what I'm telling you? I did what I did to save you." He looked at his son intently.

Michael looked at his hands. "I understand." *You did what was easy for you. It's a long ride to Kayenta. Inconvenient to spend a day with the child you didn't want.* Looking up, he said, "Is the coffee ready?"

Lawson smiled and brought his son a mug with a police logo on it. "Do you want cream and sugar?"

Michael shook his head.

The Lawyer stood over Michael, smiling like a dog

trying to sneak a piece of meat. "I've got pictures of you —
when you were little. They're a little faded. I had them with
me while I was in the Army, and they got a lot of sunlight."
He practically bounced into the other room.

The jars on the counter looked like bears sitting on their
haunches. There were three sizes. Those bears had danced
in Michael's dreams as a child. He never thought they were
real. Getting up, he lifted the head off the largest bear. It was
filled with round, black cookies.

The Lawyer returned with a big album. "Let me show
you." He stared at the table, apparently startled Michael was
at the counter.

"How long have you had these jars?"

"Someone gave them to us for our wedding." He placed
the album on the kitchen table. "Help yourself."

Michael's breath caught in his throat. He had a flash of
his mother handing him a cookie from the squatting bear.
He stepped back, leaving the bear's head next to its smaller
friend.

The Lawyer put his hand on the album, looking at
Michael expectantly.

He didn't want to look at this man's memories. He had
his own, and The Lawyer wasn't part of them. "I'm tired. Do
you have a place I can sleep?"

"Ah, yes...sure. You must be exhausted." Lawson passed
a hand over his eyes. His mouth turned down. He glanced at
the book on the table then turned quickly. "Let me show
you where your room is."

Down a short hall, he pointed out the bathroom. A
couple feet beyond it, he pushed open the door of the room
where Michael would stay. The warm tans and burnt orange
of the walls were covered with images of cavorting cartoon
animals. The small bed had a wool blanket, woven in the

cloud ladder pattern used most often by Michael's clan mothers. A lamp shaped like a bucking horse sat on the night table. A rag rug lay on the wooden floor. Several cloth animals inhabited a shelf in the corner. Dust covered everything in a thick layer.

"This is your room. I...ah...don't come in here often. Sorry about the dust. Let me shake out this blanket." He gathered it up and scuttled out like he was carrying a stolen lamb.

Standing in the doorway, Michael's mind reeled. He knew this place, the horse and the elk on the wall above the pillow, a memory of a woman's voice... singing. Turning, he lurched into the bathroom, kicking the door shut with his heel. Michael grabbed both sides of the sink to still his trembling hands. His mouth was dry, and the coffee soured in his stomach. Turning on the water, he rinsed his mouth, splashed water on his face, and wiped it with a blue towel. The instinct to run pulsed through every fiber of his body. *Did my mother die in this house?* Michael let the water run in the sink and soaped his hands and arms, to waste time. *I'm here to help Jon. For Jon, I can do this.*

The sounds of The Lawyer in the next room dwindled. Then his voice from outside the door made Michael jump. "Let me know if you need anything." When his son didn't reply, he continued, "I'll leave some extra towels out here if you want to take a shower."

Michael heard a door opening and closing.

"I'll leave them on the floor out here."

Michael was leaning on his arm against the door. *Maybe I should leave. I can't let this place get inside me. I don't owe him anything.* He took a ragged breath. *I need him to help Jon.* "OK," Michael said in a voice he didn't recognize.

"That's great then...I guess I'll see you in the morning."

Michael heard a door close at the end of the hall. After a few minutes, the sound of water started in the back of the house. He opened the bathroom door and picked up the towels and held them against his face to catch the gulping breaths as they tore from his lungs. On the wall opposite the door, his mother gazed at him from a faded picture. The towels caught his tears.

Chapter 12

DOWNED SHEEP

THE NEXT MORNING, JON, IN HIS ORANGE CLOWN SUIT, WAS sitting in the jail's meeting room. Since they were with The Lawyer, the three men met in a regular room with tables and chairs. The walls were dirty. Grime crusted the table. The whole place smelled of sweat and hopelessness. Michael touched his cousin's hand. Jon looked at him with blank eyes, as though he was already gone.

"I left a message for your mother." Michael squeezed Jon's hand. "I'll talk to her again this afternoon."

Jon didn't react. He was so still, Michael had to look closely to see him breathe. Jon's eyes flicked up briefly as his cousin explained how the evidence they collected at the jail would be helpful. His shoulders hunched slightly at the hundred-thousand dollar bail.

His behavior reminded Michael of wild sheep who, once pulled down, would lie without a struggle while the coyotes ate them.

"Brother!" Michael wanted to reach across the table and shake a reaction from his cousin. "Quit acting like a downed sheep. You need to help yourself," he said it in Diné, a language which softens even the harshest words. Jon looked into Michael's eyes indicating he didn't believe what was said. At least it was a reaction.

Switching to English so The Lawyer could follow, Michael enticed Jon to talk about what he remembered. It came out in fits and starts.

"I thought the two men were going to have sex . . . The taller man was the one who put the knife in my hand and hit me. Didn't see what happened to the smaller man. Is he the one who got killed?." Jon leaned his elbows on the table and dropped his head into his hands. "I was really drunk. I don't even remember where I left my truck, let alone remember any details about the tall man. He could walk in here right now and I wouldn't recognize him."

"Think. Anything could be helpful, images, impressions," The Lawyer said in a soothing voice.

Jon raised his head and looked at his fingers. "I scratched the man's arm when he grabbed me."

"Did you go near the dead man?" Michael asked, realizing the dead man's spirit energy, the Chindi, might be making Jon sick.

"No, I was clear over the other side of the loading area."

He gave a sigh of relief. Jon had enough problems without trying to deal with a crazed spirit inside him. The Lawyer looked confused at the turn of the conversation. Michael didn't bother to explain how when a person died, his energy tries to find a new body to inhabit. It would try to take over any person, or animal nearby instead of spreading out into the universe as it was supposed to. It wasn't something The Lawyer would understand.

When it was time to leave, Michael hugged Jon hard and whispered in Navajo, "This man is my father. He's your uncle. I think he has magic."

Jon's muscles stiffened in their embrace. His indrawn breath was nearly a sob. He turned and walked away with the jailer. The man took his arm, as though he were a coyote dragging Jon to a den. Michael watched until they were gone.

When they left the jail, The Lawyer went off to do lawyer things, and Michael went back to the courthouse to call home. He sat on the bench by the statue of the blindfolded woman, watching people. The whirl of emotions in the crowd muted his inner chaos. He was exhausted from lack of sleep. He'd not been able to rest in The Lawyer's house. The bed was fine and the house quiet, but the images of the life he never had whirled around the bedroom throughout the night. At least the book of pictures was gone when he went into the kitchen in the morning.

Michael tried not to think. When his efforts didn't work, he tried to imagine what the people walking by did for a living. It wasn't much use. His imagination was on overdrive showing him scenes: Jon being brutalized by guards, the face of his aunt while he explained how her son might be going to prison for life. His stomach flopped when images of the murdered man flashed behind his eyes. As those horrors faded, Michael started wondering about The Lawyer. *Why did he still have pictures of my mother in his house?* Michael's jaw clenched, the story about why he abandoned his son couldn't be true.

At three, Michael got up to call Aunt Jean. The phone at the jail had some unnamable slime on it so he went into the bathroom to get paper towels. He splashed water on his face. At least his shoulder didn't hurt today.

Auntie Jean picked up the phone at the chapter house before the first ring was complete. Michael was able to get out most of the details about what was happening to Jon before she started. Her tirade included the dangers of leaving places you know and the evils of the outside world.

"Auntie," Michael said when she stopped for a breath. "I need Aunt Lila, is she there?"

He heard her still ranting as she handed the phone to Lila. "My poor boy, the police are going to kill him in jail. He's a good boy. He doesn't deserve this." Jean's voice faded.

"Yes," Lila's calm voice relaxed Michael's shoulders.

"Jon's in big trouble. I'll have to be here a long time. I'll do what I can for him."

"I know you'll do your best. What else is wrong?" she asked softly.

"Jon's lawyer, he is...the man who left me with you when I was small," Michael replied even more softly.

She waited a long minute, and the operator on the phone asked for money. The jangle of the coins dropping ran like spiders down his neck.

"This is not a bad thing. He is a wise man and he will do his best for Jon because of you." She sounded confident.

"He let me stay in his house last night. It was a regular house with a fence and a yard." Michael leaned close to the filthy wall and put his arm up against it to shield his face. The strangers in the hall shouldn't see his pain. "Auntie, he has pictures of my mother." Michael opened his mouth wide to take in air, so she wouldn't hear him cry.

"Jean and me will come tomorrow," she said.

"You don't have to come. This court thing will take a long time," Michael said, trying not to sound relieved.

"We have time. We always have time."

Chapter 13
POOR PROSPECTS

THE LAWYER GAVE MICHAEL A KEY, SO HE WENT BACK TO HIS house. It smelled like an alien creature's house, all disinfectants, plastic, and stale air. It wasn't long before he had to go to the yard in the back to breathe. The outdoors wasn't much better. It smelled thick and green. The yard was a little square of grass. It was unnatural, all that green. He'd seen sprinklers come on last night like upside down rain. Upside down was how he felt. He was out of place here.

There was the constant noise of cars and the sounds of people talking, faint ghosts in the distance trying to get his attention. Michael couldn't relax, so he went back into the house and looked around for something familiar. Even the refrigerator was an alien artifact, all square and steel with water and ice in the door. In the front room, there was a fireplace. He gathered some logs from the basket beside the firebox and set a fire. It was too hot to light it, but the automatic motions of placing the kindling and logs was calming.

Michael started to relax until he stood up. His mother's picture stared at him from the mantle. It was a picture he'd seen before. Aunt Lila had this same photo. His mother was smiling. Her red polka-dot dress bulged in pregnancy. Her eyes were even more beautiful than her sister's. Michael propped his arm against the mantle. Tears ran down his face and sobs choked breath from his lungs. He wailed for a person he barely knew. Neither the fading photo nor the silent antiseptic house offered comfort.

When The Lawyer returned, just after dark, Michael was composed and ready for him. He'd showered and changed into clean clothes, the best jeans he had, and a white shirt with faint blue stripes and pearly white snap buttons. He'd even cooked chili. Michael was ready.

The Lawyer came in smiling. "Michael, I'm glad you decided to stay."

Michael shrugged noncommittally, but it didn't dampen The Lawyer's high spirits. "You didn't have to make dinner. I was going to take you out," he said. He was smiling broadly.

"Have you learned anything more about Jon's case?" Michael asked, with no expression. He stood very straight and still. Michael hoped The Lawyer wouldn't want to show his picture album and play at being a father. He didn't need a father. His uncles taught him all the things he needed to know to be a good man. All he required from The Lawyer was help for Jon.

The bright energy the older man entered with dimmed a bit. He set his briefcase on the kitchen table and pulled out some papers. The picture of the dead man was on top. "By the way, don't tell anyone I've shown you this file. Technically, these are private court documents. Anyway, we won't have DNA results for a few days, but Jon's fingerprints were on the knife, so it still is a tough sell."

"Jon explained how it happened," Michael said.

"That won't go far with a jury without a witness to say

someone else was at the murder scene," he replied. "No one but Jon saw anyone in the alley until the police came."

The picture of the dead man kept coming to Michael's mind; an older man, with a worn, gaunt face and wasted limbs. Michael shook the sad face from his mind. He needed to read this as if it were an animal kill. Keep himself objective. Not think of it as a person. Strings of the man's intestines were in his lap. There was a lot of blood. Other pictures showed the blood that had squirted several feet from the body. The blood spray on the ground had an odd shape.

"They had to stick him from the front to gut him like that," Michael said.

Lawson shuffled some papers. "The coroner says it was an upthrusting blow."

"Was Jon covered in blood? Look at how far it spurted as the guy died. Nobody could get away without getting sprayed," Michael said.

"Good point," he said. The Lawyer shuffled a few papers. He wrote something down on a long yellow notepad. "The DA hasn't sent over the forensics on Jon's clothes yet. I'll request it. You're being helpful."

"Who was this guy anyway?"

"He was a drug dealer who specialized in meth and crack," Lawson said. He looked through the papers. "His name was Simon Ortega. He went by the street name Twitchy. Does either of those names sound familiar?"

Michael shook his head. "I talked to a Detective Garcia, and he asked if Jon did drugs."

"Does he?" The Lawyer asked. He jotted more on the yellow pad.

Michael looked right at him to let him know he didn't care for the question, but The Lawyer was still writing. His head was down and the hair he'd combed over didn't cover the bald spot on the top of his head. "Jon doesn't do drugs. Didn't they test him when he went to jail like they do if you're drunk?"

Lawson flipped through the file and grinned like a raccoon. "They didn't test his blood or the tissue under his nails. I had to make an issue about the lack of forensics. The prosecution is just as happy there is no admissible test, because what we find might help us as leverage to have Jon's case dropped. There was no police at the hospital, so the earlier evidence was tainted. The prosecution can't use it. It's a mistake that helps us."

At Michael's blank look, he continued, "This is a good thing. I am having a lab test on the blood and tissue we found under Jon's nails. It'll be a few days before the tests come back. They won't be admissible at trial, but the information can be useful for any investigation."

"How is Detective Garcia making a mistake a good thing? Is he investigating, or is he just going to go with Jon as the killer?" Michael asked.

"I imagine he wants to simply close the case with Jon, but because I'm forcing forensics, Garcia has to do his job," he replied.

"How would you do this whole thing if Jon was a rich white guy?" Michael asked.

The Lawyer looked at Michael intently, and Michael looked back right in his eyes. *He should know my look is a challenge.*

"Michael, I'm doing my best for Jon. I don't differentiate between rich and poor, Native, Hispanic, or White. The problem is I only have a small office these days, just me and a couple of other guys. We can barely afford a secretary. Larger firms can afford to hire investigators and order tests the DA doesn't think are necessary. I already forced a couple of tests that will cost a couple thousand dollars."

"I'll pay for the tests." Michael thought quickly about which of his cattle could be sent off to market. "How much would a private investigator and the other tests cost?" he asked.

"An investigator could run into thousands of dollars and still not find out anything, the tests could be the same," The Lawyer replied.

Michael looked at the series of pictures on the table, trying to make sense of them. "Order what tests are necessary. I'll pay you back." He contemplated the pictures for a few minutes. "I need to go look at the place where this happened. I need to talk to Garcia and make him understand about Jon. To find out what he knows." Michael looked up at The Lawyer. "I have to do something."

"Going to the murder scene isn't a good idea. It's a bad part of town," Lawson said. "You could get in trouble for interfering with the investigation. There's a way to have you investigate legally, but I think it's a little early to get into that."

"I have to do something," Michael repeated. "I need to get Jon out of the jail. I can tell he's dying inside." He stood up and began to pace. "My aunts are coming tomorrow. I have to give them hope."

"Your aunts?" The Lawyer asked.

"John's mother and our Aunt Lila."

"Jean and Lila?" The Lawyer's face turned even paler. "What time are they coming?"

Chapter 14

INVASION OF THE AUNTIES

AUNT JEAN WORE HER RED BOOTS AND A DETERMINED LOOK. She was decked out in half the family silver. Her plump body practically stooped with the weight of a squash blossom necklace. It crushed the velvet of her blouse and reached below the waist of her layered black skirt. Lila was the opposite of Jean, taller and slender, dressed simply in a canvas skirt buttoned up the front and a red and blue plaid collared shirt with the sleeves rolled up. Her hair was pulled back in a tail that was folded under and wrapped with blue wool yarn. Muscles in Michael's back relaxed when he saw them. He hadn't even realized he was so tense. When the third woman got out of the old Jeep, his muscles tightened again. It was Salina Tsosie. She stood silently by the driver's side door and waited for Michael to greet the elder women.

"Ah'hahlah'nih," Michael said as he clasped his aunts hands, moving from one to the other. Neither of them looked at The Lawyer. Jean spoke first. "Don't worry about your cattle. Thomas is looking after them. He has moved them to the top pasture and cleaned out the tank. The windmill is pumping good, and those calves are getting fat."

She patted Michael's hand and turned to The Lawyer. "My sister loved you. You help my boy. You get him out of the jail, now."

"Jean," The Lawyer stuttered. "I will do all I can, but it—"

"Is this my sister's house?" Jean rudely cut him off.

He nodded, wisely not venturing anything more. *He really did know Aunt Jean*, Michael thought. He didn't know why it surprised him. She was his sister-in-law after all.

"We will stay here until this is all fixed. Now, we go see my boy." Jean looked at him steadily.

Michael had to give him credit. The Lawyer didn't squirm at all. He gained a little stature in his son's eyes at that moment. Michael didn't know many people who could win a stare off with Auntie Jean. She was a force of nature. When she finished looking at The Lawyer, she turned abruptly and got back in the rusty green Jeep Cherokee with the blue passenger door.

Once Jean was in the vehicle, The Lawyer looked at Lila, at Michael, then at Salina. His eyes were wide, and his face flushed red. Lila looked directly at him and tilted her head slightly. Her calm expression must have told him something since his shoulders slumped, and he nodded in defeat.

Michael didn't say anything. He was carefully studying the clipped shrubs lining the driveway. He recognized the Jeep Salina and the aunts were driving. It belonged to Hosteen Simon up in Kayenta. It usually sat out behind his gas station. He hoped his aunts had asked before they borrowed it. He'd give Simon a call to let him know where it was, just in case.

The Lawyer was looking at the young woman by the Jeep.

Lila introduced her. "David Lawson, this is Salina Tsosie. She drove down with us to pick up her brother."

With all that had gone on, Michael'd forgotten his message about running into Sam at the Lucky Buck. "Ya'at eeh," Michael greeted Salina.

She smiled shyly and replied in English, "Hi, your aunt Jean really wants to see Jon. I'll ride with you. We can go look for my brother later."

Michael swallowed, trying to moisten his mouth for a reply.

"Michael, why don't we put the bags in the house and you can meet us at the jail, "David Lawson said with a sigh. "Drive my car. I'll ride with your aunts and Salina."

As he helped Michael get the bags out of the back, The Lawyer looked a little abashed. The aunts had literally brought their clothes in bags, more exactly, plastic garbage sacks. One smaller burlap sack held red beans. They smelled earthy and tart. Michael's mouth watered at the memory of the taste when Aunt Lila cooked them with mutton and squash. He hadn't realized how he missed the smells of home, here in The Lawyer's tidy little square house, so sterile, with green grass all around.

"I'll try to explain to them..." The Lawyer gestured toward the aunts with his shoulder as he handed Michael a bag, "...how difficult Jon's situation is when you take Salina to her brother."

Michael looked him directly in his eyes for the second time since they'd met. Lawson didn't seem to recognize the challenge. "You can try," he said, looking away, and slinging a couple bags over his shoulder.

Michael noticed Aunt Lila watching him in the rearview mirror. His scalp itched. Sweat trickled down his back. He knew somewhere in his head The Lawyer must have known his Aunts. Michael'd heard stories all his life about how close the three Yazzie sisters had been. He still didn't think The Lawyer had any idea how difficult it would be to persuade Aunt Jean of anything she didn't want to hear.

The Lawyer's car was large, and the seat was deep and made of soft leather. Michael would have liked to drive Salina in the fancy car, but proprieties wouldn't allow it with the aunts around. The radio was set to a news station. The announcer was talking about the La Niña bringing unusual amounts of rain to the high desert area and making Phoenix humid. At least he wouldn't have to worry about grass for his cattle. With plenty of rain, the forage would hold up for a few weeks before they had to be moved again. Cousin Thomas was a good boy, but he wasn't much of a stockman, and Michael's fool yellow heifer could always find a way to get in trouble. Despite having bigger things to worry about, those cows were his responsibility.

Chapter 15

LOOKING THIN

Antonia had outdone herself with dinner. Rudy sat back and loosened his belt a notch. The sear of peppers from the beef stew made his mouth tingle as he swigged his beer. Next to him his partner belched quietly, then took a long pull on his drink.

Ray rested the bottle in the curve of his sling and wiped his mouth with the back of his hand. "Antonia, you ought to start your own restaurant. I don't remember the last time I've had such a great meal."

"Ray Chamberlin, did my husband pay you to say that, or are you flirting with me?"

"I swear all compliments are from the heart, and as much as I'd like to flirt with you, I don't dare. Your husband carries a gun."

Antonia giggled. Her smile showed her dimple. She gestured to the children. "Come on, you guys. Time for bed."

The boy and girl hugged their father. Bobby, at six, wasn't too old to kiss his dad but held out his hand to Ray.

The big man's paw engulfed the tiny fingers and gave them a somber shake.

Anita, the four-year-old, climbed into Ray's lap. "Butterfly kisses," she said and put her face against Ray's jaw, blinking several times, brushing her eyelashes against his cheek. She backed off and held his face in both her hands. "Nite nite."

He patted her back gently. "Sleep tight." He held out his cast where she'd drawn a stick figure hugging a heart. "I love the picture you made me."

The little girl giggled and covered her face.

"Come, Miha, teeth need brushing." Her mother held out her hand.

The little girl obediently bounded over to her mother. "Can Mister Ray read me a story?" She looked up at her mother with wide, guileless eyes.

Ray moved his hand to his cheek where the little one's eyelashes touched. "Sure, sweetie, I'll read you a story, but you have to get your jammies on and brush your teeth first."

Antonia smiled at Ray and herded the kids down the hall.

"You got some great kids there, Rudy." Ray saluted him with his beer bottle.

"It's Antonia's doing. She keeps all of us in line."

"You're a lucky man. Don't fuck it up."

Garcia raised a good natured middle finger from those wrapped around his bottle. "So, when you coming back to work?"

"I wish I could go back tomorrow. I swear I'm going to shoot the TV if another cop show has a streetwise perp confess after two minutes in interrogation." Ray held the beer bottle to his temple.

"I know what you mean. Yesterday, I thought I had one

of those made-for-TV busts, drunk Indian with a knife in his hand. Then I start looking closer and the case is unraveling."

"What you got?"

Rudy outlined the Ortega murder for his partner, including his concerns about the lost evidence and the lack of blood on the perp. "I'm going to do more digging, but the case is screwed."

"Good riddance to Ortega. The world's a better place with fewer drug dealers. Personally, I'd give the Indian a medal, but justice must be served." Ray raised his bottle in a small salute. "There's ways to explain the lack of blood and the knife. He could have stood to the side, so the blood missed him." Ray took the final swig of his beer watching Rudy over the bottle. "He could even have had an accomplice who left him to take the rap. You're just lucky you got him before he got back to the Reservation. The jurisdiction problems are a nightmare." The big man carefully lined up his empty next to the other two on the table. "There's always ways to explain the evidence. You just have to help the prosecutor with a creative story."

Ray frowned at the last statement, but before he could comment, Antonia appeared in the entry to the hall.

"Come on Mister Ray," she said. "You've got a job to do. *Iggy the Confused Piggy* is waiting for you."

Ray heaved himself out of the chair. "Duty calls."

She reached up and patted Ray on the back as he passed her. "No more than two stories. You're such a pushover; they'll keep you reading all night." Ambling into the kitchen, Antonia grabbed a couple beers from the refrigerator. She handed one to Rudy and plopped on the couch next to her husband. They clinked bottles. "Ray's good with the kids."

"Yeah, you know he lost his son a few years back."

"Oh no, the poor man. What happened?" Antonia automatically crossed herself with the hand holding her beer.

"It was a drug overdose. The kid was only sixteen. Ray's wife left him not long after."

"That must be why he's so sad all the time. I think we should introduce him to my Aunt Linda."

"Now, don't you start matchmaking, Leave the poor man alone." Garcia saw the wheels turning in his wife's brain and thought, *Ray's a goner.*

GARCIA THREW THE TOXICOLOGY REPORT ON THE DESK. THE Indian was clean for drugs. The slam dunk case was coming even further apart at the seams. Despite what his partner said last night, he couldn't massage the facts. Jon Pete had no reason to kill the drug dealer. Nothing was adding up. Rudy slid the fingers of both hands along his temples and up through his short hair. He squeezed his scalp and mashed his eyes closed. *Why couldn't just one case be easy?* He had six more on his desk and two in trial.

At least Ray could come off sick leave to handle the court testimonies. They'd talked about it last night. It always felt good bouncing ideas off Ray. They'd sat up until nearly midnight last night going over cases and drinking beer. It hadn't been that long, but he missed his partner on the job.

After a deep breath, he reached for the report and placed it in the binder serving as a murder book on the Ortega case. Rudy scrubbed his hands through his hair again. He needed a caffeine jolt to get his brain working.

Norris stood looming over the coffee pot when he

entered the break room. Norris wore his slacks and polo shirt like a suit. A huge bruise on his forearm near his elbow was turning from purple to green.

"Hey, Norris. What's happening?" Rudy called.

"Same shit, different day," Norris said with a companionable grin. "How's your problem case coming along?"

"The more I look at it, the thinner it seems. A couple things aren't adding up. I may go out and canvas on Indian School and 17th. See if anybody saw anything the night of the murder. The Unie's canvas didn't come up with much." Garcia added four sugars to his coffee.

"Who did the canvas?"

"McCafferty and Sanchez."

"They're a good team. Do you think they missed something?"

"Not really, but as much as I hate wasting time going over the same territory --" He shrugged. "I need to go through the motions to keep the DA happy."

"Don't let the lawyers push you around. Those assholes will run you ragged if you let them. They always have some alternative theory they want you to chase." Norris looked at Garcia over his cup as he took a gulp. "Screw the lawyers. You're not going to find anybody in the area who will admit to knowing their own mother. It's not like you don't have more important cases than some junkie dealer."

"I don't know," Garcia mused. "The Lieutenant already chewed me a new one over this case. I'd better follow through." Garcia appreciated Norris's support, but he wasn't as bulletproof as the older detective.

"Follow your gut, kid. Do what you have to do. If you are determined to go down there, why don't I ride along as backup? Davis is stuck in court the rest of this week."

"I'd appreciate the company. Davis must be going stir crazy sitting in court," Garcia said. Phil Davis, Norris's partner, was notoriously active. He had the highest arrest record in the department.

"Let me know when you're going out. I'll ride along with you. Indian School Road isn't a neighborhood you want to be wandering around on your own. Hell, even the Unies only go down there in pairs." Norris patted Garcia on the shoulder and stalked out of the break room.

Garcia sipped his sweet brew thoughtfully. He must doing something right to be accepted by a detective as high ranking as Norris. He left the break room whistling.

Chapter 16
OPEN EYED TRUTH

SALINA OPTED TO WAIT IN THE JEEP RATHER THAN GO INTO THE daunting edifice of the county jail. Michael didn't blame her. He wouldn't come to this dreary place unless it was absolutely necessary. He was glad she stayed in the Jeep. Jon looked even worse than yesterday. His face was bruised. His left eye was nearly swollen shut. His lip had a crack on the left side as if someone had slammed him against a wall.

Michael looked at The Lawyer and let him see the I-told-you-so in his eyes. He glanced at Aunt Jean waiting for the explosion.

Jean was expressionless for a moment. She took a deep breath and smiled her best sunshine day, life is good, and spring is here smile. "You look bad, boy. You get drunk and fall on your face?"

He looked at her wearily.

"Don't you worry now, we got a way to get you free soon," she said heartily. "Davey here," she clapped her hand on The Lawyer's shoulder, "is your Uncle. Did you know that boy?" Both Jon and Michael were startled when she used The Lawyer's name while he was present. Neither of us ever heard Jean be so rude. Maybe it was because she was trying to sound White for The Lawyer.

Now Jean was wearing a coyote grin. "Him and your cousin will fix everything, so quit feeling sorry for yourself. You'll be home soon. You got work to do. The sheep shed didn't clean itself just because you're gone. It's waiting for you, boy. Maybe next time you come to town you going to remember not to get drunk. You come on home and do chores like you're supposed to."

Michael winced inside, and stared toward the door, thinking how little Jon needed a tongue-lashing from his mother right now, but when he looked back at Jon, his cousin had actually perked up a bit. Jon must have thought if his Mom could yell at him about a little thing like getting drunk and not doing chores, things couldn't be as bad as he imagined. He looked at Michael. There was a faint smile on his cracked lips as he gave his cousin the eternal look of the long-suffering son. Michael smiled back at him as encouragingly as he could.

The Lawyer and Jon talked about what happened. Jon wasn't very forthcoming with his mother standing there. No, he couldn't remember anything more. He didn't know what happened to his truck, either. Jean asked about the food, and Jon said he'd prefer her fry cakes, which made Jean laugh. The Lawyer caught Michael's eye, and told Aunt Jean he needed to talk about special law stuff, so they should all wait outside.

Jean held her smile until the interview room door closed and they walked out of earshot. She turned to the wall, hiding her face with her hands. Her voice sounded almost normal. "I wonder about the statue in the lobby where we came in," Aunt Jean mused. "Why do they have a statue of a lady with a bandage on her eyes?"

Michael had wondered the same thing and had asked The Lawyer, as a way to avoid talking about other things, the second night he stayed at the house. "They call the statue Blind Justice. They say she is supposed to weigh the truth without being prejudiced by emotions," he told her.

"Humph," she snorted. "How can the truth be prejudiced? The truth is the truth. The way things happened." She wiped her eyes with her hands as she turned to them.

"I want the truth seen with eyes open," Lila interjected. "Not with a blindfold on."

"It's one of those ways of thinking that got my boy in trouble in the first place," Jean said, nodding her head wisely. She looked at Michael. "Boy, you go out tomorrow and look at the place where the man got killed. You don't go with a blindfold like the police. You keep your eyes wide open, and you see the truth about what happened. Then you go tell the police. They will believe you with your yellow hair." She folded her arms over her plump belly and gave a short nod of her head, as though it would be the end of the whole situation.

Michael was raised to avoid telling people bad news. He didn't know how to let Aunt Jean know the legal system didn't care how white he looked. So far, his yellow hair hadn't done much good with the police, but he couldn't bring himself to say the words and let her down. Aunt Lila looked at Michael with her calm, wise eyes. She always knew what her nephew was thinking. She gave Michael a tiny smile, just the barest corner of her mouth curving up for less than a second.

Michael sighed. "Ho'lah, auntie. I'll go look. I'll do my best."

Jean patted Michael's hand, "I know you will boy, you always do your best."

Chapter 17

THE LAWYER'S LAIR

THE LAWYER GAVE THE AUNTS KEYS TO HIS HOUSE. HE SEEMED resigned to the inevitable. Salina agreed to help the aunts get settled before they went to look for her brother.

Michael rode back to his office with The Lawyer in his comfortable car. "How did Jon get hurt?" he asked when they were alone.

"Another inmate attacked him, but the guards broke it up. He wasn't hurt too badly. Don't worry." The Lawyer patted Michael shoulder.

Michael tried not to flinch.

"I wasn't able to get Jon protective custody. They did move him to the medical wing." At Michael's alarmed look, he continued. "Jon will be all right. It is just a precaution. The second smack to his head might have made his concussion worse."

"Why would someone attack him?"

"There is an Indian gang, The Warrior Brotherhood, who wanted Jon to join. He didn't want to, so they roughed him up. It happens. He's safe now." The Lawyer drew out a white handkerchief and rubbed the back of his neck. The man sounded as if he was trying to convince himself.

Michael resisted the urge to hit something. He was useless just following The Lawyer around. He said, "I need to go find Jon's truck and see if there's anyone who saw Jon that night."

"I understand," he said. "I'll file some papers telling the court you are an associate investigator for my office. That way the police won't be able to give you a hard time."

The Lawyer's office was in a nondescript building. The inside was made up of a collection of small offices that had apparently been put together by a drunken carpenter. It was all corners and closed doors.

"I share this office space with two other lawyers. We're in and out a lot," The Lawyer said as they entered the hallway.

A single dirty window looked out on an area between buildings. It was filled with orange dumpsters. Michael's shoulders tensed as they walked the short hallway. He was jumpy as if he was tracking a wounded bear, waiting for it to charge from the brush. This whole city with its sharp corners made him wary. He'd spent the past few days with too many angles. Michael favored the round hogán where he'd grown up, or the curves of nature, smoothed by wind and water. This city didn't have enough curves. He couldn't hear danger around sharp corners.

An older white woman wearing a pink blouse sat at a cluttered desk. Her features suited the geometric chaos of the building. A variety of machines and file cabinets lined the wall behind her. She slid her glasses down her nose to look at the two men. Her grey hair was pulled back in a severe bun. "Mr. Lawson, you have six messages." She held out a handful of pink papers. The Lawyer took them, thanking her.

"Martha Jones, I'd like you to meet my son, Michael." In reply to her raised eyebrow, he continued. "He's in town helping me with the Jon Pete case." If anyone asks, he's working for me as an associate. I'm going to file the letter today."

The woman stood. Curiosity came off her in waves.

"You look a lot like your father." She held out her hand.

"That's what I've heard, ma'am. It is nice to meet you." Michael shook her hand, conscious of his work-hardened palm against her smooth skin. She smelled faintly of violets. Violets don't grow in the desert. He knew the smell, because his third grade teacher always smelled of violets. She'd shown him a picture of the delicate plant.

Michael followed The Lawyer into a rectangular office with the dimensions of a foaling stall, twice as long as it was wide. The tops of the walls were made of frosted glass which let in light from the old lady's area. The Lawyer switched on an overhead fluorescent which hummed softly with the sound of distant bees. The worn carpet once had a green and brown geometric pattern. There were no windows. Piles of papers and thick books covered every surface. A narrow path led to the desk. It smelled dusty and frantic at the same time. The Lawyer sat his briefcase on the floor and removed a stack of papers from a chair and gestured for Michael to sit.

Michael stood by the door.

"I'm a little behind in my filing," The Lawyer said. "I have to answer these calls, and send that paper to the court."

"Why does the court have to think I'm working for you?" Michael was wary of the unfeeling court knowing his name.

"It will give you a legal standing to help investigate Jon's case. If you aren't my associate, it's illegal for you to go to the crime scene, or question witnesses. As my agent, the police can't give you as much grief."

Michael nodded without expression.

"Martha, could you fill out a Letter of Association for Michael?" He raised his voice a bit.

"No problem," she called from the other room.

"Here is Jon's file." He handed Michael a good sized box full of papers. "They've sent over some more details since you last saw it. They added the forensics reports. Later, we can set you up on a computer to look at the digital photos. As usual, they sent over several hundred," The Lawyer said. "If you want some coffee, there's a pot in the main office by Mrs. Jones' desk." He picked up the phone and began dialing.

Figuring he could fend for himself, Michael took the box along as he searched for coffee. When he looked at Jon's growing file, the air seemed to be getting thinner in the room. There were five times as many papers as when he saw it at The Lawyer's house. Ms. Jones eyes tickled his neck, even though the *tick-tack* of her typing didn't slow. Michael didn't want to go back into the sad dusty room with The Lawyer. There was an empty table near the window next to the coffee machine.

"Can I work out here by the window?"

"Sure, honey, pull up one of those comfortable chairs. What is your full name for the Associate letter?"

"Michael Yazzie."

One of her perfectly drawn eyebrows raised.

"I don't have a middle name." A flush crept up Michael's neck as he realized why she was surprised. He knew not having your father's last name was significant among white people. He didn't really understand why, since your mother was the parent you *knew* you were related to. That's why, among the Navajo, a woman's brothers made sure her children were raised properly. Father's last names weren't a big deal in The Nation. Clan relationships were what counted. Heck, every time you introduced yourself in Navajo, you practically explained your whole bloodline.

Mrs. Jones didn't follow his train of thought. She just said, "Mmm hmm," and went back to typing.

The Lawyer could tell her whatever he wanted. Michael wasn't going to discuss his life with a stranger. Pulling a chair up, he purposely sat with his back to her. A sip of coffee jump-started his fuzzy brain enough that when he opened the file, it didn't shock him as it had the night before. A sketch of the crime scene was at the front.

Labels explained the body was found on a cement loading dock at the back of the Soledad Bodega. A crudely drawn shape labeled with Jon's name showed where he had sprawled unconscious on a pile of trash bags forty feet across the parking area. Nowhere did it say the name of the murdered man. The Lawyer had mentioned it, but Michael couldn't remember. He flipped through the file until he found the name, Simon Ortega. It was important for him to put a name to the other sad little shape drawn on the diagram.

Michael steeled himself and laid out the printed pictures from the file. The photos of the body weren't any easier to digest the second time. He spent some time examining each photo. Coffee churned in his stomach. Jon was photographed lying on trash bags next to a dumpster. He looked asleep. In another picture Jon looked terrible, he was half sitting, slumped over, blood sticking his hair to his face and neck. Eyes half open, he looked barely conscious.

In the photos Michael least wanted to see, the dead man's wounds gaped through the slashed Dallas Cowboys

Tee-shirt. His eyes were open, as though he were accusing the camera. He seemed ready to rise and avenge his death. A shiver ran over Michael's neck and shoulders. He looked away from the gaunt corpse's gaze and studied the rest of the photo. The blood pool in front of the body still didn't look right. His first impression hadn't changed. Someone had to be standing in front and a little to the right of the man who was killed. Their left shoe and pant leg would have been covered with blood. Going back to the photos of Jon, it was obvious no blood stained his faded jeans. Michael wrote a note about this on a long yellow pad Ms. Jones placed on the table beside him.

He put the murder pictures aside. The Lawyer said there were several hundred more. Michael couldn't imagine what else pictures could show.

There were several pages of notes in someone's tidy handwriting. The body had been found at 6:30 am behind the Soledad Bodega. Store clerk Fred Dunwoody found the dead man when he went out to have a smoke before he opened the store. The police arrived at 6:50 a.m. The patrolmen (McCafferty and Sanchez) found Jon holding the knife a short time later. Detective Garcia arrested Jon in the hospital when he woke at 11:15 am. He was noted to be uncooperative during his interrogation, refusing to speak English. They noted he was some sort of Indian. There was nothing in any of the reports to explain Jon's head injury.

Michael added some questions to the yellow pad. Why would Jon want to kill this man? Where was Jon's truck? How did he get to the Bodega? Were there any surveillance cameras in the area? Why didn't the report say why Jon went to the hospital?

Jon's hospital report said he had a mild concussion and a scalp laceration. Michael added, "Who hit Jon?" to the list of questions. He had no drugs in his system, but his blood alcohol was still measurable thirty hours after the crime. Michael scribbled more details on the notepad. The official chronicler wrote how an amount of the victim's blood type was found on Jon's left hand and cuff of his shirt. His picture showed that. No blood was recorded to be on Jon's shoes or pants. A single drop of the victim's blood type was on the right side of his shirt. There was a note about which photo showed that specific drop.

Michael asked Mrs. Jones to use the computer. He hadn't used one since high school, so after much fumbling, he found the picture of the blood drop. It was small and round, like a drip off the end of the knife. Michael visualized it falling on Jon as the real murderer placed the knife in his hand. Most of the blood on Jon's clothes was from his head wound. A hand-written sticky note said the DNA was being matched to the other blood samples found on Jon, per the defending attorney's request. Jon had tissue under the fingernails of his right hand. It was also being DNA typed, although the blood type was B positive, as was both the victim and Jon.

Dust sparkled in the light streaming through the window. Michael got another cup of coffee and contemplated the alley outside. A fat rat poked through the refuse heaped around the dumpster. *At least there are some living things that flourish in this city.*

Sitting again, he found a very official looking autopsy report. Simon Ortega died between 4:00 and 5:00 a.m. on the loading dock of the Soledad Bodega. The cause of death was described as exsanguination from an upward-thrusting knife wound that pierced his heart and opened his abdominal cavity. Michael almost asked Mrs. Jones for a dictionary to figure out the word exsanguination, but reading on, he realized it meant he lost a lot of blood. An attached diagram showed the blow had pierced the right side of Ortega's heart causing massive bleeding. The comment section said there were no hesitation marks and the blow was from lower right to upper left indicating a left-handed assailant.

Jon was right-handed.

Michael jumped up and went to The Lawyer's office. The older man was on the phone talking intently. Michael was too well raised to interrupt, so he backed out of the door jittering slightly.

"Good news?" Martha Jones inquired.

"I think so, ma'am."

"Is he busy?"

Michael nodded.

"He is one of the hardest working men I know. He has helped a lot of people. He never gives up." She had the set jaw of a person who believed what she said.

Throughout his childhood, Michael was taught to respect the experience of older people. He didn't want to disagree with the gray-haired lady. However, deep down, some evil part of his soul wanted to tell her The Lawyer gave up at least one time. He'd abandoned his child on a dusty road and never looked back.

Instead, Michael nodded respectfully, went back to the table by the window, so she couldn't see the muscle jumping in his jaw. He continued reading the reports. Simon Ortega's toxic screen was pending. The report repeated the cause of death due to the penetrating knife wound to his heart. Michael couldn't find any mention of scratches on the victim. Jon must have scratched the real murderer. He wrote that on his list. He didn't know why, was he going to run around Phoenix checking the arms of tall men until he found one with a scratch? Michael took a deep breath. He needed a plan.

Michael's butt was getting sore. He could still hear The Lawyer on the phone. Looking around, he saw a sign to the men's room. The corroded handle on the sink was rough against his hand. The pipes groaned before water sputtered out. He let it run for a moment before splashing his face. A handful of water rinsed his mouth. Michael enjoyed the clean taste before spitting it out and leaned on both hands to let the water drip from his face into the stained sink.

How can I help Jon? Right handed, left handed, who cared? It wasn't enough. Jon was an easy catch for the police. They would make sure he stayed in jail. How could he convince Detective Garcia his cousin was innocent. The detective didn't even believe Michael was Jon's family.

The Lawyer came in. "Is everything OK? Martha said you had an inspiration."

"Jon is right-handed, but the autopsy said the murder was done by a left-handed attacker," Michael said. "Didn't Detective Garcia notice that?"

"I think I should pay the District Attorney a visit. Detective Garcia hasn't been doing his job." The Lawyer's mouth was a thin line against his pale face.

"Before I meet Garcia again, I need to find Jon's truck and look at the place where the murder happened," Michael said.

"We have the crime scene photos."

"They aren't enough. I have to get the feel for the area. Talk to people and look for cameras."

The Lawyer gave Michael the address where they found Jon. "It's a bad area after dark, but it should be safe enough to walk around during the day."

They decided Michael would take his car and come back

later that afternoon. He could take Salina to find her brother before dinner.

"You might have trouble finding the place where the murder happened," The Lawyer said. "Let me get you a map of the city." Back in his office, he rummaged around one his desk and brought out a book with a wire spiraling through one side. On the cover was a sunset behind a spindly cactus with the words '*Greater Phoenix Area*' emblazoned on it.

"Is that supposed to be a Phoenix map?" Michael asked.

"Well, yeah," The Lawyer replied, looking puzzled. "It says so right here on the cover. You can read, can't you?" Michael made his face blank and said, "I can read," in the flattest voice he could manage.

"I'm sorry," Lawson sputtered. "It's just that the cover says--"

Michael rudely interrupted. He didn't care if this man thought he was raised poorly or not. *He thinks I'm a dumb Indian who can't read.* "I know what the cover says, but the picture is of a cactus that grows in the Chihuahuan desert. Phoenix is in the Sonoran desert. That cactus can't grow around here. The picture is from someplace else."

"Oh," The Lawyer said. "I didn't realize. I'm sorry. I just can't seem to say the right thing with you, can I? There is so much I don't know about you that I'd like to."

Michael looked him in the eye for a second. "I'd better get going." He went outside, slid into the man's comfortable car, and drove off.

He couldn't help but notice David Lawson standing at the window, watching him the whole time.

Chapter 18

CHINDI IN THE WIND

THE DRIVE TO THE MURDER SITE SHOWED MICHAEL PARTS OF Phoenix he'd never seen; not that it was much different from the parts he had seen. Television always makes cities seem so glamorous. He didn't watch television much, but what he did watch gave him an idea how big cities should look. Phoenix and Durango didn't resemble the towns on the TV at all.

Michael never really cared to spend time sitting inside, watching a machine. The family only had electricity in the winter when they moved the sheep down on the flats, and there were only two channels to watch in that area. Once he got the weather and the farm reports, Michael generally had work to do. His uncles watched basketball, but Michael always preferred to be playing the game himself. He imagined when he got old he'd probably enjoy watching TV more.

The aunties watched reality shows about white people. A few minutes of those stories were plenty for Michael, although the aunts went on for hours about the goings-on of people they'd never met. He never understood their interest in those folks, but since it made the aunties happy, who was he to judge?

Michael crossed the canal, a man-made river that stole water from the pastures to the north. The sun reflecting off the water made him squint. Even though it was high summer, the canal was full of life-giving water. Grandfather Jay told Michael when he was a boy, even the small rivers up north, like the San Juan, had water in them nearly all year long. Michael didn't remember seeing any river other than the Colorado, down in the Grand Canyon, with water in it more than a few months a year. Yet, here was this canal, a river to nowhere, diverting the life's blood away from his people.

He turned onto Indian School Road and passed miles of apartment buildings, trailer parks, and strip malls accented by an occasional Circle K or a 7-Eleven. Michael passed under the I-10 freeway and turned onto 17th Street. Parking wasn't a problem in the area behind the buildings where the murder actually happened. It was a dreary place even in the bright sunshine, a sorry place to die.

Several rats picked through trash piled along the fence. City rats were dark, heavy, and lumbered laboriously as they foraged. They showed little resemblance to their quick, tan desert cousins. The rats brazenly ignored Michael. He was in their territory. If a man posed a threat, they were confident of escape. Michael wished he were back on his own terrain where he knew how to find what he needed, where he was confident of his escape routes.

The reeking alley consisted of hard surfaces, dirty cement block walls, and the concrete docks behind the stores. Noise from the freeway a few streets over echoed eerily. A ten-foot high fence of corrugated tin was topped with barbed wire. Filthy, scarred dumpsters hemmed the back loading area of the businesses along this strip. For at least fifty yards, there were no gaps between the buildings. There were no trails to follow, nothing to track.

Everything is changed, Michael thought. All the trash is still here, but the trash bags have all been moved, scattered around. Someone was looking for something. Could the killer have dropped something? The police had found the knife. What else could he have lost?

A fat rat, carrying a piece of bread, scuttled into its nest in a pile of sticks and trash next to the fence separating the loading dock from the U-Haul storage lot. Another rat scuttled by and disappeared into the nest. Michael had an idea. Rats are always hoarding things they find in their nests. He walked over and pulled out a tire iron from behind the seat of his truck. Using the metal bar, he beat on the rats nest. A half dozen creatures scuttled out and ducked under the fence into the U-Haul lot. Michael flipped the main part of the nest over to expose the central chamber of the structure, A few more smaller rats ran out, disappearing under the fence. Using the iron he stirred the items the rats had collected. Most of it was filthy with rat excrement but a shiny piece of metal caught his eye. He gingerly reached in and pulled out a religious medallion, St. Anthony. The inscription on the back said, "Riley, know you are loved." He couldn't tell if it was what the killer had been looking for, but he put it in his pocket just in case. He'd ask The Lawyer about it, but he needed more. Michael began a spiral search in this strange wilderness. He went about it as though he were looking for the blood trail of a wounded animal, starting at the doorway where the body was found. It was the only way he could think of to find some trace or pattern to make sense of what happened.

He hoped the Chindi, the evil spirit of the dead man,

had fled the area by now. Maybe Chindi trying to possess a person was superstition, but a physics class in high school described a science law that said energy never could be destroyed. The energy that made a person alive needed to go somewhere when they died. Michael figured that energy was what the Diné called a Chindi. In any case, he held his breath in case the dead man's energy still lingered.

It looked as though someone had thrown a couple buckets of water and spread out the blood, but not really cleaned it up. The brown stain was obvious against the nearly white cement. Michael turned slowly, visualizing what Jon described to him, cool dark before dawn, silhouettes against bright light. The angle of the buildings hid the murder location from the nearby street. Unless they were actually in the loading area, no one could have seen the attack. At least Jon had been far enough away from the body so the Chindi wouldn't have invaded him and made him crazy...one less thing to worry about.

The bright sun glared off the cement loading dock and blocks of the buildings. There were doors staggered down the alley. Only two of the nearby doors had lights. At night, there would have been a lot of overlapping shadows. The pile of trash where Jon laid would have almost hidden him from sight. It looked just like the pictures the police took. The attack happened near the lighted doorway. Would the killer have been able to see Jon in the darkness beyond the light? Michael doubted it. Jon must have done something to draw the murderer's attention.

Michael started walking, testing doors along the alley as he passed. Most of the businesses were stores. Trying to get an idea of which direction the killer came from was useless. There was no way to tell while he was still behind the buildings. Reaching the street, he turned right and circled the block. Resettling his ball cap from the Tractor Supply in Tucumcari, Michael stopped and considered the area. There was a dead raccoon in the storm drain with big green bottle flies buzzing around. The fronts of the businesses were as dreary as the backs. A check cashing place, a liquor store, the Hair We Are beauty shop, and the Soledad Bodega faced a row of dusty apartment buildings. The only plants were some chickweed growing in the cracks along the edge of the street and an occasional spindly palm tree. No cars passed while he continued his trek. Michael could see the freeway over the tops of the buildings to the east. The roar of traffic was like the constant hum of angry bees.

His first stop, the Soledad Bodega, was a shabby place, cluttered with boxes full of cans and faded display cards. A rack of magazines featuring nude women graced the front of the counter. The clerk lounged on a chair watching a tiny TV. He couldn't have been more than twenty. Scraps of paper and stubbed-out cigarettes littered the floor at the clerk's feet. His face held a lot of metal--silver pins through his eyebrows, multiple rings in his nose and ears. Angry black and red tattoos covered his arms and hands.

Michael waited until two old Hispanic women waddled out of the store, and he was alone with the clerk. He bought some gum, and while the pincushion man made change, he asked, "Were you here when they found the body out back?"

The clerk absently scratched at the skull tattooed on the shaved side of his scalp. His clothes were crusty and dirty. Michael could smell his acrid stench from across the counter. "Yeah, I found him when I stepped out for a smoke. I liked to shit myself. I was out of there so fast I didn't even see the Indian they caught. I was lucky he didn't come after me." He scratched his collarbone with determined fingers. "What a mess. I had to clean up the dock after the cops got done. The owner went bug shit. You'd think I'd murdered the asshole."

"Nasty job. Did you move the trash bags and stuff when you were cleaning up? I noticed they were all shifted around like somebody lost something."

"Aw, Fuck. Was somebody digging in the trash and left a mess?"

"Looks like. Did you know the dead guy?"

"I seen him around. He was a junkie. They're always coming in to buy candy when they start jonesing."

"Uh huh." Michael wasn't sure what he meant, but the stinky guy wanted to talk.

"Junkies are always dying around here. This neighborhood's a black hole for junkies." His scratching had moved down his neck and centered under his AC-DC T-shirt in the vicinity of his left shoulder. "Everybody stumbles over a dead one, eventually."

Michael was starting to itch just looking at the guy. He resisted scratching. "Do you know who was working late the night of the murder?"

"Nobody was here. We always close up by ten when the real creepy-crawlies start coming out. It cuts down on robberies. Why do you want to know? You some kind of cop?"

"No, I was just wondering, because the police are framing my cousin for the murder. I'm trying to figure out who really did it, to get him out of jail."

"I thought it was the drunk Indian who did it? Is he your cousin?"

Michael nodded. "He didn't do it, but he was too drunk to remember what happened."

"That's fucked up, man." The clerk's scratching stopped, and he started to pick at his teeth.

Michael offered him a piece of gum. "You got any idea who's been killing the junkies?"

He took the gum, and shook his head. "I try to stay away from the crap out on the street."

"It's important I find something to help my cousin. He isn't doing well in jail."

"I'd like to help you, but I don't know nothing. I work seven to four. I'm out of here by the time most of the shit starts happening." He picked a scab on his arm. "You might try the guys at the liquor store or the bar a couple blocks over."

Before he left Michael pulled the metal medallion from his pocket and held it out to the clerk. "You see anybody wearing this?"

"Is that a St. Christopher?" The guy leaned over the counter and looked.

"I think it's St Anthony. It has the name Riley on the back," Michael said.

"Nah, I don't pay much attention to that religious stuff. I don't know anybody named Riley."

Michael thanked him and walked out into the hot sun. The State Liquor store was on the west end of the alley. It was probably where Jon got his bottle the night of the murder. The bottom four feet of the building's front was painted a dark red. The windows, screened by bars, had brightly colored posters advertising different beverages. Michael thought the simplest one was the prettiest. It had a goose silhouetted against a grey background. After admiring the poster for a minute, he pushed open the barred entryway and walked into a room walled with bottles. A cooler full of beer hummed along the longest wall. A short, round man lazed behind the counter opposite the beer. He looked Diné, but his surly glare and greasy thinning hair made Michael doubt The People were part of this man's heritage.

"What you want?" The man's accent was from considerably south of the Mexican border.

"Sir, I was wondering if you were working four nights ago when the man was murdered behind the Bodega?"

"Why the fuck do you want to know?" He rubbed his hands down the front of his pale yellow shirt, feeling the ribbed design.

"Well sir, they are accusing my cousin of the murder, but he didn't do it. I was hoping someone here saw him and could let the police know how drunk he was when the murder happened." Michael thought he'd try honesty, since he lacked any detective skills.

"We get murders around here all the time. We don't see too many white boys."

"My cousin is Navajo."

"Fucking dirty Indians! Piss on my walls. Puke on the floor. Let the cops have the fucker. He probably did it."

Goosebumps rose on Michael's arms. They had nothing to do with the air conditioner rattling in the window behind the counter. His right fist clenched. He had to consciously relax his muscles. It would do no good alienating this nasty little man. "Were you working the night of the murder?"

"Fuck no, I don't work nights. I own the place. You think I'm going to be here, a target for the assholes who come in here after dark?"

Michael looked around to calm himself. The light on a video camera winked at him. "Could I get a copy of the video tape from that night?"

"We got robbed the same morning. The cops got the CD." The little man narrowed his eyes. "Fucking police, they don't come down here till ten. Cletus called them at six. If they came right away they'd probably caught the bastard going down the street with my money. They don't care I get robbed. They are just as happy when the scum around here kill each other off. They..."

Michael cut him off before the rant could go any farther "Could you tell me who was working that night? Maybe I could talk to him. See if he remembers seeing my cousin."

The clerk's name, Cletus, came with another outburst of profanity describing the man in question's parentage and personal hygiene. Michael'd never heard anyone who wasn't drunk swear as much as this unpleasant little man. He decided to come back later to talk with Cletus.

Michael continued his search pattern determined to find Jon's truck. The next corner brought him to the opposite end of the strip mall, 17th Street. Apartments flanked a U-Haul rental lot which backed up to the fence behind the businesses where the murder happened. Two dead palm trees graced the entry to one of the apartments. There was more traffic here, and the fumes made his head ache. He finished his circuit of the block without the truck or any new insights. Conversations with a few people in the stores and an old woman he passed on the street yielded no information that would help Jon. Everyone he spoke to commented on how many murders happened in the neighborhood.

He walked a few more blocks in an ever-widening circle and worked his way into an area of shipping terminals and gas stations. A shabby bar stood alone in an empty field which served as its parking lot.

Jon's dusty truck sat parked at an angle to the building. Michael wondered how his cousin had walked so far when he'd been drinking. The bed of the truck contained dozens of beer cans and a couple of drained vodka bottles. Fast food containers littered the cab. The space under the seats was surprisingly empty, with only jumper cables and a lone beer can there. Michael hoped Jon hadn't gotten his tools stolen. He found the keys up under the springs of the seat where Jon usually stashed them. The engine chugged and died when Michael tried to start the truck. The gas gauge read empty. That explained why Jon had gone walking.

Trudging back toward The Lawyer's car, Michael wished he could hear the wind over the traffic noise. Heat waves made the mountains south of the city waver in an inviting way. He'd much rather be in the mountains than on the hot flats of the city. A buzzard drifted on the thermals over the nearby hills. He had an itchy feeling between his shoulder blades, as though someone were watching him. He stopped and looked around. *Who would be watching?*

A truck cruised by with a big, familiar looking man in the driver's seat. Michael shrugged and kept walking. His mouth tasted like it was full of greasy wool. If he were in the hills, he'd put a pebble in his mouth to draw some spit. None of the things lying along this road looked wholesome enough to taste, so he decided to stop and get something to drink.

Chapter 19
PROBABLE CAUSE

THE DARK COOLNESS OF THE SHABBY DINER WAS WELCOME after the city's reflected sunshine. A couple glasses of water and a Coke helped Michael rehydrate. He was deciding what he would say to the guys at the U-Haul before he went to pick up The Lawyer. The face of the man in the truck popped into his mind. He was the guy that bumped into him at the court. The one The Lawyer talked to. He wrote "What is the Lawyer's friend doing out in this part of town?" on his notepad.

It would have been nice if Salina were there. She could always find some reason to laugh, and her laugh made him happy. He needed something to give him joy these days and was glad she came with the aunts.

He dug the medallion out of his pocket and examined it closely. It was shiny and clean. It couldn't have been in the rat's nest more than a day or so. It was heavy for its size and looked to be gold, not a cheap piece of jewelry. He couldn't remember the significance of St. Anthony, but the name Riley could mean something.

The bell over the door rang. Detective Garcia and a tall

lean man with iron gray hair cut flat on top came in. Garcia's shiners were fading to yellow and green around the edges. He looked like a comic book bad guy. The two police sauntered over and sat across the table from Michael. The medallion lay on the table.

"Mr. Yazzie, fancy meeting you here." Garcia said.

Michael waited.

"What are you doing in the neighborhood?" the other man asked without introducing himself.

"I'm looking for my cousin's truck. I figured it would be in the area."

The men looked at each other trading some silent idea. "I heard you're working for Lawson. You know, I can arrest you for misrepresenting yourself the other night." Garcia rubbed behind his ear. "What does that carry, Tom? Six years for obstruction?"

"Yeah, if not more," the tall man drawled. He leaned back in his chair. He had a nasty looking bruise on his forearm.

Michael kept his face totally blank. Lawson said they couldn't arrest him if he were The Lawyer's agent. "I hadn't even met Lawson when I talked to you."

"Yeah, right. How are you related? You look enough like him to be his son." Garcia had narrowed his eyes, and his shoulders were set in a rigid line. Michael thought that expression must hurt with his two black eyes. The other man was relaxed in his seat, watching Michael like a fox at a gopher hole.

"I guess my relationship with David Lawson is my own business. I'm working with him now is what should concern you." Michael boldly looked Garcia in the eyes. "He tells me, once you finish investigating, you'll figure out my cousin didn't murder anyone."

"He tells you that, does he?"

"I'm sure you already read the report and noticed the murderer was left-handed and my cousin is right-handed." Michael threw that out to see how they reacted.

Garcia's back stiffened. The tall man didn't move. He was looking at the medallion on the table.

"I'm working as Lawson's agent, now. Maybe I can help with some of the details to catch the person who really committed the murder." The Lawyer actually told Michael that Garcia was incompetent, but he didn't think repeating it was going to win him any points with these guys. He scooped St. Anthony off the table and slipped it into his pocket.

The two detectives looked at each other and grinned. "You're going to help us?" The tall one smiled a coyote smile.

"If I can. Would it help you to see Jon's truck?"

"You found his truck?" Garcia looked skeptical.

"It's out of gas at the bar by the shipping terminal, a couple streets over." Michael couldn't help but add. "It wasn't hard to find."

He rode with the police in their unmarked car. A couple of buzzards circled lazily overhead as they went through Jon's truck. The tall one, whom Garcia finally introduced as Norris, worried him. He had a slick air.

"Well, well, it looks like we found probable cause here." Norris stood holding a small square cellophane packet. "I guess we'll need to get this checked out. Mr. Pete must have been buying. It was laying right there under the seat."

Michael's jaw muscles began to ache. That packet wasn't under the seat. He'd have seen it. He shouldn't have brought them to Jon's truck. They had their minds set. They'd decided to make up the evidence to convict Jon. "Wouldn't he have had it on him if he had been buying from the guy who got killed?"

"He probably made the buy and followed Ortega to rob him of the rest of his stash," Norris returned.

"Did you find drugs on the dead man?" Michael avoided using Ortega's name. He knew there were drugs on the body. Norris was making things up, so he must be desperate.

Garcia gave Norris a strange look. He was frowning. "I'll get the truck towed to the forensics lab. If we get Ortega's prints of it, Jon Pete is going down, no matter how much Lawson complains."

Chapter 20
DINER WITH JEAN

Michael told The Lawyer there was no drug packet when he found the keys.

"Son-of-a-bitch," Lawson shouted and slammed his hands on the desk. "I didn't think Garcia would stoop so low as to plant evidence."

"It was the tall detective, Norris, who said he found the drugs."

The Lawyer paced the narrow path through his office. "Norris is a seasoned detective. I don't know why he would plant drugs. Are you sure there was nothing when you looked?"

Michael nodded. "I shouldn't have shown them the truck. They weren't even looking for it. I don't want to go back to tell my aunts I'd made Jon's case worse."

"No, you did the right thing. Since you were acting as my agent, and I'm an officer of the court, you were obligated to report it. There was no way you could know they would plant drugs in the cab."

"How can we prove Jon innocent if they create evidence? Is this how the blind justice works?" Michael wanted to break something, but settled for clenching his fists until his fingers cracked. "I need some open-eyed justice."

"This pisses me off, too, but I can't just accuse Garcia of planting evidence without proof. It ends up your word against theirs, and you aren't credible because you're related to Jon. I can make a fuss about them threatening you in the restaurant...six years for obstruction, my ass. The case is far from over. We have the left-handed assailant issue and the lack of drugs in Jon's system. If we could prove Jon wasn't the only one behind the building, we should have more than enough reasonable doubt." "Another thing is, if Jon didn't have money for gas, how would he have money for drugs?" Michael said.

The Lawyer rubbed the back of his neck with one hand. "It would be normal behavior for a junkie or an alcoholic. I kind of like that you don't know that." He gave a grimace that passed for a smile. "I'll request the tape from the liquor store to make sure nothing on it will hurt the case. I have to petition for a court order to get it turned over, since it's evidence in another case. We just need to look at it. If the victim was in the store around the same time, it might look bad, as if Jon was stalking the guy." He sat back at his desk.

The Lawyer shifted to look at Michael more directly, and continued, "I doubt anything on the tape will be useful. Jon being there drunk doesn't help us. We need anything that can add to reasonable doubt that might give me enough to get the DA to drop the charges."

"I found this." Michael pulled out the medallion. "It looked like someone moved the bags Jon was laying on to look for something, so I looked around." Michael explained about the rat nest.

The Lawyer said, "I couldn't use this in court. It probably has nothing to do with the case." The look of disappointment on Michael's face must have registered with his father, who continued: "It was a good hunch though. Even if it can't be used in court, show it around. It might be a lead. You never know." "I'll go back tonight and talk to Cletus at the liquor store. Then, talk to more people in the area tomorrow. Maybe someone saw something that will help." Michael could feel the muscles in his shoulders forming knots as though he'd spent the day roping calves.

The Lawyer said, "You're right, nothing we can do right now. I'll write the petition to drop the case first thing tomorrow. Now, let's go home and see what your aunts have been up to."

The smell of mutton, squash, and bean stew met them as they got out of the car. Michael breathed deep, letting the familiar smell chase away the tension of the day. The Lawyer wrinkled his nose. The house was alive with bustling women.

Aunt Jean looked behind them expectantly as they entered the kitchen.

"Where's Jon?"

The Lawyer and Michael both looked at their feet.

Lila said, "Jean, you have to give them some time. You know how things work in the city. It always takes time."

"I'm going to talk to more people later tonight, Auntie," Michael said. He wasn't going to tell her he'd made things worse. He'd bear the burden on his own. "Try not to worry. I'm sorry I didn't do more today."

Jean hugged Michael briefly around his waist. Michael realized she only came up to his chin. She had never felt so tiny before. She quickly backed off and patted his cheek. "You sit, eat some good food." Then she smacked him on his shoulder. "And don't tell me what to do. I'll worry if I want to."

Salina, who was cutting chilis at the table, ducked her head to hide her smile.

The Lawyer was trying to sneak into the living room. "Davy," Jean said without turning.

He froze, briefcase in hand. "Yes, Jean."

She folded her arms and gave him "the look." Michael'd seen bucking horses go flat-footed from Aunt Jean's look. The Lawyer held up pretty well. He only cringed. "You come eat some stew and tell me when my boy is coming home."

"I...I have to wash up. I'll be right out." He fled to the bathroom.

Auntie Lila and Michael looked and each other and stifled grins.

Michael washed his hands in the kitchen sink and dished up a big bowl of stew. His eyes closed involuntarily as he chewed. The sweet goodness of the squash overcame the gamy, slightly bitter mutton. The beans and chilies stung his mouth in such a familiar way, tears welled behind his eyelids. Love in a bowl of stew. The aunts had made this alien place feel like home; just as they had made Michael a home his whole life.

The Lawyer didn't do a very good job of reassuring Jean. He just started talking lawyer language until her eyes glazed over. He praised her stew and took seconds, which surprised Michael. Most Belagáana he'd met disliked the taste of mutton. They preferred the sweet young lamb. He always thought it was a waste to eat lamb. An adult sheep has a lot more meat on it, even though mutton from an adult sheep tastes different.

"It's good to get a home-cooked meal," The Lawyer said. "It's been awhile." He sat back, rubbed his stomach, and belched.

"Maybe you can take Jon some stew in the jail tomorrow.

He'll get sick eating jail food." Jean didn't wait to hear if The Lawyer could do it. She bustled around preparing a bowl and covering it with foil.

The man looked at Michael, who just shrugged. He was in favor of anything to make Aunt Jean feel useful. He got up and put his bowl in the sink.

Salina washed the dinner dishes. Her habitual smile was present, but she'd been a lot quieter than Michael ever remembered. She gave him a raised eyebrow look, and tilted her head toward the door. She wasn't going to ask any questions in front of a strange white man, even if he was supposed to be Michael's father. She'd heard of the ghost man father.

Michael slipped out the door into the early dusk. The sky was streaked with pinks and oranges blending in a riot of momentary beauty. The thick green smell of the yard made him wrinkle his nose. A few minutes later Salina came out and stood beside him.

"How are you doing?" she asked. "Your father seems nice enough."

Michael shrugged. "I just need him to help Jon."

"Yeah." She touched his hand without looking at him.

"We should go look for Sam. When I saw him the other day, it seemed like he didn't want you and me together."

"He's not a happy drunk."

"Is anybody?"

Salina sighed. "We should try to find him before he gets too drunk. If he's too far gone, I'll never get him home."

"You'd drive back tonight?"

She shrugged. "Sam needs to be home. And I should get Hosteen Simon's Jeep back to him."

"I'm glad you came. I'm really worried about Jon." Michael stepped closer to her so his arm was touching hers.

She leaned into him and put her head on his shoulder. "We should get going."

"Yeah."

They stood together, not moving until the brilliance of the sunset faded to a soft glow. Without a word they went back into The Lawyer's kitchen made homey by the bustling presence of his aunts.

"Salina and I are going to look for Sam," Michael said. "Then I'd best go down to the liquor store and talk to the guy who might have seen Jon the other night."

"I'll go with you," The Lawyer jumped up like a prairie dog smelling a fox. "I'd hate for you to get lost. We can take my car."

I thought he was really trying to avoid being alone with Jean. Aunt Lila hid her smile behind her hand. She must've had the same thought.

Jean nodded wisely. "You go on with them, Davy. We don't need to lose any more youngsters in this big city."

Chapter 21

CORONER'S TAKE

GARCIA YAWNED AND RUBBED HIS EYES WITH CLOSED FISTS. He'd skipped breakfast, and the small office barely contained his pacing. The coroner's report on the Ortega murder gave him more questions than answers. The Indian's truck didn't have any of the victim's prints, and he had a bad feeling about the drugs found under the seat. He'd noticed how clean the floor of the truck was when they'd started the search. He'd looked under the seat. He could have missed the packet. He must have missed it. Norris was a great cop. He was a legend on the force.

Garcia's excess energy shoved him toward the coffee machine when he heard Norris' voice. "The dammed drug dealers are the reason this city is going to hell. I'd just as soon give the Indian a knife and send him out to get another one."

Hearing the senior detective talking about his case, Garcia smiled. He wouldn't have planted the dope. He just wished the case didn't have so many holes in it. He needed to tie up some loose ends, or the DA would be up his butt, and he didn't need another nick on his record. What he needed was an objective opinion.

Fortified with coffee and camaraderie, he walked the couple of blocks down Jefferson, to search out his friend Sally. As a medical examiner, she had a good eye for details. He trusted her judgment. Besides, she had no dog in his hunt like Norris and the other detectives who seemed to want to make the evidence fit, no matter how thin it was.

The Maricopa County medical examiner's morgue was a series of nondescript rooms one floor below the airy, glass front, arched ceiling entry. The architect's reason for the lofty entrance escaped Garcia. Maybe it helped with the ventilation upstairs. While he waited for Sally, he tried to breathe as little as possible. No matter how much they disinfected the place, it always smelled of corpse. He loved how on cop shows, the coroner was always in the same building as the precinct. He'd attended the autopsy of a guy who had been fished out of the canal. The smell was so bad he couldn't get it out of his clothes, even after they were dry cleaned. He had to throw them out. Wouldn't that be a wonderful smell to have in the precinct every day? On the other hand, it might be a way to deter drunks and nuisance complaints.

Sally had the face of a teenage cheerleader, curly blond hair, a button nose, and phlox blue eyes. The smile she bestowed on Garcia was the stuff of dreams. However, below the chin, she resembled the Michelin man, with rolls of fat jostling for position as she waddled down the hallway.

"Rudy, my Latin heartthrob, have you decided to leave your wife and take me away from all this glamor?"

"You know you're my best girl, Sally. If it weren't for the kids, it would be you, me, and a beach in Tahiti." Garcia's smile was genuine.

"I just love a man who's full of shit." Sally smiled wearily back. "What can I do for you today?"

"It's about the Ortega case. I need your inestimable opinion on what happened. You know, the stuff you can't put in the report."

"I did the autopsy, but I've had a half-dozen since his. Come to my office. I'll pull the file." She lumbered to her cubicle.

Following her, Garcia thought, not for the first time, what a shame the rest of her doesn't match the face. As much as he loved Antonia, the beach in Tahiti would be tempting.

"Are you sure it was a left-handed assailant? Could it have been a righty using his left hand?"

"It was a clean, sure stroke. I don't see any way it was a right-hander." She frowned. "I remember thinking this was a practiced blow. The guy you're looking for knew what he was doing."

"You think it might have been somebody in the medical field?" Rudy asked.

"Probably not. A half inch to the right and the doer would have missed the artery and there wouldn't have been as much mess. But, the way he pulled the knife out eviscerated the guy. I'd lay odds he'd done something like this before."

"How about the evidence from the suspect?"

"Well," she said flipping through the crime scene photographs. "I'm not a blood spatter specialist, but I'd say the assailant had to have a lot of blood on his or her lower legs." She held out a photo. "Your perp has the victim's blood on him." She picked up another picture. "It looks as if the blood dripped on him rather than spattered from the victim. These pictures say he wasn't close to the actual murder."

"What do you mean he wasn't close to the murder? He was holding the bloody knife." Rudy rubbed a hand through his hair.

"We have a clean set of his prints on the knife. They were right-handed, but the prints were upside down on the handle. There is no way he made the death blow. If you ask me, he was there, but what we have doesn't really support this guy as the murderer. What did he see?"

The cute wrinkle between her brows that accompanied her inquiring look was lost on Garcia.

Shit, shit, shit, Garcia thought. "He didn't see anything. He was drunk on his ass."

Chapter 22

A FEELING IN THE BONES

MICHAEL WAS SO DEPRESSED AT BREAKFAST, EVEN AUNT Jean's special fry cakes and the sight of Salina fresh from the morning couldn't cheer him up. The Lawyer chatted with the aunties as though the three of them ate breakfast together every day.

Last night was a total bust. They couldn't find Sam Tsosie at any of the bars Navajo usually frequented, so they'd dropped Salina back at The Lawyer's house. On the way to the liquor store, The Lawyer and Michael had a long, awkward ride in the dark. The Lawyer tried to chat and be Michael's buddy. Michael didn't give him anything but yes and no answers. Even so, the older man kept talking. Michael figured he was trying to get in his head to suck out his soul, so Michael kept his mouth shut. It wasn't going to happen.

At the liquor store, they met Cletus the night clerk. He was a huge moose of a man with skin so dark he looked blue-black in the store's harsh fluorescent lights.

Cletus' voice vibrated Michael's bones as much as his ear drums. "We got robbed about six in the morning, just before I was supposed to get off. I was out from the cage putting out stock and a son-a-bitch come in with a shotgun. I gave him the cash. I ain't risking nothing for the old greaser who owns this place."

Michael agreed how bad he thought it was, and how Cletus did the right thing not trying to stop the thief. The Lawyer showed him a picture of Jon.

"I remember seeing a half dozen Indians that night. Can't say for sure if one of them was your cousin." Shown the picture of the dead man, he denied seeing him as well. The big man shifted from foot to foot and looked at the floor, only glancing at Michael when his gaze shifted around the room.

The more Michael thought about it, the less he believed Cletus. The man answered too quickly, as if it was something he'd rehearsed. Michael wished he knew how to coax the truth from people. The Lawyer was no help. Cletus kept glancing at him out of the side of his eyes. They said their good-byes when a customer came in.

The evening's final stop was the bar where he'd found Jon's truck. No one remembered Jon, and the bar's video camera only looked at the cash register. To top off the evening, while they were inside, a drunk threw up in the bed of Michael's truck.

The next morning after breakfast, Michael washed the puke out of his truck. He didn't need the sun to bake it on permanently. The muffler needed looking at too, so he crawled underneath to re-wire the can to the rusted pipe. He didn't speak when he heard Aunt Lila talking to The Lawyer. They were in the little yard behind the house and couldn't see him.

"He's afraid of you. His only memory is you driving away and leaving him."

"You know why I didn't come around, Lila. I was a mess when his mother died. I wasn't doing him any good. Then the Army sent me to Germany and law school. Time just slipped away."

"Maybe that was a reason then, but you've been back for years. He needed to know you. He's a good boy. He would have understood. You didn't give him a chance."

"I know. It breaks my heart. I went and watched him at school. I couldn't bear to talk to him. He has his mother's eyes."

"He has her good heart, too. You have lost as much as he has by not getting to know him."

"I have nobody to blame but myself."

"That's true."

Aunt Lila was never one to mince words.

Chapter 23

DOING LUNCH

Michael fiddled around under the truck until The Lawyer drove away. The day was already heating up, so he went inside. There was nothing to do except think of the dozen or more chores that needed doing back home. Plopping down at the kitchen table, he shook out the sports section of the Phoenix Sun. What the Dallas Cowboys were doing didn't cheer him up. Basketball was more his game. There was no mention of the Mesquite Rodeo. Switching to the business section, the livestock prices were even more depressing. Michael couldn't keep his mind off of the conversation he'd overheard outside.

Salina was airing out the dusty baby room, the bedroom where the women were staying. Jean was scrubbing the kitchen. "Our sister would never keep her kitchen like this. Davy should be ashamed. Look at this oven," she grumbled as she clattered around the room, banging pots and slamming cupboards.

The smell of beans cooking made Michael's mouth water. She would simmer them all day, occasionally adding spices. He wasn't hungry, but his stomach made an involuntary noise at the thought of their fiery goodness.

He neatly folded the newspaper sections he'd finished and passed them to Lila to read. He sat up a little straighter when he started the main section of the paper. "This article says there have been a lot of drug dealers and prostitutes getting killed in Phoenix," he said to his aunt.

The reporter was thorough. She'd even included a little map showing the locations of the dead girls and dealers. There were twelve little X's clustered around the west side of the central city. Most were within two miles of the bar where he'd found Jon's truck. All of the people were killed with knives. None of the murders had been solved. The point of the article was that the police didn't seem to be doing much to find the killer, or killers, because the victims were poor and lived in a bad area.

"The boy at the Bodega said a lot of junkies were killed in the area," Michael said. "If they were killed with a knife, maybe the same person who killed them, murdered the man they blamed on Jon."

"I bet it was the same person. He made it look like my boy killed that man," Jean chimed in from the kitchen. She'd raised five kids and a passel of strays like Michael. Jon and he used to joke she had bat ears. She never missed a thing.

Lila gave him a look with raised eyebrows and he handed her the article.

"I wonder if it would be a good idea to talk to the lady who wrote this?" Michael asked.

"It couldn't hurt. Let's ask your father during lunch," Lila replied.

"We're having lunch with The Lawyer? What time is he coming?" Michael wished the aunts would fill him in when they made plans.

"We are meeting him in the Star Diner," Jean chimed in from the kitchen. Eating in a restaurant was a treat for her.

THE DINER WASN'T CROWDED WHEN THEY ARRIVED. THERE were only six people scattered at the tables in front of the counter. The Lawyer was waiting at one of the back tables. His briefcase was beside his chair. He rose as they walked in and gestured for them to join him. Lila sat next to Lawson, Jean and Salina sat across and Michael pulled up a chair on the outside. Jenny was their waitress and she smiled at Michael when she brought menus. "Welcome back," she said.

He should've introduced his aunts and Salina, but she rushed off to pour coffee for a fat woman wearing orange pants.

"So, Davey, when can we bring my boy home?" Jean started as soon as she sat down.

"Jean, we talked about this. It will take some time. I was able to get a court date to start his trial." The Lawyer took Jean's hands in his. Her rough brown hands with their wrinkles and distended veins were a sharp contrast to The Lawyer's smooth, soft white ones. "But, it won't be for another two months."

"What?" Jean shouted, attempting to jerk her hands away. The Lawyer held on. He probably knew Aunt Jean well enough to realize there were too many available projectiles on the table. Aunt Jean was a thrower. Michael heard Jon often say the family had no plates left from his childhood, because Jean'd broken them all when she got mad at his dad. Jon always said it was a good thing she had a bad aim, or he would have been orphaned at a young age.

"Isn't there any way to make the trial sooner?" Aunt Lila asked with concern in her voice. "Jon has already been hurt in jail. I'm worried he can't last two months."

The Lawyer still held Jean's hands, but now he was rubbing them gently with his thumbs. Tears ran down the stoic faces of both the aunts.

They both turned away when Jenny came back with menus. They wouldn't let a stranger see their tears. When she asked for drink orders, Michael said, "We'll all have coffee." He made a circling gesture around the table.

"Sure, I'll be right back."

Michael watched her bounce off, ponytail bobbing.

Salina scrutinized the interplay and gave Jenny's retreating back a look that should have caught her hair on fire.

Michael pulled a few napkins from the dispenser and set them in the middle of the table. "They have really good pie here."

"That's right," The Lawyer chimed in. He released Jean's hands. "Their soups are good, too."

The napkins disappeared, and the aunts surreptitiously rubbed their eyes.

"Jon's a tough boy. He'll do what he has to do," Jean said, with an air of finality. "I want a cheeseburger and some of those sweet pickles. What is a key lime pie?"

Michael smiled at Jenny as she came to take their orders. She put her hand on his shoulder as she leaned in to place cups of coffee around the table. Jean and Lila both gave her their most disapproving looks. She was lucky her hair really didn't burst into flame under the elder women's gaze. Jenny noticed the glares and straightened to take orders. Salina made a snorting noise through her nose and pointedly looked out the window.

"I'll be right back with your meals." Jenny hurried off.

"You and Michael should go talk to the reporter who wrote this story," Jean said, shoving the newspaper in front of The Lawyer. "Her name is Carol Kowalski. Is that a Pollack name?"

The Lawyer shifted like he had gas.

Lila put her hand on her sister's arm. "Jean, Pollack isn't a nice term."

"So what, it's just a word for a description of a person from Pollackland. They call us Indians, and we're Diné. I never been to India. But, you remember the boy from India who ran the 7-Eleven in Shiprock? He looked Diné, so I see how people could think we're Indians."

Aunt Jean could circle a topic like a buzzard.

Lila stopped her in mid-flight. "I remember him and you're right. Regardless, the country is Poland, and...David, what do they call the people from there?

"Polish."

"Pollack is not a nice word in English, so don't use it."

We were lucky Aunt Lila was there. Without Lila, Auntie Jean would have probably started a tirade that took in all non-Diné, as well as their associated ancestors.

The Lawyer picked up the paper and scanned the article. "It might be a good idea to go see her," he said after a few moments. "Let me call a friend I have at the Sun." He pulled out his cell phone. He left the table for a few minutes. When he returned, he said, "We're going to meet the reporter for dinner tonight."

"Good," Aunt Jean said. "We going to eat here, again? The service isn't so good." She said it loudly enough, Jenny stiffened as she set plates on the table next to ours.

Michael blushed like a scalded hog. "Auntie."

"I embarrass my nephew," Jean said, leaning back and poking the old white man at the table behind her.

"That's what we're here for, to embarrass the young folks," he said.

Jean gave a cackling laugh and slapped the table.

The aunts started reminiscing about how the clan treated The Lawyer when he started dating Michael's mother. Michael let his attention wander, so he was looking right at the door when the cops, Garcia and Norris, walked in with another man who was nearly as tall as Norris. The unknown man had hard eyes. They tracked around the room, classifying everyone there. Norris said something to the third man and his laser eyes met Michael's. By habit, Michael seldom looked into another man's eyes, but he met this man's gaze as though it were a challenge. If he'd been a dog, his hackles would have risen involuntarily.

"What is it, boy?" Aunt Lila's voice lowered with concern. Jean was continuing a story about Frank Asanie, the Ute, who tried to win her sister away from The Lawyer.

"Nothing, Auntie."

"Hmmm?"

"The policemen who are investigating Jon's case just came in."

"Who are they?" Jean dropped her story in mid-sentence. She was as alert as a beagle. She stood and looked around.

Michael tried to sink into his seat.

The Lawyer turned his chair to survey the room. "The tall one with the gray hair and the Hispanic guy," he said. His smile was the widest Michael'd ever seen. He stretched in his chair and slung his arm over the back.

Jean narrowed her eyes assessing the three men. "The tall one has a flat head. Order me apple pie. I'll be right back." She marched over to their table, a freight train bearing down on an unsuspecting steer.

Michael tried not to watch, but like anyone seeing a wreck, he couldn't stop himself.

Aunt Lila sighed and took a sip of her coffee.

Jean snagged the extra chair at Garcia's table. "You arrest my boy?" She plunked herself down.

The men looked at each other.

"Who's your son, ma'am?" Garcia asked.

Norris gave Michael a look that should have seared his skin. The other man ignored Aunt Jean and gestured to the matronly waitress who was serving that end of the diner.

"He's Jon Pete. Someone framed him for a murder. When you going to figure out who did it and let my boy go home? He's got chores to do." She waited patiently while Garcia squirmed his way to an answer.

"Ah, Mrs. Pete, I'm afraid I can't discuss your son's case. Why don't you talk to Jon's lawyer?" He raised his chin toward our table. The Lawyer smiled and held his hand up and waved by wiggling his fingers.

"I talk to David plenty. I'm talking to you now. Why you think Jon killed that man? He was too drunk to walk. How's he going to kill some guy? You don't find drugs in Jon, why would he mess with a drug dealer?" She stood up and put her hands on her hips. "It don't make sense my boy killed anyone. You aren't looking for the real murderer because an Indian boy who was too drunk to see straight is easy. Don't be lazy. TV police figure out who really kills somebody in one hour, why you taking so long?"

Norris spoke up, trying to calm my agitated aunt. "Now, mother, most boys have secrets from their moms. Maybe you don't know everything your son was up to."

Michael heard Aunt Lila's intake of breath. The Lawyer's

coyote grin got wider, and he chuckled quietly. Salina put a hand over her eyes.

"Don't call me 'mother.' I wouldn't own a child like you." Jean puffed up like a horned toad. "Maybe your momma didn't know you, but I know my boy, and I got some common sense. How about you? That man was gutted like a pig, and Jon didn't have no blood on him. Did you even see if the man you think my boy killed was like the other drug murders in Phoenix? Big story in the newspaper. Don't you read? All those murders happen, and my Jon is no place near Phoenix?"

Garcia rolled his eyes at Norris. Michael winced in anticipation of what was coming.

"Don't you roll your eyes at me, boy. You treat your momma like this? You should be ashamed. You and Flat Head here are embarrassed because you know I'm right. Be big men and make faces at an old lady."

Both men found things around the room to look at. The third man watched Jean intently.

She ignored him. "You finish your lunch and go figure out how to let my Jon out of jail." Jean stalked back to their table. A scattering of applause broke out from a couple people around the diner. Michael noticed a uniformed policeman smiling behind his hand.

"Where's my pie? I told you the service was no good here." She flounced into her chair.

"I'll get it." Michael jumped up and caught Jenny at the counter. "Could I get a couple pieces of apple pie? She's a little upset. Please don't take what she says personally."

"Don't worry. I'm used to it." She handed him little plates of pie. Jenny's smile was one of the nicest things about her. Michael tried to lose himself in her smile, but as he turned, the quiet man with Garcia and Norris was watching him. A shiver ran down his back.

Chapter 24

A FEELING IN THE GUT

After the Indian woman was finished, Garcia was quiet through the rest of lunch. She reminded him of his grandmother, a sensible woman who had never suffered fools. *Am I a fool?* The little round lady had touched almost all of his qualms about the Ortega murder. His mood didn't get any better as she gave him a scalding look on her way out.

"Don't let the old lady get to you," Norris said as he patted Garcia on the shoulder. "She was with Lawson. He does all the bleeding heart stuff for the Indians. He probably sent her over to mess with you."

"Did you notice how much the blond kid looked like Lawson?" Phil Davis asked. They watched the lawyer's group leave.

"Damn, partner, you must be an honest-to-God Detective to notice a detail like that," Norris replied. "The kid's working with Lawson, doing background for the Ortega case. He's an amateur."

"He came in to check on Pete before the arraignment. Said he was Pete's cousin." Garcia mused. "He found Pete's truck."

"He and our killer were probably running buddies. Pete told him where the truck was," Davis said.

"Yeah, Lawson's just throwing shit at the wall to see what sticks. He's running the kid as a distraction, trying to shake up the DA's case." Phil Davis tried to reassure the younger detective. He stood up and pulled out his wallet. "Come on, Garcia, we need to get back to the salt mines. Make the taxpayers happy."

They left a nice tip for the waitress and filed out. Garcia was getting a feeling in his gut which had nothing to do with the food from the Star Diner.

THE AFTERNOON STAFF MEETING WASN'T AS BORING AS USUAL. The article in the Phoenix Sun had the Lieutenant chewing everyone a new asshole over the drug dealer murders. None of the homicide detectives were spared his wrath. Almost everyone had at least one unsolved case from that pile.

Phil Davis was doing court for another few days, so the Lieutenant officially paired Norris with Garcia and put them in charge of a small task force correlating all the drug-related murders.

"You have three days to give me something to satisfy this reporter's accusations. Make it a priority."

The group routinely went through the major cases. It seemed as if a lot of crimes were being solved. Rudy was looking down when the boss finally turned to him. "Garcia, how's the Ortega case?"

"After reviewing the coroner's report, I have some questions about my perp." He still didn't look up from his notes. "The evidence is getting thinner. I need a long talk with the DA, and I need to put a rush on the DNA that was collected." He glanced up briefly.

"You're bringing up this crap now?" The Lieutenant's eyes nearly disappeared in his frown. "Do you have any alternative suspects?"

Rudy's neck ached. "Not at this time. I'm going to go back to the scene and see if I can come up with new leads."

The Lieutenant's frown lines deepened perceptibly.

"Sounds like a plan that should have been implemented before the guy was indicted. Get it done."

GARCIA CLOSED HIS DOOR GENTLY AND DELIBERATELY. He didn't want to get the reputation for being a hothead. Slamming his door once in a week was plenty. Closing his eyes and breathing deeply wasn't doing much to calm his jangling nerves. He jumped when the phone rang. *Some kind of fearless defender of the public I am.* The moment he heard the voice on the phone, his muscles relaxed.

"Mi amor, don't forget, I invited Ray for dinner again tonight. I worry about him being alone so much."

"You have the best heart, my wife. That's why I love you so much."

"Sweet talk isn't going to get you anywhere with me, darling. You still need to be home by six."

Antonia's mellow voice, along with the sound of the kids squabbling in the background, worked a miracle on Garcia's peace of mind. He could handle anything. "I have some news, mi Corazón. They put me on a task force."

"That's wonderful. They are finally smart enough to see what a great detective you are."

"I think it's more like they didn't have anyone else available."

"It will give you a spotlight."

Rudy nodded to the phone. "Maybe. Or maybe it's just going to be more work."

"Wait until Ray hears. I bet he's going to be jealous."

"I want to talk with him about it. It's a big case, he should have some insights. I know he's going stir crazy at home. He won't mind me bouncing ideas off him." Garcia's mind was already evaluating how to organize the information from the multiple murders. "Don't worry, dear, I'll be home early tonight."

Chapter 25

U-HAUL

AFTER LUNCH, MICHAEL TOOK THE AUNTS BACK TO THE Lawyer's house and he and Salina went searching for her brother. He seldom knew what a woman was thinking, and Salina's silence as they made their way to the truck made him wary.

"Sam might be staying with relatives. Do you have any family living down here?" he ventured.

"My father's cousin stays over by the Salt River. We could try their house."

She and Michael consulted The Lawyer's map and started off.

After a few miles they turned onto the highway.

"There sure are a lot of people in this town." Michael said.

"It's a city. Cities have lots of people. That's why they're called cities." She folded her hands primly in her lap.

"Mmhmm. Do you want the radio on?"

"No."

"Are you mad at me? Did I do something wrong?"

Michael glanced at her sitting rigidly in the seat, her back straight and stiff.

"Who's that girl at the diner?"

"Huh?" He didn't understand the topic shift.

"The blonde you were flirting with."

"Jenny? She's just the waitress. I wasn't flirting. I was trying to be polite because Aunt Jean was so rude to her." He felt heat rise in his face when he remembered his musings the first time he ate at the diner.

Salina snorted a rude sound. "Looked like flirting to me."

"I was just being polite." His eyebrows pushed his cap up. "I'm always nice to waitresses. They have a hard job."

"So you always flirt with waitresses?"

"I wasn't flirting! That girl is no different than the waitress back home." He couldn't imagine flirting with Mrs. Martinez, the waitress at the Kayenta Truck Stop Restaurant. She was as wide as she was tall and always smelled of chewing tobacco.

"If you say so."

"I say so."

They continued the drive in silence. Michael concentrated on driving, occasionally throwing glances at Salina. She pointedly looked out the passenger side window.

They turned onto a street full of ramshackle houses. Someone had whittled the number of her father's cousin's house into a post near the road. The low-roofed cinder block building was all sharp angles, from the walls to the two-bar covered dusty windows. The sun beat down on the patch of land devoid of trees. Two cars in various stages of disrepair lay canted in the front yard. A scattering of plastic children's toys strewn randomly around added color to the sun-washed scene. A yellow mongrel dog lay in the meager shade of the car missing the most parts.

"I don't see Sam's car anywhere," Michael said.

"He rode down with Jon. When we find him, I'll drive him back in the Jeep."

There was no distinction between the road and the yard, so Michael pulled in facing the black hole of the open door. The dog didn't look up. A curtain fluttered in the right-hand window. Michael turned the car off as Salina fanned herself with a newspaper. After a more than polite ten minute wait, a squat woman waddled out of the door leaning on a cane. Her grey-streaked hair was pulled back in a tail and bound with blue yarn.

"This is the right place," Salina said as she popped the door and climbed out to greet the woman.

Michael followed, slowly, giving them a few moments to catch up. He greeted her in Navajo, and gave his name and lineage as was the custom.

"You're a nice boy, polite. We don't see that so much here in the city. Come in. We'll sit." She shuffled back into the maw of the house.

Inside, furniture, boxes, children's toys, and piles of clothing covered most available surfaces. A trail wound through the clutter ending at a sagging sofa, a mismatched chair, and two child-sized pallet beds. A radio mumbled barely audible mariachi music in another room. A nimble girl brought in glasses of coke and silently handed them to Michael and Salina before scampering out. A different girl with squinty eyes brought a plate with three fry cakes. Mrs. Tsosie offered the cakes, and they declined.

Michael sat patiently, waiting for the conversation to move from family matters and general gossip to a possible location for Sam. When the third offer for them to eat the fry cakes came, Michael was happy to have something to do. He took the flat pastry and shook off the excess sugar. The women's conversation faded to the background in anticipation. He loved fry cakes. The first bite of this one, though, made him gag involuntarily. He turned it into a cough, and surreptitiously spit the cloying mass into his hand. It tasted bitter. He couldn't imagine how anyone could mess up fry cakes. He excused himself and went outside, pretending to control his coughing. Out in the yard, he crouched and pretended to pet the dog while slipping the mutt the remaining cake. The dog didn't seem to mind the flavor and it wolfed it down in a flash.

A ball rolled to his feet, followed by a toddler of undetermined gender in a sagging diaper.

"Hello, little one," Michael said still balancing over his heels. "Is this your ball?" He picked it up and handed it to the child who stepped back and regarded him solemnly.

"Ba"

"Jush," Michael said in Navajo.

"Juh," the kid said.

The ball flew at Michael's head. He caught it and tossed it gently back to the little one and received a smile showing two teeth and a lot of drool. They tossed the ball back and forth for a few minutes before the toddler lost interest and wandered toward the house.

When he stood up, he saw Salina climbing into the truck. He quickly joined her.

"Sam's been staying here with our aunt and working on a construction site over on Baseline road. We should be able to find him there." She handed Michael a map scrawled on an oil-stained paper plate.

"Do you think he'll come home?"

Salina looked out the window at the sad houses and

barren sun drenched dirt. "I don't know." Her fists were balled on her thighs. "Would you talk to him?"

Michael bit his lip and steered around a low-slung car driving ten miles an hour and blaring heavy metal music. "I'm not sure he wants to listen to me. The last time I saw him, he told me to stay away from you."

"He what?" Salina's back straightened.

Michael shrugged. "He was pretty drunk."

"Who does he think he is, telling you to stay away from me?"

Michael didn't risk answering. Uncle Leon warned him about poking sleeping bears and venturing opinions to angry women. In either situation, a fella was likely to lose a hand.

"He better hope it was drunk-talk, because if he thinks he can decide who I see, he is going to find out first-hand how I can take care of myself. Then he's going to be looking for his teeth." She pounded her thigh. "He's always been so bossy. He's my brother. He doesn't own me."

This was a side of Salina Michael'd never seen before. People told him she had a temper, but she'd always been sweet and accommodating when they were together. Some guys might think a woman flushed with anger is sexy and exciting, but not him. He concentrated on his driving and tried to think of a way to change the subject. "Did your uncle get Sam the construction job?"

"Sam's probably drunk up all the money he made. My aunt says he didn't even bring any food, and he's been there a couple of weeks."

"I hear jobs pay better here in the city. I imagine Sam is doing OK." Michael turned onto Baseline Road and craned to see the landmarks drawn on the scrap of paper. They passed the Circle K and the hotel with the waving cowboy.

"Sam better be making good money. Mr. Simon's Jeep uses a lot of gas and we had to stop twice to put oil in it when we came down." She gnawed a hangnail on one hand, and pounded her thigh with her other fist.

He needed to break Salina's negative attitude, to help her find Hozoh, the beauty in the world. Her angry comments poured salt on his already wounded soul. The problem was, there was nothing in sight remotely beautiful. His gaze centered on a couple of birds circling in the cloudless sky. "Are those Harris hawks?" he asked. "I heard they mate for life and always hunt in pairs."

Salina craned her neck to look at the birds. "Those are just buzzards. Something must be dead over behind those buildings. Oh, look. There's the place Sam's working." She pointed to a half-finished building with a crane. Men in hard hats swarmed like ants.

Michael sighed and turned into the construction site. He sure didn't want to be Sam Tsosie right now. Maybe the buzzards had foreknowledge of impending doom.

Salina was out of the truck as soon as it stopped. She strode through the workers, making a bee line for Sam, who was carrying a stack of two-by-fours. Michael got out and leaned against the fender trying not to look at the scene playing out between brother and sister. He failed, along with most of the men on the job. Sam let the ends of the boards settle on the ground behind him and balanced the long ends on his shoulder. Salina, hands on hips, stopped in front of him. Her mouth moved furiously.

Michael heard the occasional low vowel sound. She was speaking in Navajo which makes it hard to sound truly nasty, but from her expression, she was making a good effort. Sam visibly withered, his shoulders hunched, his head hung. Michael was glad he wasn't in the line of that verbal barrage. The work crew, mostly white guys, were going about their business casting curious sidelong glances at the angry, but beautiful, girl.

Sam nodded repeatedly, never looking at his sister. His head hung lower with each nod as if the weight of her anger were crushing him. The boards on his shoulder splayed like a giant feathered headdress. He turned away from her to straighten them. Salina threw up her hands, turned on her heel, and stalked back to the truck. She got in without a word. Michael tilted his head to Sam, who stood, flat-footed, watching his sister. He waved a hand at Michael and hoisted the boards back to his shoulder. He was on his way up the stairs into the building when Michael started the truck.

Salina had an ugly set to her mouth. "He says he wants to stay here. Can you believe it?"

"Well, he has a job. There's not much work back home this time of year."

"He's probably got some white girl he's courting. He'll break our mother's heart."

"I didn't see him with anyone the other day."

"Then he's going to spend all his money drinking and die a drunk. What will our mother say?" She rocked forward and back. A tear rolled down her cheek.

Michael pulled into a 7-Eleven parking lot and shifted into park. "Sam's a grown man. He has to make his own way in the world." He reached a tentative hand toward her shoulder.

She shrugged his hand away. "He's got no more sense than a frog." She dropped her face into her hands. "I promised Mother I would bring him home. She couldn't bear to lose Sam. Not after what happened to our other brother." She wouldn't speak the name of their younger brother, who froze to death two winters ago, lest she draw his spirit.

Michael took a deep breath. "Maybe he'll do OK. He has a chance to make some good money. He'll come home when he's saved enough for a truck of his own." Most guys Sam's age wanted a truck.

Salina put her hands up and turned her face to the side window. Michael put the car in gear and drove back to The Lawyer's house. He tried to get her to talk, but she just shook her head.

At the house, she got out. "Thanks for helping me, even if my brother is a big stupid."

"I wish I could have done more," Michael offered.

She walked away without looking back. Michael shrugged and drove away. The aunties would do what they could for Salina. He was useless when it came to dealing with an upset woman.

He drove back to the murder scene. The sky was littered with clouds, but it didn't smell as if it would rain. He parked and climbed to the loading dock and stood looking for a window where someone might have been able to see the loading dock. No windows were visible in any of the buildings he could see, but a box just under the awning of the U-Haul behind the fence might be a camera.

The man running the U-Haul shop was busy when Michael walked up. He was hitching a trailer to an old Chevy Suburban. The trailer was so small you couldn't even stuff a small cow inside. Michael couldn't imagine what the elderly white guy with the big suburban was going to use it for.

When the customer drove off, the man turned to Michael, eyeing him suspiciously. Michael marveled at how the man's khaki shirt and pants were starched and tidy even though he had been on the ground. His wrists and neck barely filled his collar and cuffs. Michael couldn't guess his age. The patch below his left shoulder said, "Chet." Michael introduced himself, and asked if Chet knew about the murder behind his parking area a few nights ago.

"Ayah, I heard about it. We have a lot of murders hereabouts, seems like," Chet said.

Michael'd never heard an accent like his and wondered where the man was born. "Do you have any cameras looking out on your back lot?"

"Ayah, we got one. What you want it for? You a reporter?"

"No. No. I'm not a reporter. I'm trying to help my cousin. The police think he's a murderer. If I can find a video showing someone else was there the other night, the cops can't keep him in jail." Michael hoped he didn't sound too crazy and held his breath waiting for a response.

Chet looked Michael up and down. "Well..." He rubbed behind his right ear. "I guess we best go look at the tape."

Michael's breath rushed out. "Thank you so much, sir."

"Now, I'm not saying there'll be anything to see, mind you. But, I guess it can't hurt to look." He led Michael into a ravaged metal building. The office had walls of unpainted plasterboard. An air conditioner rattled in the fly-specked window. A small television on a shelf changed images every ten seconds. It flipped through pictures of the front entrance, the garage bays, and the back parking lot where the trailers were stored. A radio in the corner was playing country music.

Chet sat on the metal chair and pushed buttons on a machine tucked into the corner of his metal desk. The TV screen stopped its travels between cameras on the back lot. In the upper right corner of the screen, the top half of the

Bodega's back door was visible. Michael could see it over the back fence. Adrenaline rushed through his veins.

"That fella was killed on Monday, wasn't he?" Chet rhythmically pushed a button on the machine and images flashed and changed: trailers moved, darkness came and went, people moved through the scene, and the date stamp changed. "Do you know what time it was?"

"The police say it happened between four and five on Monday morning," Michael said.

Chet punched the button a few more times, and the screen grew dark. "There you go, four in the morning." The light over the Bodega's door shone brightly in the picture over the top of the back fence.

The picture changed without Chet doing anything. "The camera takes a picture every thirty seconds." Chet smiled.

A bell dinged in the other room announcing a customer. Chet showed Michael the button to stop and start the tape and left to take care of his customer.

Michael was alone twenty minutes later when the shadows appeared at the Bodega's door. He almost shouted for Chet to come and confirm what he was seeing. The man-shaped forms, one taller and one shorter, could just be seen over the back fence of the U-Haul lot. Their arms moved. They got closer together. Then the shorter form dropped out of sight. The other turned and disappeared from the video. He must have walked down the stairs. Sweat poured out of Michael despite the wheezing air conditioner. He watched another twenty minutes, and nothing happened in the corner of the video feed.

Michael remembered the button Chet had used to fast-forward the video. He scanned ahead to 6:00 a.m. Fifteen minutes later the Bodega door opened. A figure moved in the doorway. The door slammed shut. He fast forwarded again, and more forms crowded the area around the door. Michael assumed it was the police arriving.

He stopped the video and went out to find Chet. "Could I borrow your phone?" Michael couldn't keep the tremor from his voice. He could see Chet start to refuse him on general principals.

"Do you think this is a phone booth–" When he saw Michael's face, his voice softened. "Eh, go ahead. Just don't call China."

"Thanks, sir, I won't take advantage. I appreciate your help." Michael was uncomfortable asking a favor of a white stranger, although he wouldn't have worried about asking anyone from home. "Besides, I don't know anyone in China."

Chet smiled and waved Michael back into his office. The bell dinged, indicating another customer.

Michael's first call was to The Lawyer. Lawson said he would call Garcia and meet Michael at the U-Haul.

Rather than pace the small office, he went out and helped Chet hitch a huge trailer to a Chevy S-10 pickup. As the customer drove off, Michael asked, "Does he know he doesn't have enough truck to pull such a big trailer?"

"Ay'up, I told him, but he knows better. Won't do any good though, he'll come a-yelling when he gets the bill for his dropped transmission. They all know better than me what's been doing this for forty years." He rubbed the back of his neck. "That's why I have them sign a waiver."

They chatted about trucks and how people abuse them until Detective Garcia arrived, followed by The Lawyer. Neither man was impressed with the video.

"You can't make out any faces. It just affirms what we already know," The Lawyer said.

"Ortega is the short one. The guy with him is a good six

inches taller and he's bulky. Jon isn't more than a couple inches taller than Ortega and he isn't near as wide. Besides, can't you use computers to make the faces show?" Michael asked Garcia.

"There is a limit to what we can do. This isn't the best equipment." Garcia shrugged. "I'll send it to the techs, but I can almost guarantee it isn't going to tell us much."

Michael bit his lip. He felt as bad as when he missed roping a calf in front of Salina Tsosi at the last rodeo.

"If they can give us the height of the two people it could rule out my client." The Lawyer was looking directly at Garcia as if he didn't believe him. He was a lawyer, but Michael was worried that, if he were challenged, Garcia would cause more trouble for Jon.

"I'm sure the detective will do his best," Michael said.

The Lawyer gave his son a funny look, but didn't say anything more.

Garcia rubbed his neck. "Tell Mrs. Pete I'm doing everything I can to solve the murder."

Chapter 26

A REPORTER'S EYE

Michael was the only person wearing jeans in the fancy restaurant. Even The Lawyer looked a little out of place in his rumpled suit. At exactly seven, Carol Kowalski strode in as though it were her own home. Her heels were so high she couldn't even walk like a regular person. She strutted on her toes with her behind stuck out. Michael wondered if all reporters dressed so uncomfortably. He thought her feet must hurt.

The Lawyer and Michael stood and exchanged greetings. The reporter's skirt was so tight she had to squirm her long legs into the booth when she sat down. Michael kept his gaze on the wall behind her. His face flushed, as he thought of what was happening under the table.

The Lawyer explained Jon's case. Michael studied Ms. Kowalski. He had a hard time thinking of her as Carol as she'd asked. She was about The Lawyer's age, with wavy reddish-brown hair that made a halo around her face. She smelled like a city woman, exuding more chemical than human odors. Her face was carefully painted. He wondered what she was hiding behind her painted mask — was it fear, pain, or something else?

"My son, Michael, is helping me with the investigation."

The reporter turned her attention to Michael. He'd seen a hawk watch a rabbit with the same expression. "How long have you been an investigator?"

"About a day and a half, and I've still found more than the detective in charge of my cousin's case," he said.

"How so?"

The Lawyer warned him not to give her too much information about Jon's case. Before they got to the restaurant, they'd agreed on the facts she could know. Michael explained about finding the truck, and how Garcia didn't interview anyone around the murder scene. The reporter sucked in a breath when he told her about finding the video at the U-Haul, because the cops had never checked. "I have no way to prove it, but I think Norris may have planted the drug packet in Jon's truck," he finished.

"That's off the record, of course," The Lawyer added.

The reporter was completely still. Michael could almost see her brain pulsing behind her eyes.

"Tom Norris and his partner Phil Davis were involved in at least a few of the series of murder cases I've been investigating. So were Garcia and Chamberlin," Carol said as the shiny red nail of her index finger absently tapped the table. "It may not mean anything. The department is small enough, a team would probably pull multiple cases." The red nail tapped like dripping blood. "Your cousin's case is similar to the murders in my story. All the victims were disreputable people, drug dealers, or predatory, diseased prostitutes."

Michael knew the word predatory but had to think for a minute about disreputable.

The restaurant door opened and an older man with broad shoulders entered. He stood a head taller than most of the men in the room and a blue-clad cast covered his arm. He spoke to the hostess, who led him to a table in the corner.

"Well, speak of the devil and he appears," Carol said.

"You got that right," The Lawyer agreed, watching the big man.

"Who is he?" Michael asked.

"That's Ray Chamberlin." The Lawyer said. "He's Detective Garcia's partner. This is a strange coincidence."

"I don't much believe in coincidences." Carol said without looking at the man in the corner.

Michael was facing Chamberlin, but the man seemed oblivious to their presence. He was looking at a menu. "I saw him at the courthouse after Jon's arraignment. Do you both know him?"

"We are on the same bowling league," The Lawyer said. "He probably didn't notice me when he came in."

"I know who he is, but I've never had dealings with him." Carol took a drink of her wine. "Let's get back on track. I did some research after you called. Simon Ortega was a nasty piece of work. He was a suspect in several murders, and he peddled dope laced with poison. If the murders are all connected, Ortega definitely fit the profile."

"It sounds like someone is feeling the need for a little vigilante justice," The Lawyer tipped his head toward the broad shouldered man and raised an eyebrow.

"That's the theory my editor wouldn't let me print. He didn't want to disturb the public. Personally, I think our bloodthirsty public would be happy someone is cleaning up the streets."

"Is that what you think?" Michael asked.

Tap, tap went the blood nail. "I know these are bad people who are getting killed. I can't say I would miss any of them, but the courts should deal with them. What worries me is the police don't recognize that there's a problem. That someone has decided to treat my city like it was the Wild West."

"The grapevine says the department is setting up a task force to look into your allegations," The Lawyer said. "At least you made them take notice."

"Maybe," she said. She took a sip of her drink. "I don't trust a task force made up of guys who are checking up on their friends. It's too easy for a bad cop to slip by them."

"Who else would want to get rid of the disreputable people?" Michael asked.

Both The Lawyer and the reporter went very still.

Michael continued, "Your article said the courts didn't have enough money to prosecute complicated trials. I could see that would make people want to take things into their own hands. It might be why they wanted to use Jon as a scapegoat."

"He was an easy collar, until I made a fuss about forensics," The Lawyer mused. He shifted in his chair.

"An extra cop on the scene wouldn't be noticed. And he would be easy to rule out if his DNA showed up in forensics," Carol said. She narrowed her eyes as if she was looking into the distance.

Michael wasn't sure what Carol was thinking. The Lawyer was nodding as though he had a clue.

"If they lied about Jon, could they have done it to other people?" Michael asked. Carol focused on him, an owl after a mouse.

"It wouldn't be hard to research court records. They are all public," The Lawyer said.

"My boss has me on another story. He won't let me spend too much time on this one now that it's published. I could use some help finding something to get me back on the story. Michael, could you come to my office tomorrow? You could look for connections in the court records and the newspaper morgue." The reporter's eyebrows rose.

"How would that help Jon?" Michael asked. He wasn't sure what the morgue where they kept dead people had to do with the newspaper. The Lawyer must have noticed his confused look, he said, "Going through the news files you might spot connections with Jon's case since you are the most familiar with the people involved.The things you find might lead to more reasonable doubt to take to a jury. We can use all we can get."

"I could look at your nephew's case file?" Carol's red lips curved in a smile so obviously phony, even Michael could see through it.

"You know that can't happen." The Lawyer shrugged. "After we get him acquitted, you can have a look."

"Can't blame a girl for trying." Now, her smile was real. She had a dimple in her right cheek. Michael wondered how she looked when she didn't paint her face.

As they were leaving the restaurant, The Lawyer's cell phone rang. He stopped, and Carol and Michael continued out the door.

"I'll see you tomorrow, Mike." She ran her hand down his arm and looked him right in the eye.

Michael was deciding how to react when he noticed The Lawyer off to the side. He still had the phone to his ear and was looking at his son. His free hand clasped his forehead. His shoulders slumped.

Carol caught Michael's expression. "What is it?"

He tipped his chin at The Lawyer, who waved Michael over.

"We'll be right there." He closed the phone. "We need to pick up your aunts and go to the hospital."

Chapter 27

A DANGEROUS PLACE

HOSPITALS ARE DANGEROUS PLACES. ALL THE ANTISEPTIC cleansers in the world can't completely remove the smell of sickness and decay. The walls are always painted with bright colors, and happy pictures are scattered here and there, but people die in hospitals, trapped in a building their energy can't spread out through the universe as it should. The decorations can't hide the flickers of the lost souls wandering the building, Chindi, trying to be people again.

The aunts held each other, huddled together on the couch. They hadn't moved in hours. The Lawyer paced and fumed during those hours. He talked to nurses, doctors, and anyone who wandered past. Michael listened as he found out Jon's intestines were perforated and there had been massive blood loss. The inmate who stuck a home-made knife into Jon had practice doing maximum damage. He was part of the Aryan Brotherhood, who had special enmity for anyone who wasn't white.

Michael stood at the window with his back to the scary, comfortable room. He clutched the tiny buckskin bag around his neck. It contained pollen, cornmeal, and a stone he'd found during the ceremony which confirmed he was a man of the Diné. He hoped the power of the ritual would protect him in this alien place. Michael hoped the universe didn't require Jon's life.

Silently, Michael sang the song to greet the morning. The ritual took some of the tension from his shoulders. He watched the dawn creep over a distant mountain. It glowed eerily in the slanted morning light. It bothered him he didn't know this mountain's story. He knew the names of the mountains in the Navajo lands, Chi'oolii, where white shell woman was born, and Tsoodzil, the Turquoise Mountain where the Great Snake perpetually guarded Turquoise Girl. Raised in the shadow of those peaks, Michael knew where he fit in when those mountains encircled him. He didn't have a place among the lonely nameless mountains surrounding this city. Even so, he'd rather be in those ragged hills than in this terrible place. He knew in his soul that if he walked on any of those nameless mountains he could find the peace that eluded him in the stench, angles, and noise of this city.

The Lawyer jumped up when a man came in wearing an outfit made of thin green fabric. There were white paper covers over the man's shoes and a tight paper cap on his head. Michael thought this couldn't be the doctor. His cap had pictures of cartoon cats printed on it. The cats were holding hands and kicking their striped legs. He focused on the dancing cats and didn't hear what the doctor said. The Lawyer's heartfelt, "Thank God," told him what he needed to know.

Auntie Jean appeared at the doctor's side. "I'll go see Jon, now." She wasn't asking.

"He'll be in recovery for an hour or so. You can see him

when he's transferred to his room." The doctor turned to leave.

"I'll go see him, now," Jean stepped in front of the doctor. She didn't raise her voice, but she gave the doctor the look. He went flat-footed, as if he'd been punched.

"I'm sorry, the family isn't allowed in the recovery room," he stuttered a bit on the 'f' in family.

"I'm not family. I'm his mother. I'll go see him. Now."

"I'll...ah... see what I can do." The doctor with his silly cat hat fled the room. Jean was right on his heels.

The Lawyer pushed his glasses up onto his head and was pinching the bridge of his nose. He took a deep breath. Aunt Lila patted his shoulder gently.

"You couldn't have known this was going to happen. At least he's out of the jail now," she said. "I'll stay here with Jean. You and Michael go find out who murdered that man. Make sure Jon doesn't have to go back to jail."

Chapter 28

A KIND WORD

Michael left The Lawyer at his office. The man wanted to write some letter to the court, asking to get Jon's charges dropped. It had some legal name that didn't matter. He said it probably wouldn't work, but he needed to get it on the record. Records and papers and legal rules...Michael just wanted to smack something. He didn't ever remember being so angry. He didn't know who he was mad at, himself for not protecting Jon, the person who hurt him, or the whole city of Phoenix. Uncertainty wasn't helping his peace of mind. Anger tightened every muscle in his neck and back. His hands kept forming fists that he had to make an effort to unclench.

He needed to burn off some energy and decided to go ask Garcia what the police were doing about the guy who tried to kill Jon. He doubted they were any more efficient than they'd been when they were investigating Ortega's murder behind the Bodega.

At the police station, a fat desk sergeant told Michael to wait. He sat on the same lonely bench as the first night he'd come to the jail looking for Jon. The place was as haunted during the day as it was at night. It seemed worse with the bustle of all the people and the ringing of phones.

Michael took out the little medallion he'd found in the rat's nest. He needed something to do with his hands. After a few minutes of fiddling with it, he dropped it and it rolled under the swinging half-door that separated the waiting area from the police desks. Watching it roll, he got up to fetch it and looked into the eyes of the hard man from the diner. The one who'd been with Garcia and Norris. He felt the hair on the back of his neck rise.

The dangerous man picked up St. Anthony and flipped him over. He read the inscription and his eyes met Michael's. "Where'd you get this, kid?"

"I just found it." Michael held out his hand.

The man dropped the bit of metal in it, his eyes never leaving Michael's. He turned without further comment and walked away. Michael tucked the medallion in a pocket and sat back on the bench feeling as though he'd just faced down a bear. He leaned back and watched the hard man leave. The bit of gold glinted in his fingers. Maybe it was important..

A tall woman with extremely black skin and cartoon character red hair strutted to the desk on eight-inch high heels. Her red skirt barely covered the curve of her butt, and her shapely legs had white net stockings held up by little straps which hung down from under the skirt. Michael knew there was a name for those straps, but his sleep-deprived brain wasn't functioning well enough to remember the word. When she turned around, her white blouse barely concealed her ample chest. She sashayed over to the bench and sat down next to Michael. He leaned forward and rested his arms on his thighs. He didn't bother to unclench his fists.

"Don't you just hate the wait?" she asked. Her voice was very deep for a woman.

"Yes, ma'am." He rubbed knuckles across his eyes and stifled a yawn.

"You look awful, honey." She leaned down to look at him.

"I was up all night. My cousin was hurt."

"This is a tough town. What happened?"

"He was framed for murder. Last night someone stuck a knife in him in the jail infirmary." Michael's eyes filled with tears. It wasn't his way to talk to strangers about personal things. He wasn't raised to have another carry his burdens. Michael didn't realize how much emotion he'd been holding in. His aunts had enough to worry about without adding his concerns to theirs. By burying his emotions, he was trying to protect the women who loved him. A deep breath helped clear his head. What was the harm sharing thoughts with another person who wasn't emotionally involved?

"I need to talk to the detective who's doing my cousin's case." He dropped his head into his hands. Michael rubbed his hair and scrubbed the moisture from his eyes. "He isn't doing anything to find the real murderer."

The woman patted his shoulder with her red and blue manicured hand. "You been up all night?"

Michael nodded, not looking up.

"You need to get some rest, baby. I seen this before. If you go talking to the cops now, you're just going to make more problems. Go get some sleep." She gave his shoulder a gentle shove. "Go on now, before you end up in jail, too."

Michael looked at her. His eyes blurred a bit. He took a deep breath. "You're right." He got up to leave. "Thanks, ma'am. Can I ask your name?"

"I'm Paula Michelle, cutie. When you get rested up, you come down to the strip and ask for me. I'll put a smile back on that handsome face of yours. I do love blond-haired boys." Her laugh was deep and wholehearted.

On his way back to his truck it hit him, Paula Michelle was probably a prostitute. He'd never met a prostitute. Michael heard rumors about how some of the women who lived in the government housing made most of their income. He'd also seen some sad-eyed girls wandering around the truck stop in Cow Springs, but never talked to any of them. Despite his weariness, Michael felt rather worldly.

Chapter 29

MIXED MESSAGES

RUDY GARCIA SAT WITH HIS FEET ON HIS DESK, LOOKING AT the whiteboard in his office. Last night after the kids had gone to bed, he'd spent a couple of hours discussing the multiple murders with his partner, Ray. He felt more muddled than ever. Ray had an alternative for every one of his theories. He felt as though he were a rookie again.

Garcia got up and started to pace the four steps back and forth across his office. He'd argued his points with his partner. Garcia knew his ideas were valid. Was he kidding himself that his theories were better than a guy with twenty-five years of experience? He wrote a couple of his partner's ideas on the board.

He leaned against the wall, contemplated what he wrote, and shook his head. Ray's ideas wouldn't fly. They set a strange rationale for Jon Pete being responsible for more than one case. The veteran's ideas were too big a stretch, with no corroborating evidence. He scrubbed Ray's theories off the board with quick jerks of his hand.

The old lady from the diner wouldn't get out of his head. Her son was looking worse and worse for the Ortega murder, let alone any of the others. The video from the U-Haul showed a guy well over six feet tall on the loading dock with the victim. Jon Pete, wearing cowboy boots, was five eight at best. But, other than the grainy image, there was no evidence anyone else was at the scene.

Garcia sighed, flopped into his chair, and started sorting through the pink message slips on his desk. "What the f..." his feet hit the floor. The Pete kid got shanked in lockup and was in surgery. He should have been called with this message. He strode out of his office with his jaw clenched and stopped at the secretary's desk. She was about twenty with mousy blond hair. Sitting sideways in her chair, she was chewing a large wad of gum and filing her nails.

After a few more passes of her file, she looked up. "What?"

"Didn't you see this priority message?" He waved the pink slip at her.

"I took the message yesterday," she said without missing a chew on her gum.

"Why wasn't I called?"

"I put it in your office like I always do."

Garcia's voice dropped an octave. His children would recognize the tone, and would have gotten as far from him as possible. "The case detective is to be called when there is a priority message."

"You'd gone home already." She popped another stick of gum in her mouth.

He sighed and closed his eyes.

PHIL DAVIS WAS FILLING HIS INSULATED COFFEE MUG WHEN Garcia came in an hour later. "I heard the perp in the Ortega murder got shanked in the lockup." He ripped the top off four packets of sugar and poured them into his cup. "Saves the taxpayers a trial."

"The kid's going to live." Garcia filled his mug from the pot. "But, I'm not sure he's going to trial. Lawson won't plead out, and the D.A. says he doesn't have much of a case. He wants me out on more interviews. I'm supposed to find somebody at the bar who saw Ortega and Pete together."

"No shit, the D.A. needs to grow some balls. He has enough to get the Pete kid."

"I've got a bad feeling about this one. I was talking to Ray the other night, and he's thinking like you, but I'm not sure." Rudy shook his head.

"Ray's been helping you even though he's off." Phil's eyebrows raised over his mug while he took a sip of his brew.

"My wife keeps having him over for dinner. You know women, they always figure a single guy needs company. I think she is planning to fix him up with her aunt." Garcia rubbed his aching neck. "We watched the game and talked shop all night. I know he wants to get back to work, but until the cast is off he can't qualify on the firing range."

"Sounds like Ray's got the old war horse syndrome. Maybe he can talk them into letting him back on the desk. Did you know Lawson's kid found a St. Anthony medallion with an inscription -- 'Riley?'" Davis looked intently at the younger man.

"Where did he find it?"

Davis shrugged. "I saw him with it down in the bullpen this morning. Not sure what it means. If you see Ray, ask him if he knows a Riley."

"Sure." Garcia said. He ran a hand over the back of his neck. "I don't know how I'm going to get a canvas done, and go over the murder books for the dead dealer task force. I need to keep chasing the Ortega murder."

"Don't worry. I'll get started on trying to make sense out of the deaths of the great unwashed. You go canvas Indian School Road." Davis sipped his coffee, frowned, and reached for more sugar.

"Thanks, Phil. Tell Norris I'll be back as soon as I can."

I'm finally getting accepted in the squad, Garcia thought. *But Davis is a weird sort of guy. He's always giving me the fish-eye. I'm glad I drew Ray as my partner instead of him.*

Chapter 30

EVERYBODY COMES TO WALMART

THE SOUND OF AUNT LILA MAKING COFFEE WOKE MICHAEL about one in the afternoon. The wonderful smell brought him off the couch. Shambling into the kitchen, He realized he couldn't remember sleeping during the day since he was a little kid.

Aunt Lila handed him a mug. "Salina called, the Jeep broke down in Cow Springs. Charlie Kootenai gave her a ride home."

"Charlie's a good guy."

"You going to spend more time with Salina when we get home?"

"I don't know, Auntie. She's a strong woman and I...I got to think about helping Jon right now," Michael said in rush.

She pointedly scrutinized her nephew before continuing, "David called the reporter lady. You don't have to go look at her papers today."

Michael tried to memorize the tabletop while he took his first sip. The heat and bitter goodness of the coffee reminded him he was alive. He felt guilty for forgetting about doing research with Ms. Kowalski today as well as not being able to help Salina, or Jon. Guilt was becoming his go-to emotion. *Who am I going to let down next?*

Lila talked while frying eggs. "We have to pick up Jean at the hospital. She wants to get some things for Jon at the store." She put bread in the toaster.

His stomach growled at the smell of the eggs. "Where's The Lawyer?"

She frowned fiercely. "Your father is at his office. He had to work today, unlike some people I know who sleep on the sofa and snore like a drunken pig."

"I don't snore."

"Eh, how do you know, if you're asleep?" She wiped her hands on the kitchen dish cloth and picked up her purse. "Your father snores, too. A woman can't hardly get any sleep around this house with two snoring men."

Michael ate his eggs in silence. Lila was his little mother, she raised him. He knew she wasn't really talking about his snoring. He rinsed his plate in the sink, picked up the truck keys, and headed out the door.

Lila was painfully quiet on the way to pick up Aunt Jean. He could feel her wanting to talk to him about The Lawyer. It was as if waves of heat were blowing across the truck bench. He drove with eyes straight ahead and a set jaw.

She didn't speak until they reached the hospital.

"Things aren't like you imagine. You think too much, boy."

AUNT JEAN WAS IN HIGH SPIRITS. JON WAS CONSCIOUS AND alert. She wanted to make him a special meal, so they went to the Walmart for supplies. Light glared in the afternoon sun, reflecting off the walls of the buildings, heating the city like a mirrored room. The store was about halfway between the jail and the hospital. Michael found a parking spot close to the door and followed the aunties as they moved inside. Two brown women in a sea of white faces, they didn't seem to notice how they stood out in this city crowd. Chattering away in Navajo, they were making observations about all the strange things white people spent their money on. Of course, they remained polite by not speaking English. Michael smiled when he heard Jean compare a large trash can to a sheep dip tank.

A skinny white man with a big Adam's apple, and who wore his ball cap on backwards, was walking behind the aunts. He was only a few inches taller than Lila. His hunched shoulders and clenched fists drew Michael's attention. He started over to place himself between the ball cap guy and his family. Before Michael reached them, the man spoke loudly. "Hey lady, you're in America. We speak English here. If you want to speak Mexican, go back to Mexico."

Jean stopped and gave him a look that should have made the man frizzle like a moth in a fire. Michael was near enough to protect her if need be, so he stopped when Jean held up her hand. In a perfect, accent less voice she said, "We are speaking Navajo, properly known as Diné Bezaad, a Native American language. I think if you are worried about people speaking English, perhaps you should go back to England." She turned on her heel and clomped off followed by Aunt Lila.

The man stood flat-footed. People around him waited to see what he would do. Ball Cap watched the aunts for a few seconds then he spit on the floor, and headed toward the checkout line. Michael couldn't read the expressions on the faces of the watching people; couldn't tell if they agreed with Aunt Jean or the skinny man in the ball cap. The flow of the crowd started and he was able to relax.

Michael followed the man to make sure he didn't double back to mess with the aunts. Ball Cap picked up a Slim Jim and a Monster drink. He got in the checkout line. Michael moved over to the in-store Subway and bought a sandwich. He didn't understand why he was still hungry. He hadn't done enough real work to break a sweat since arriving in Phoenix. The insulting man walked by as he left the store.

After paying for his meal, Michael rifled through his wallet counting the bills. His bingo winnings were dwindling rapidly. He folded a ten and a twenty and tucked them in the billfold's inner pocket to be sure he had gas money to get out of this city when he was ready.

There were little tables scattered around near the Subway, so Michael sat. Chewing the turkey sandwich slowly, he tried to think of what to investigate next. The Lawyer was looking into legal connections. Not speaking legal, there wasn't a lot he could do to help him. Michael didn't think he was going to be much use to Carol the reporter tomorrow, either. He had no idea what she meant by doing research. Since the U-Haul video wasn't useful, he was running out of things to scrutinize.

The coffee washed caffeine through his body. It was like a sack coming off his head. This trip was opening his eyes in a lot of ways. *People should travel more*, Michael thought. Some people try to attribute special powers to Indians. They think all Native Americans have magical, psychic powers; that they can read the weather, and are able to track and hunt without learning how. Didn't Michael wish that were true? Special powers his ass. He knew guys from the government housing in The Nation who had never been out of town. They were Diné, but didn't know which end of a sheep to feed.

Michael's uncles taught him about nature and how to work. They taught him by living close to the land. One thing about a traditional Navajo, they appreciate and learn from their elders. That's how Michael knew what he knew. His uncle Leon blamed the movies for all the misconceptions about Native people. He might be right, but Michael thought a lot of Diné have wrong ideas about white people, too. Uncle Leon once told him Belagáana have no sense of reality, because they live all the time indoors and need to watch movies to know how to have sex. Leon was a well-traveled man. He'd been to the ocean during World War II.

Michael used to believe everything his uncles told him. Having spent this time in the city now, he wasn't so sure. He was beginning to understand how the elder's wisdom was limited by their time and experience. Much of what they taught him wasn't doing him much good here in the city.

Most of his life, Michael hadn't had much to do with city people. He worked with some ranchers and cowhands, but that was work. They didn't usually talk much, because he always had his Navajo friends around. He met country folk at the rodeos, but honestly all they did was exchange howdy-dos. Occasionally, tourists would wander into a Squaw dance, or show up at the chapter house trying to get what they call the real Native American experience. They didn't spend time talking to a blond guy like Michael.

Other than school, he didn't remember having more than a few words with any of the Belagáana strangers who passed through his life. There was never any reason to. They were always on Michael's home ground. He was confident in his world and the foreigners didn't really affect him. Now that he was in the city, he wished he'd paid more attention to those alien strangers. All his life Michael learned stuff by keeping his eyes open and listening to people with more experience. He realized that's what he needed to do here in town. He was in alien territory now. He needed guidance.

The faces of the people Michael'd met in the past few days flowed through his mind. Most of the ones he thought he could trust wouldn't be able to help him understand a murderer. The others, reporter Carol, Detective Garcia, and The Lawyer, Michael didn't quite trust to help Jon, if helping him interfered with their own ambitions.

His mind kept returning to Cletus the liquor store clerk. Michael had a feeling the big man knew more than he was telling. Trying to figure how to get him to open up, strained Michael's brain.

Michael was thinking deeply, not dozing, when a deep voice startled his eyes open.

"I thought I told you to go home and get some rest? What you sleeping in the Walmart for?"

"Hello, ma'am." He nodded a greeting to Paula. "You look great this afternoon." She was wearing a different outfit since this morning. The red fishnet stockings matched her hair. Her skin tight dress had a waving geometric pattern of dark purple on a red background. Her lipstick was white to match her platform shoes.

"How lucky am I meeting such a sweet blond boy twice in one day?" Paula carefully folded herself into the chair opposite him. "Baby, you still look like somebody stole your puppy. Please don't tell me your cousin died." She patted Michael's hand.

"No, he's going to be all right. I just don't seem to be any use at getting him out of jail." He stretched his neck and rolled his shoulders. "My aunts are shopping, so I thought

I'd wait here." Remembering his manners, he said, "Can I get you a cup of coffee?"

"You're a darling. I could use a cup."

Michael bought her some coffee and brought it back to the table. "What are you doing here at Walmart, if you don't mind me asking?"

She added three sugars, took a sip while closing her eyes, and inhaled deeply through her nose. "That is what I needed." Her eyes opened and she smiled showing a lot of teeth. "I chipped a nail and needed to stop by the salon to get fixed up." She held out her hands, knuckles up, and wiggled her fingers showing of off the newly lacquered red and white nails. "I got some time while I wait for a...friend. Why don't you tell me all what's going on with your cousin?" She sat back and crossed her legs.

Michael thought about making an excuse to leave, and realized he had nowhere to go. Besides, he could start learning from people with more experience right now. Miss Paula had already given him some good advice. "I've been trying to find information to help him, but nothing seems to work. I'm out of ideas. You were right about not asking the police what's going on. I'd have just got in trouble."

"You seem to be a bright boy. I bet you got something up your sleeve."

"There's a guy in the liquor store over on 17th Street who might know something. I talked to him once, but I think he was put off, because the lawyer made him nervous."

"Darlin', lawyers always make everybody nervous. That's why they get paid so much."

"I'm not good at talking to people here in the city."

"You're talking to me."

"You're different, you're easy to talk to."

"Why thank you, baby, if you only knew how different." Paula smoothed her hair.

"I just don't know how to get the liquor store guy to help me." Michael dropped his head into his hands and ran fingers through his hair. "I think I'll go talk to him again tonight, even though he probably doesn't know anything anyway."

"17th Street is pretty rough at night. What's the fella's name?"

"Cletus. He's the night manager at-"

"Oh, sweetheart, I know Cletus. He and I socialize on a regular basis." She sipped her coffee, holding the cup with both hands. "Cletus knows everybody, that boy do get around." She tilted her head back and laughed loudly.

Michael noticed she had an Adam's apple. So, Paula was a man. He mentally shook himself. She had been kind to him when she didn't have to. It wasn't any of his business how anyone wanted to present themselves to the world. Michael looked white and felt brown. Who was he to judge?

Paula reached over and patted his hand. People walking by looked at her strangely. "What you looking at?" Her voice was strident. She started to get up.

"I think they aren't used to people dressing so nicely at Walmart." Michael said.

She sat abruptly. "You're so sweet. Such a sweet, sweet boy." She watched him from under her extra-long eyelashes. "I'll go with you to talk to Cletus. If he knows anything, he'll tell me." She poked at her hair with a manicured nail.

"That would be great. I really appreciate your help."

The aunties were finishing at the check-out. Michael waved them over and stood when they arrived. "Aunties, this is the woman I told you about, the one who helped me at the police station this morning." He didn't want to be rude in front of his aunts by using Paula's name while she was present. "She's going to help me talk to some people about what happened to Jon." He turned to Paula. "This is my aunt, she's Jon's mother, and my other aunt who raised me." He indicated Jean and Lila in turn. Michael held his breath, hoping Aunt Jean wouldn't say anything to hurt Paula's feelings.

Jean looked at Paula, who sat back and crossed her legs. Paula tilted her head, narrowed her eyes, and looked up at Jean.

"My name's Jean. It's good you're helping Michael. He needs somebody to show him how to talk with them crazy white people." Jean plopped on the empty chair next to Paula.

Paula laughed and sat up, primping her hair again. She introduced herself.

I pulled up a chair for Aunt Lila. "I'm called Lila. How did you meet Michael?"

"I talked him out of doing something foolish at the jail this morning." Paula got out a little mirror and reapplied her white lipstick.

"Michael, go get us coffee." Jean ignored Michael and turned to Paula. "How do you keep them white shoes from getting scuffed up?"

Aunt Lila raised her eyes in a long suffering look. Michael went and got more coffee.

Chapter 31
TASK FORCE

THE WHITEBOARD SPANNED THE LENGTH OF NORRIS'S OFFICE. Pictures of the murdered drug dealers and prostitutes lined the top of the board, laid out in chronological order. Details of each murder were written neatly under the pictures. A map on an adjoining wall had pushpins showing the crime scene locations. The pins clustered around the northwest part of the central city. Piles of fat binders covered every available surface.

Garcia stood in the doorway where he could take in the whole room. "This is a little 'old school' isn't it?"

"It's been working for me and Phil for a lot of years," Norris said from behind his desk. "Your gold-bricking partner stopped in a while ago."

"Yeah, I saw him. He had a couple ideas, but I don't think they'll pan out, nothing worth throwing up on the board."

Norris laced his hands behind his head and rocked back in his chair. "Can you see anything, kid? Even Ray's ideas might be worth a try. I've been looking at this mess for hours and can't find any new pattern."

Garcia leaned against the doorway. "Other than the

obvious connections of location, being killed with a knife, and the fact they were all low-life trash, I don't see a thing."

Rudy closed his eyes and perused the board in his mind. "Ray had an idea about a drug connection, but at least three of the victims had no connection to the drug trade. Maybe, if we did timelines for the week before each murder, we can look at known associates to see if they intersect."

"It's worth a try, but all you'll probably get is the victims buying and selling to each other."

"At least it would be something. The Lieutenant's antsy for some results." Rudy scraped his fingers through his hair.

"Don't worry about the Lou. He's always antsy about something. That's why he makes the big bucks." Norris took a legal pad out of a drawer. "You might have something with the victims. Why don't you do the timelines, and I'll work on known associates."

Garcia nodded absently. He perused the board again. "I'm going to throw the Ortega murder into the mix. It fits the pattern. The Indian is looking worse and worse as the perp."

"Don't tell me the old lady got to you the other day."

"No, she didn't." Rudy shook his head, a frown crumpled his face. "It's the evidence. I can't tie the Indian to Ortega. I'm not happy, and neither is the DA. Lawson is pushing to get the charges dropped, and it's probably going to happen."

"What's going to happen?" Phil Davis said from behind.

"Jesus, don't creep up on me like that." Garcia clutched his chest. "You nearly gave me the big one."

Davis grinned wolfishly. "Suck it up, Buttercup."

"Rudy thinks the DA is going to toss the Ortega case," Norris said.

"I thought the Indian was next to the body with a knife

in his hand." Davis moved some papers off a chair and plopped down.

"The Indian's lawyer has been riding the DA hard. And the evidence is thin. The prints are on the knife upside down and in the wrong hand. He didn't have any blood on him, either." Garcia scrubbed his hair with both hands. "None of the local interviews put the Pete kid and Ortega together. It's frustrating. There aren't any other leads."

"What about the drugs you found in Pete's truck?"

Garcia shrugged. "We can't connect it to the victim. No prints, and the crap Ortega peddled is chemically different." He shook his head. "This is getting me nowhere. I'm going to start those victim crosschecks." He headed out the door, but grabbed the doorframe and leaned back into the room. "I'm doing them on the computer, instead of using markers like you dinosaurs."

NORRIS GAVE HIM A MIDDLE FINGER SALUTE AS HE LEFT. PHIL Davis sat without any expression and watched him go.

"I saw Lawson's kid in the precinct today," Davis fiddled with a pencil. He looked up at his partner. He said he found a gold medallion. One with the inscription, 'For Riley.'"

Norris nodded solemnly, "I wonder where he found it?"

"Only one place I could think of."

"You know, Ray Chamberlin came in today to look at the board," Norris said.

"Yeah, I saw him. I mentioned the medallion."

He and Davis exchanged knowing looks.

Four hours later, Garcia's phone rang. He groaned looking at the clock. "She's definitely going to turn me in on a newer model."

Sound blasted out of the receiver when he picked it up. "The kids and I have eaten. Ray, your partner, our guest, was here and gone." His wife's voice was about an octave higher than usual. "Are you ever coming home?"

Rudy tilted his head back and closed his eyes. "Me Corazon, I'm sorry, work got away from me."

"The kids don't remember what you look like. Are you going to see them before they go to bed?"

"Probably not tonight, I have another couple hours on task force business. Honey, you know this is a big chance for me. Tell the kids I'll see them tomorrow. I'll come home early, so I can play with them."

"Oh, Rudy, you're working on a Saturday?"

"Sorry, sweetheart, crime never sleeps," he said, using his best Bogart imitation.

"Hey, Bogey, bring some milk when you finally get to come home." Her voice softened. "Don't work too late, honey. Ti amo." She made a kiss noise before she hung up.

Chapter 32

COYOTE CLEVER

PAULA ENDED UP COMING HOME WITH THEM. AUNT JEAN insisted the tall woman needed a good meal. When they got to The Lawyer's house, Michael went to the front room to see if he could get any new ideas from Carol Kowalski's article. Paula and his aunts went to the kitchen. They were talking about fashion and television shows while they fixed a meal.

"I never have time to cook," Paula said. "My kitchen is so small, I have to go outside to change my mind."

The Aunties both laughed. Jean repeated, "Go out to change your mind."

I'm going to be hearing that line for the rest of my life, Michael thought. He shook wrinkles from the paper.

Lila took Paula's hand. "How do you do anything with those long nails? Are they good for peeling potatoes?" All three of them shrieked with laughter. Hearing the aunties in high spirits warmed Michael's heart. Paula didn't seem to have any issues about spending time with Indians.

She was in the bathroom fixing her makeup when The Lawyer came home about five thirty.

"Everything smells wonderful," he said, opening the pot of stew. He reached for the stirring spoon.

Aunt Lila grabbed the spoon and slapped his hand. "Wait till it's on the table."

His smile practically split his face. "I could get used to home cooked meals on a regular basis."

Paula walked into the kitchen. The Lawyer's face went blank. His mouth was open.

Michael was putting dishes on the table. "David Lawson, I'd like you to meet Paula Michelle. Paula this is my cousin's lawyer, David Lawson." He figured it was all right to introduce them white person style.

"He's Michael's father, too," Jean chimed in. She handed her nephew silverware to put on the table with the stew bowls. "Davy, close your mouth, you're going to catch flies."

"Pleased to meet you, counselor." Paula walked across the room rolling her hips with every step. She held out her hand, fingers down, with her wrist bent.

The Lawyer looked at Lila, at Jean, and finally at his son. Michael raised his eyebrows. The Lawyer turned to Paula, took her hand, and shook it. "Pleased to meet you, Ms. Michelle, are you joining us for dinner?"

"She's too skinny. We're going to feed her up." Auntie Jean said. "Then she's going to help Michael talk to people."

"Ah, that sounds like a plan. I'd better get cleaned up." The Lawyer retreated down the hall to the bathroom. To give him credit, he didn't rush.

Dinner conversation was mostly about television. Michael watched silently. Paula and the aunties talked about the Real Housewives of Atlanta. Jean insisted the women were useless as wives because all they did was eat in restaurants and go shopping.

"Honey," Paula said. "Those women have a duty to spend their stupid husbands' money."

The Lawyer chimed in with stories of some rich people's divorces he'd handled.

Aunt Jean changed tracks suddenly. "Don't get too comfortable, Davey. You have to take me back to the hospital tonight. I made Jon some soup. It should help him remember who hit him." Jean placed her dirty silverware on her plate. "I'm going to stay at the hospital with him tonight."

"I'm not sure they will let you do that, Jean."

"You make them police see some sense. What is an old lady like me going to do, hit someone over the head and make a prison break?" Jean patted The Lawyer on the cheek.

He sighed and raised his eyes to the ceiling as though he were counting. He finally looked at Jean and said, "I'll see what I can do."

Michael was pretty sure that if she thought she could get Jon out safely, she wouldn't hesitate to hit someone over the head. With strangers in the room, he kept the thought to himself.

MICHAEL WAS SURPRISED THAT PAULA, IN HER TIGHT SKIRT, didn't have any trouble climbing into his pickup truck. Their first stop was at the liquor store where Cletus worked. Paula followed him in and started looking at labels. They didn't see Cletus, so Michael went to the counter. The nasty little man who owned the place was there.

"Boy, what you doing here this time of night, you're going to get mugged," he said.

"I'm looking for Cletus. Will he be in tonight?"

"The motherfucker quit on me. Left me high and dry after all I did for that son-of-a-bitch."

Paula strode up. "You didn't do shit for that man and you know it. He worked his ass off for you, and you never gave him so much as a kind word, you little bastard." She smacked the glass protecting the counter.

"Get off the glass, you faggot. Go fuck somebody. You don't need to be in here if you ain't buying." He reached down and picked up a shotgun.

Michael backed up. "There's no need to get upset. We're just looking for Cletus. If he's not here, we'll be leaving." He gently took Paula's arm and steered her toward the door.

"I thought you was a good kid. What you letting that faggot suck your cock for? Don't come back here." The greasy little man waved the shotgun as he yelled.

Paula started to turn back. Michael gripped her arm more firmly and whispered, "He's just a bigoted asshole, don't let him upset you." As Paula looked at him, he realized he was blushing bright red.

She shrugged his hand off her arm, made a rude gesture to the store owner, and stalked out the door. Michael followed without looking back.

They climbed into his truck and sat quietly for a minute. Paula was staring straight ahead. She was breathing hard.

"Don't let him upset you," Michael said, and started the truck.

"I had such a nice day today. Now it's ruined."

"He's a nasty old man. Don't let him get to you." He didn't put the truck in gear.

"He's right, you know." At Michael's confused look, Paula continued, "My original name is Fredrick Mitchell."

He didn't know what she was trying to tell him, so Michael didn't say anything.

"You and your family...it was so nice to feel accepted. Not to be judged as a freak because of who I am."

"Why would we think you're a freak?"

"Honey, don't you get it, I'm a woman in name only. I got a man's plumbing."

"Well, heck, I know that, I knew it since Walmart. I'm sure my aunts know, too. What does that have to do with anything?"

"Sweet, sweet boy, if only you knew." Paula's mouth scrunched up, and her eyes glistened with tears.

Michael patted her shoulder. "People are what they are. You're a good person. You helped me when you didn't have to. That's a rare thing." His brow was wrinkled, and he raised his shoulders. "Why should your feeling like a woman bother me or my aunts?" He let his shoulders drop.

Paula started sobbing into her hands. Michael fished around on the seat and found a paper napkin and handed it to her.

She kept weeping for a few minutes, shoulders shaking and breathing in gasps. As she wound down, she blotted her face, sniffing and gulping down her sobs. When she was finished drying her tears, she took a deep breath. "I haven't let go like that in years. I must look a mess." Paula got some things out of her purse and began to apply them to her face.

The only thing Michael recognized was the lipstick. He cracked the door, so the overhead light came on.

"Thanks, Hon, I need to spend more time in the company of blond Indians," Paula said, her eyes wide while she drew a line under her lashes.

Michael watched the people along the street. The neighborhood was much busier after dark. There was a constant stream of people in and out of the Bodega and liquor store. Most of them stayed in the shadows. Their scuttling travels reminded him of the rats near The Lawyer's office. The people on the street knew this territory and had escape routes embedded in their nature. Many were moving shadows, identified only by the golden spark on their cigarettes flickering through the dark. A few of the street's denizens strutted in the light, shouting at passing cars, accosting possible customers. A hulking shape stood almost invisible in the shadows beside a dumpster. The broad-shouldered shape seemed to be watching the action on the street.

Michael followed the direction of the phantom's gaze as a woman in a dress tighter than Paula's climbed into a car with two men. She was tiny, like a child in grown up clothes. Paula noticed the direction of his gaze and stopped her facial prepping.

"Is she safe going with those men?" Michael asked.

"Probably, but it don't matter. She's got to make a living."

"There is so much I don't understand about the city." "That's why you have me as your trusty native guide." Paula patted his shoulder. "Let's go find Cletus. I know some places where he hangs out."

Michael looked around. The large man had faded into the blackness of the night. They drove off, leaving the predators and prey of 17th Street and Indian School Road to deal with what was natural…in their world.

Paula said she recognized Cletus' ancient Cadillac at the Bar where Jon had left his truck. Motorcycles lined the front of the building. Michael parked out near the road.

"I can't go in," Paula said. "With the motorcycle gang in there, it won't be my kind of place tonight. Could you go in and tell Cletus I need to talk to him? Once he comes out, you make yourself scarce."

Michael tilted his head and looked at her.

"Those gang boys hate my kind. They'd stomp me to a bloody spot." Paula examined her long nails. "Come to think of it, they wouldn't be too happy to know your family history, either."

"I imagine a lot of people wouldn't be happy I'm related to a lawyer."

Paula laughed and slapped her thighs. "Something like that," she said. "Now, Cletus, he won't be as willing to talk to me if you're around. He's not a trusting man."

"But he'll talk to you?"

"We have a close acquaintance."

Michael nodded. He wasn't sure what to make of Paula and Cletus' relationship, but he guessed it was none of his business. "Talking with Cletus won't cause you trouble, will it?"

"Darling boy, where were you when I was younger?"

Michael got out of the truck.

"You be careful." Paula warned. "I don't want to explain to Jean and Lila how I got you hurt."

He headed into the bar trying not to look as if he were related to a lawyer. The place wasn't quite as filthy as the Lucky Buck, but it was close. Acrid cigarette smoke burned his eyes. The noise was nearly a wall. He couldn't make out individual words, just a roar of consonants and vowels. Most of the bar was inhabited by boisterous men wearing black leather and faded jeans. They had angry tattoos with a general theme of skulls, knives, and chains. Michael kept his head up but didn't make eye contact. His uncles taught him not to show fear around predators. This place was full of them.

As Michael stopped to survey the room, a few bikers watched him. Despite the air conditioning, sweat prickled out all over his body. Cletus was in a booth at the back of the bar. Michael made his way to him, skirting the central commotion by hugging the walls. He resisted the temptation to hunch his shoulders and scuttle like a rabbit. Don't act like prey, he told himself.

Cletus watched Michael as he approached. The big man's hands engulfed a mug of amber liquid. Michael could smell beer and another mild pungent scent.

"Mr. Cletus, I don't know if you remember me. We met at the liquor store a couple of days ago." He stood at the edge of the booth, trying to keep an eye on the rest of the bar.

"You look nervous, kid. You best sit down."

Michael slid into the booth opposite him. "This isn't my kind of place."

"No shit. Damn bikers got kicked out of their dive over on Camel Back Road, so they moved over here." He hawked and spat on the floor. "Totally ruined the ambiance."

Michael nodded as if he had a clue what Cletus was talking about. He needed to make a list of English words he didn't recognize. "We have a mutual friend."

"That so?"

"Yeah, Paula Michelle, she's outside in my truck. She sent me in to let you know she wanted to talk with you. You can understand why she didn't want to come in herself."

The big man grunted, pulled himself up, and drank down the rest of his beer in one gulp. "Let's go out the back." He threw some money on the table.

Michael followed him down a hallway, past a reeking bathroom with no door and out into the clean night air. Michael pointed out the truck. "I'll leave you to talk."

Cletus strode away without comment.

Michael started walking. It was only a few blocks from the busy Indian School Road, but he saw no people. The area wasn't any more interesting at night than it was during the day. A coyote slinked through a warehouse parking lot. He didn't cross Michael's path, so he kept moving. He tried to decide if the coyote was some kind of omen. Some people worried about black cats crossing their path. Michael figured it was the same problem as a coyote, but didn't know the legend behind the cat superstition.

He'd grown up on stories of Coyote, the trickster. During the winter, when everyone moved in together, Auntie Jean would tell the Coyote tales. Coyote always got the woman he wanted, caused problems for other animals, and for white men. Michael's favorite story was about Coyote, Porcupine, and the elk. Coyote thought he'd tricked the Porcupine out of his elk meat, But porcupine hid the meat up a tree. That was how slow old Porcupine, who didn't see too well, was able to outwit the sly Coyote who couldn't climb. Everyone has their own special skills. Michael always thought it would be better to be the quiet Porcupine than the clever Coyote. He felt like the half-blind porcupine here in the city. His special skills weren't much use.

The chill of the desert night seeped through his jacket, so he hurried his pace to warm up. He must be getting soft, being in the city so long. Normally the temperature didn't bother him so much.

Real coyotes are cunning. Michael had a heck of a time with them in the spring when they were after the new calves. Coyotes adapt to living just about anywhere. He thought about acting like a coyote, and just adapting to Phoenix. Then he remembered the Porcupine, as well as some of the crude Coyote jokes he'd heard and changed his mind. In the city, he'd be better off as a badger. Badgers were fierce and never gave up once they started something.

While Michael walked, his mind wandered to his little

ranch. The cattle were on his mind. At least the news said there was plenty of rain up north. There would be good grass. The windmill on the upper pasture was pretty shaky. He'd planned on adding some supports and greasing the gears this week. He hoped it would hold if there was a storm. When he got back home, he needed to vaccinate the calves. His cousin Thomas shouldn't have to do the heavy work. He was a good kid, but the cattle were Michael's responsibility, and his future. If something happened to his herd, he'd have to go back to being hired labor as a ranch hand. He could lose everything he'd worked for since he was a kid.

By city standards, Michael guessed his life wasn't much. He had his truck, a sturdy shepherd's wagon to live in, four good horses, twenty cows, and twenty-four calves. All things considered, he was doing pretty well. The section of range he cared for wasn't the best in the Navajo lands, but he was starting to make a decent living. A few more good years and he'd be able to build a house. He had the perfect spot at the base of Tall Man Butte beside a little spring amid some poplar trees. The location was half way between the aunties' hogáns. He might even get one of those solar panels so he could have electric lights and a television all year. Michael's imagination kept switching between Salina Tsosie and Jenny from the diner being the woman looking from the window of his house.

Michael's musings took up the time while his feet led him back to the bar's parking lot. He didn't see Paula in the truck. Cletus sat very straight in the passenger seat. His head pressed against the headrest, and he was holding the frame of the open window. Michael looked around for Paula. Her head popped up next to Cletus' chest. The heat of his blush fought against the cool night air.

Michael turned away and found a lamp post to lean against at the edge of the parking lot. He contemplated the stars while he waited for Paula to finish...talking. The stars looked funny. They were twinkling like they did during a dust storm, even though there was no wind. Thinking about it, he realized it must be the pollution from the city that caused the flickering.

Michael spent time picking out some friendly constellations. The tiny group of The Planters was guarded by the Big Slender One. The Great Snake wandered across the sky. He'd heard other cultures had different interpretations of the patterns in the stars. Dinè legends said the First Man had thrown the stars across the sky. He guessed every culture wanted to make sense of things so much larger than they could comprehend.

After a bit, he heard the sound of Paula's high heels on the uneven parking lot surface. He took his gaze from the stars and nodded to her. He didn't want to think about where her lipstick disappeared to, but he did. His blush returned.

Paula gave him a big toothy grin. "Michael, I'm going to go home with Cletus. I need a little more time to find out what he knows about your cousin." She pulled her skirt down about a quarter of an inch. "Why don't we meet for lunch tomorrow?"

Michael did a fast calculation about how much cash he had left from his bingo winnings. He figured he could afford lunch. "Do you know where the Star Diner is?" he asked.

"Oh sure, honey, how about I meet you around one o'clock?"

"I'll see you then."

"Paula, you coming?" Cletus's voice rumbled across the

lot. He was standing next to a big Cadillac town car that had seen better days.

"Oh, I love a commanding man." Paula leaned over and gave Michael a quick kiss on the cheek. "See you tomorrow. Give your aunts my love." She trotted off.

By the time she turned, Michael must have been glowing in the dark.

Chapter 33

MILK RUN

GARCIA DECIDED TO DRIVE HOME BY WAY OF INDIAN SCHOOL
Road. It was nearly eleven. His Chevy chugged and wheezed
its way through the night. *At least my car fits in down here*, he
thought. He was here out of guilt. Using uniforms to canvas
in the Ortega murder was sloppy. He should have talked to
people himself, but there was no way to do a one-man
canvas of a neighborhood like this. Who was he kidding?
Nobody in this neighborhood was going to give a cop any
useful information.

Rubbing his eyes, he rehashed his day. He'd checked and
cross-checked the movements of the victims on the final
week of their lives. The information was thin. The only
thing connecting the victims was the fact that they had all
been released from custody for one reason or another
within a few days of their murders. If they had a common
associate, he might have killed them because he thought
they were informing to the cops. It was a small lead. He'd
have to look into it tomorrow, when he reviewed the known
associates list Norris accumulated.

He watched the people on the street, hoping to gain

insight. After he saw two drug buys in as many blocks, he shivered. *What am I doing down here?* Rudy cruised another few blocks until he saw a carryout. He'd better not go home without some milk. Parking right in front of the door, he hurried inside. The cashier wore a tightly-wrapped turban and was watching soccer on a tiny television. Rudy pulled a gallon of milk out of the dingy cooler. The whole place smelled of mold. He checked the seal on the milk. It was intact, so he put the container on the counter.

A display of Pez candy dispensers near the window caught his eye. His kids loved those things. He was deciding between Donald Duck and Darth Vader when a motion across the street drew his attention. A man ducked behind a dumpster and crouched down in the dark. If he hadn't seen him move, Rudy wouldn't have known the guy was there.

Garcia scanned the area. Two girls, flaunting their wares, were chatting with a guy in a pickup truck. One of the girls wore a fluffy pink jacket that ended well above her waist. The effect was that her already ample chest was accentuated to the grotesque. Apparently, the driver was of the same opinion because pink jacket was left on the street, and her friend rode off in the truck. The guy behind the dumpster watched the scene without moving.

Rudy frowned as he paid for his purchases. Throwing the bag into the passenger seat, he told himself it wasn't any of his business. Even so, he turned wide as he pulled out of the parking lot. His lights hit the man behind the dumpster. The man stood up with his back to the light and quickly stepped around the corner of the building. For a second he was in profile. *He kind of looks like Phil Davis,* he thought, but shook his head. "Nah, I need some sleep."

IT WAS NEARLY MIDNIGHT WHEN GARCIA FINALLY GOT HOME. He put the bag with the toys on the counter and practically sleepwalked to the refrigerator with the milk. A plate covered in aluminum foil sat on the shelf. He pulled it out, silently blessing his wife. Sure she complained, but that was just her way. She was his touchstone, keeping the turmoil of his job outside their home.

Since she found out he was on the task force, Antonia, despite her grumbling, was being especially understanding about his coming home late. She said administrative types turned her on. Garcia suspected she was glad he wouldn't be on the street as much. He'd have to do something special for her soon. He didn't want to be one of those guys who took his wife for granted. He knew too many divorced cops. Look at Norris and Phil Davis, all they did was work. Twenty years from now, he didn't want to be in their position. Davis was probably still out on Indian School Road watching hookers instead of heading for a warm bed and a loving woman. Not that Garcia was in any better shape tonight. He was so exhausted; he didn't have the energy to do his loving woman any good. Maybe in the morning.

Garcia rubbed his eyes, wincing as he bumped his sore nose. The last time he'd looked, his black eyes were fading to green and yellow. He looked strange enough to scare the kids if he accidentally woke them when he kissed them goodnight. He needed to make time for the kids, too. He didn't want to be a dad that gave them presents instead of attention. His eyes strayed to the sack on the counter. "Oh, shit."

Chapter 34

LONELY MOUNTAIN

AT SIX-THIRTY, THE SUN WAS JUST BREAKING THE HORIZON. Garcia balanced a toaster strudel and a cup of coffee as he fished in his pocket for the keys to his car. Antonia had offered to get up and make him breakfast, but he told her to sleep in until the kids got her up. It was the least he could do for her. He found his keys just as a gray pickup pulled over to the curb by the end of his driveway.

"Hey, Rudy, ride in with me," the driver said, waving him over.

"What the hell you doing out this early in the morning?"

"I have an appointment at nine, but I wanted to show you something for the task force murders. Ride with me, I'll bring you back for your car." He reached over and popped the passenger side door.

Garcia climbed in. "Want half?" He held out the strudel.

"Nah, I'm good." They pulled out and headed down the silent street. As the sun rose higher, the street lights winked out in their wake.

"Is this going to take long? I wanted to get home early

today. I need to spend some time with the kids." Garcia took a big bite of his strudel.

"This shouldn't take too long." They merged onto the freeway.

"So, what you got?" Garcia savored a sip of coffee and looked at the driver over the cup.

"I wanted to get your fresh eyes on a scene I worked up in South Mountain Park back a few years ago."

This one's here on his time off, Garcia thought. *And Davis was still working when I got home. Thank you, Jesus I have a life. I don't want to be like these guys when I'm old.*

Driving with one hand on the wheel, the detective half turned to Garcia. "How you coming with organizing the task force data? As useful as it is, I hate doing the computer stuff."

"They say that's a generational thing. I was raised with computers, so I don't mind doing the data-driven work." Garcia took another sip of his coffee. "I'm just starting to get into the correlations. Right now, the only thing I have on the first few murders is that someone on the detective squad busted all the victims at least once. Obviously, that doesn't mean anything. Half the cops on the force must have busted most of that trash at one time or another. I have paper on two of them."

He savored the last bite of the strudel. "The other thing that looked odd is that they all died within a week or so after being released by the court due to some technicality. That's why I'm going in this morning. I thought I'd look at the cases and see if there were any individuals linked to all the victims or threats from relatives of people our victims killed."

"You might have something there. I took a look at the murder board yesterday. A fine bunch of scum we're wasting our time on. The world's probably better off without them."

They turned south onto freeway 10. "If it weren't for that damn reporter, we'd both be sleeping in today."

"Maybe so." Garcia licked the pastry crumbs from his fingers and took a swig of coffee.

"How about your other cases, you keeping up?"

"Most of my cases are pretty well wrapped up. The only one that's a problem is the Ortega murder. The Indian is looking worse and worse for it. The DA is riding my ass for more evidence, but it isn't there. I went out yesterday to canvas Indian School Road again, and came up empty." Garcia yawned widely.

"Canvasing that neighborhood is a waste of time. Nobody down there would tell you the time of day."

"I had to jump through the hoops. I told you how the DA is bugging me about the case."

The driver nodded his understanding. Traffic started to pick up as they made the big curve headed east. Garcia flipped his visor down to dampen the rising sun's glare. When the road turned south again, they exited on Baseline Road and headed west.

"What are we doing out here?" Garcia asked. "I thought all the murders we were interested in were in the center city?"

"All the murders the reporter spotted were in town. I thought this site might be another in the pattern, maybe the first of the series."

"How old is it?"

"About five years, from back when you were still wet behind the ears."

The hills of South Mountain Park sent shadows reaching toward the road. Garcia felt a pang of disappointment when they turned on Dobbin's Road. He'd hoped they would be going past the Stone Palace. He and Antonia had gone there on one of their first dates. The road was starting to curve to the south when they turned off on a dirt track behind some houses.

Garcia put his hand flat against the roof, holding himself in place, as the truck rattled and bounced through an arroyo. "I guess this what they call off the beaten track. A good place for a body dump," Garcia said.

"Almost as good as Tortilla Flats."

They continued through the scrubby mesquite for a couple miles. The screech of branches on the truck's sides jangled Garcia's nerves. "Are we still in our jurisdiction?" A frown was developing on his face.

"Yeah, the road twists around." The driver was half turned toward his passenger, relaxed in his seat. Despite the roughness of the road, he still only had one hand on the wheel. "It took some time to figure out who was in charge of the site. They had everybody but the Mormon Tabernacle Choir here for a while, finally some bright boy decided to look at a map and they dumped the case on me and my partner."

With brush still scraping its sides, the truck rounded a rocky outcrop. Garcia wasn't sure they were still on the park road. Finally, they bumped to a stop.

"The scene's nearby."

Garcia got out and looked down the hillside, south toward the city skyline. "Wow, if you have to die, this is a beautiful spot."

"I'm glad you like it." He walked up behind Garcia.

"I'll have to bring Antonia and the kids up here someday." Garcia took a deep breath, enjoying the crisp morning air and the acrid scents of sage and mesquite. "Where is the scene?"

THE MAN SHOT HIM, JUST BEHIND HIS LEFT EAR. GARCIA dropped like a deflated balloon. A tiny line of blood dribbled out of the hole. The man methodically placed his gun back in his belt holster and used his foot to maneuver the young detective's body to the edge of the hill. "Sorry kid, you were getting too close." He looked at Garcia's face for a moment. "The body dump is down there." He kicked the limp corpse over the rim. The carcass rolled and bounced, limbs flopping until it came to rest among some rocks next to two jumbled skeletons.

The dappled shadow of a manzanita tree hid Antonia's husband's body from the morning sun.

Chapter 35

RESEARCH

MICHAEL'D BEEN UP SINCE DAWN. EVEN THOUGH HE'D BEEN out late, waking with the sunrise was a habit that was hard to break. At eight o'clock, he found Carol Kowalski at her office in the building that housed the Phoenix Sun. The Sun was a good description. The large room that housed about twenty open-topped cubicles was so bright from the overhead lights, it made his eyes ache. There were no windows, no shadows. No natural sounds. Voices echoed around the room, bouncing together until the people sounded like birds flocking in the fall.

"Michael, it's good to see you. How's your cousin?" Carol was wearing a skirt so tight she had to take tiny steps as she came to greet him by the elevator.

"He's holding up. They say he should make a full recovery. At least he's safer at the hospital." Michael was getting used to the Anglo way of referring to people by name even though they were present. "I'm sorry about not coming yesterday."

"Don't worry about it, I understand completely." Carol led him to her three-sided box of an office. It housed a computer, a phone, and several filing cabinets. She had no pictures or personal items in the sparse area. He leaned against the corner of her desk while she answered the ringing phone. For the next few minutes, she said "yes" or "no" into the receiver. Her red fingernails tapped an impatient beat on the desktop. The walls surrounding them were covered with sticky notes, most containing names and numbers. Some had cryptic phrases like "couldn't see the top," or "unknown subject has a basement."

Carol swiveled her chair toward him. "Michael, I have an emergency meeting, but let me call downstairs and Jim will set you up so you can start going through the archives." She took off one of her earrings and held the phone with her shoulder. "Hey Jimmy, I'm sending a young man, Michael Yazzie, down to you. He's doing some research for me. Can you set him up with a computer and get him started?" She typed on the computer in front of her while she talked. "Yeah, I understand. He's a curly blond, about six foot, very fit, with a great tan. He's wearing a gray plaid collared shirt, faded jeans, and genuine cowboy boots." She waited a few moments. "Yes, Jim, he's a real cowboy, so keep your hands to yourself. I got dibs." She smiled up at Michael who shifted his stance. He'd seen that smile on women before. It made him nervous. She was old enough to be his mother.

"Mike, I'm going to have you go down to the morgue, our archive room. A little round man named Jim will help you set up a public records search. I'd like you to try to find any information about these police officers and detectives." She handed him a list of five names on a long yellow lined notebook. "Make notes about their lives and any notable cases you come across. See if you can find any patterns in their behavior, or any cases they had where the criminal went free on a technicality."

The archive room had long rows of shelves that disappeared into the dark beyond the dim lights. File cabinets made a wall behind which there were a few desks with computers. Jim was a smiley little man about as round as he was tall. His bald head barely came up to Michael's shoulder.

"Hi, Mike, I'm Jim, the keeper of the files," he said when Michael introduced himself. "You are a morsel. No wonder Carol called dibs."

"I'd better get started." Other than that one time at The Lawyer's office, Michael hadn't used a computer since high school. He hoped it was like riding a horse, something you remember instinctively.

Jim started the computer and found the public records website for him. Michael managed to get Detective Rudy Garcia's name in the search space, and a half dozen documents showed up. He disregarded his birth certificate and marriage license. Garcia'd been in the police department ten years. The other articles talked about court cases where he'd been involved. Michael took a few notes. He didn't see how any of this would help. There wasn't much information for the names of the other people who weren't victims.

The victims from the news article yielded more information. He started a list of their crimes next to their names. Most of the women were not just prostitutes, they'd been arrested for selling drugs, assaults, and in three cases they had trafficked in child prostitution. Michael's stomach heaved when he read about the woman, Tiffany Castain, who had been caught helping a man rape a four-year-old child. She wasn't prosecuted because she gave evidence against the parents who provided the child.

His stomach continued to churn. He could hardly

believe the list of terrible things the murdered people had done. How could people live with so little compassion for others? Michael wiped a hand over his eyes. Every one of the murdered people had been tried for their crimes, then released. How could the court let these horrible people go free when Jon, who never hurt anyone, was nearly killed in jail?

He pushed back from the computer with a sigh.

Jim looked up from his work. "Having trouble?"

"I just don't think I'm finding anything useful. I wish I could compare the names Ms. Kowalski gave me to the murder victims."

"I think we can manage that." Jim came over and called up another program. He leaned very close and put his hand on Michael's shoulder.

For all his smiles and jovial demeanor, the man had an oozy air about him. There was something behind his eyes, like a Gila Monster's pretty pink color hiding its poison bite. Michael shifted in his chair but wasn't able to escape Jim's moist grasp. He stood up to get away and offered him his seat in front of the computer. Jim slid in, still smiling. Michael had the feeling that his discomfort made the little man happy.

"Try this, you can put the names in and cross reference them. Good luck." Jim got up, patted Michael on the cheek, and went back to his desk.

He rubbed his face where Jim touched him and slid back into the chair. Cross-referencing Simon Ortega, the guy Jon was supposed to have killed, with ten names Carol had given him showed some promise. Ortega showed up in relation to Tom Norris, Phil Davis, and Ray Chamberlin. He checked his notes and found that Phil Davis was Norris' partner and Chamberlin was Garcia's. All three detectives had arrested Ortega several times through the years. Most recently, Ortega had gone to trial for selling heroin laced with rat poison. The article said five people died. Ortega got off because they couldn't connect him directly to the drugs. He was killed a week after he was released. Michael put the names of the people who died from Ortega's heroin overdose on another page of his notes. He'd go back and see if any of those people were related to any of the murdered people's victims.

Chapter 36

LUNCH DATE

It was getting on past noon. Michael needed to meet Paula. He told Jim he'd be back, and left his notes next to the computer. Dodging fast-walking people, he found his way out of the building. The clatter of hard shoes on the polished floors made his nerves jangle. It sounded like a herd of cattle on the highway. He didn't see one person with a smile on their face. A lot of them had telephones to their ears, carrying on conversations as if no one else were around.

Coming into the sunlight from the artificial world of the newspaper office, it took Michael a minute or two to realize he'd come out on the other side of the office block. He could see a big antenna to the left. Getting his bearings he noticed the big curved building that wasn't far from the diner and decided to walk rather than go back to try and find his truck. The glare off the curved building's windows made him squint. It had some type of coating that reflected the sun. He wondered how many cubicles were in that huge place.

Men were mowing the grass that surrounded the curved

building. The noise of their machines further rattled Michael's nerves. There were too many unfamiliar noises and smells. The juicy smell of the cut grass made his nose wrinkle. He'd been inside too much lately. He tried to figure out how they kept the grass from drying up. He kept his eye on the ground and finally spotted a little black squirter like The Lawyer had at his house. He shook his head at the waste. The grass in the yards around the center of this city could feed a couple dozen cows easily.

Jenny was working at the diner. She was behind the counter and held up the coffee pot with a smile when she saw Michael. He nodded, and she poured him a cup. He took a booth in her area.

"Do they ever let you go home?" he asked when she brought his drink and a menu.

"I'm here so much, I have my pillow and a teddy bear in the back." She had two dimples when she smiled. "What can I get you?"

"This coffee will do for a start. I'm expecting another person. She should be here any minute."

"I'll get you another menu," she said with a slight frown. She turned on her heel and left with her back stiff and shoulders square.

A few minutes later Paula strode in on six-inch high heels. Today, she was wearing blue jeans so tight they looked painted on her legs. Her white shirt had ruffles in front that accentuated her chest. Red lipstick and earrings matched her nails and shoes. Her hair was black today. Michael stood as she sashayed over to the booth.

"Hey, sweet boy, have I got news for you."

"Hello, you look extra nice today."

"Why thank you. I just got up a little while ago and threw this outfit together. It's not up to my usual standards."

Michael grinned. "You don't have to work for compliments with me. You're the best-dressed woman I know."

Paula leaned across the table and patted his cheek, the same place round Jim had. "How are your aunts?"

"They're still chuckling over what you said about the 'Real Housewives.' Thanks for giving them something to laugh about." It occurred to Michael that he didn't feel the need to wipe his face when Paula touched him.

Jenny came over to take their orders. She had a slight frown on her face. Paula leaned back in her chair and appraised the delicate blond woman. Her lips pursed, and her eyes squinted a little. If the two of them were dogs, they would be circling with their tails low. Michael ignored their posturing and looked at the menu. "I'd like a chicken basket and a piece of pie. We'll just need one check."

Paula gave Jenny a big toothy smile with her order and batted her eyelashes as she handed over the menu. Jenny set her shoulders and marched back behind the counter.

Michael longed to be back among women he understood. Then he thought of Salina. At least, ones he thought he understood.

Paula watched Jenny until she was out of earshot. She leaned in close to Michael and whispered. "Cletus thinks a cop is the one killing all those drug dealers and hookers."

Michael leaned in and kept his voice low. "What makes him think that?"

"Cletus is an observant type of guy. He's seen this cop called Norris in the neighborhood the day of every murder."

"Wouldn't he be there for the murders? He's a cop, after all."

"Yeah, but Cletus, he seen that Norris and another big cop he don't know, hanging around before almost every murder, too." Paula was nodding with her words. "He got no business on the street without no murder happening. They wasn't down there getting their ashes hauled either. I asked around."

"Ashes hauled?" Michael raised his eyebrows.

"Norris wasn't with no prostitute, male or female. Neither was the other one."

"Maybe they were buying drugs," he said.

Paula shrugged and leaned back in her chair. "Me and Cletus don't travel in those circles, so I wouldn't know."

"Was it just those cops? He didn't see any others?"

"There are always cops sniffing around, but Cletus said only Norris and the other big cop was always there when there was a killing."

"Why didn't Cletus tell someone about seeing those men at the murders?" It seemed a natural thing to do.

"Baby, in our world, you mind your own business. Cletus ain't going to stick his neck out for a bunch of dead trash. All those people needed murdering. They was all bad news. Besides, my man knows it's best not to mess with cops. That way you don't end up behind a Bodega with your throat cut."

A chill shivered down Michael's back. "Paula, you be careful. If a cop thinks you or Cletus knows something, you might get framed like my cousin, or worse."

"Don't you worry. I got plenty of friends who'd give me an alibi or protection if I need it."

Michael'd seen enough movies to know that an alibi wasn't always enough and said as much to her.

Paula patted his hand. "As the cowboys say, this ain't my first rodeo, but you're sweet to worry."

The diner's door dinged as it opened, and a large group of uniformed cops came in. Michael raised his chin and pursed his lips toward the group. "So Paula, are you from Phoenix originally?"

She smiled, "You're getting the hang of this city shit, ain't you?"

Michael smiled. Maybe he was.

Jenny brought their food, and they spent the rest of the meal chatting about everyday things. He invited Paula to supper, but she said she'd missed so much work she had to get busy. Michael tried not to think about all the chores he'd left undone back home.

After Paula left, he sat thinking about what she'd said. He needed to run an idea by The Lawyer.

Jenny came over to fill his coffee cup and clear the plates. "You come in with the most interesting people," she said.

"Yes, ma'am, I guess I do. It's the city broadening my horizons. Back home, I'm pretty boring."

"I doubt that." Her dimples brightened her smile.

"Miss Jenny, are you flirting with me?" He tilted his head up at her.

"I might be, but I wouldn't want to upset your girlfriend who just left."

"Paula's not my girlfriend; she's just helping me get information to help my cousin."

"That's good to know." She dimpled again.

Despite Salina's concerns about flirting with waitresses, Michael was getting ready to ask Jenny to sit down when police radios squawked from several nearby tables. He didn't hear what was said, but the reaction of the men and women was nearly identical. They stood up, threw down money, turned, and hurried out. He looked at Jenny with eyebrows raised.

"Something big must be happening," she said. "I'm going to have to get busy cleaning up."

Michael nodded and got up to pay his bill at the register. Mentally kicking himself, he thought, *What am I doing flirting with a girl when Jon is sitting in jail?*

TO MICHAEL'S RELIEF, THE BASEMENT OF THE NEWSPAPER office was empty. He didn't have the energy to figure out what it was about Round Jim that made him uncomfortable. Jim wasn't any stranger than many of the people Michael'd met here in the city. It was probably because Jim's actions didn't seem honest. An involuntary shiver shook his shoulders when he thought about the little man touching his face.

Sitting at the computer, he had to think a couple of minutes about how to do the comparison search that Jim showed him. After a few false starts, the computer finally gave him Tom Norris' relationship with each of the murder victims. There were a lot of connections. Michael wrote down the dates and the crimes that were committed by the murdered people before they died. In every case, Norris had arrested them at least once, although it wasn't necessarily his trials where the victims had been set free.

Michael was starting to see what The Lawyer and Carol were talking about at dinner the other night. Maybe Norris was unhappy about those horrible people going free. To be thorough, he put the other names Carol had given him in the computer and ran the same search. Phil Davis, Tom Norris, and a Ray Chamberlin were the only ones who had as many connections to the victims. Other police detectives had arrested a few of the victims, but no one else, besides Norris, Davis, and Chamberlin, had been in contact with almost all of them.

Michael ran another search looking for knife murders. There were sixteen in the past five years. Nine were either bar fights gone bad or husband and wife murders. Two were still unsolved. The rest of the victims were released by the police a few days before their deaths. Three were drug dealers, another, a woman who was a child molester. A couple of men got convicted for those murders. Michael wondered if those guys were as innocent as Jon.

Shutting off the computer, he stood and stretched. Trying to be polite, he wrote a note to thank Jim for his help. As Michael headed toward the cubical farm to find Carol, he met Jim as he came down the stairs.

"How's the sleuthing coming along?" Jim asked.

"I think I found everything I need. Thanks for your help with the computer. I haven't used one in a while."

"Anytime. Did you find out anything good?"

"I'm not sure. I need to talk to Ms. Kowalski before I make any conclusions. I'd best get going." Michael continued up the stairs. His neck itched. Jim was watching him until he went through the door. The man wasn't threatening in any way, but his look still made Michael twitchy. He was like a fox watching for a chance to take a new lamb. Michael didn't like the feeling that he was the lamb.

Carol wasn't in her cubby. The man in the next box told Michael she was out of the building. He didn't know when she'd be back. He watched a guy making copies on a machine near the elevator. It looked simple enough, so he made a duplicate of his notes. Michael left the copies and a note to call him at The Lawyer's office on Carol's desk. Once out in the bright sunlit afternoon, a deep breath cleared the building's artificial smells from his lungs.

Chapter 37

A SHOT IN THE DUSK

THE LAWYER'S OFFICE SEEMED EVEN OLDER AND SHABBIER after Michael's visit to the fancy building housing the newspaper. Mrs. Jones was at her desk. She looked up from her typing when he came in. Her hair was still tightly wound in a bun, but she was wearing a blue blouse today. The smell of violets clouded around her.

"Ma'am," Michael said, feeling as if he should wipe his feet or something.

"Good afternoon, Michael. He's in his office."

"Thank you." Michael rapped on the door. "It's your investigator." He heard a grunt that sounded sort of affirmative, so he went in.

The Lawyer was hunched over his desk typing on a computer. He looked up briefly and, using his chin, indicated a chair that was clear enough to sit on. Michael'd been in a chair more the past few days than he usually was in a month. Instead of sitting, he leaned against one of the file cabinets. Anxious as he was to show The Lawyer what he found, he couldn't interrupt the man. Patient courtesy was the way he'd been raised. Michael might give up some of his manners after dealing with the city people, but he had limits. He would no more bother the man until spoken to than he would do a hoochie dance with Mrs. Jones.

Fishing around in his pocket, Michael pulled out his notes. He couldn't find any new patterns on his second read-through. The more he thought about it, the more he realized he needed to understand the predators in this city. He knew why a bear or coyote went after its prey. Michael needed to figure out why a person would decide to kill strangers. He needed to do more research.

The Lawyer quit typing and cleared his throat. "What did you find out?"

"I have a couple of things. Carol was gone when I finished, so I didn't get a chance to tell her. There was a connection between all but one of the victims and the detectives Tomas Norris, Phillip Davis, and one named Raymond Chamberlin." He waited for The Lawyer to comment. He knew Chamberlin was The Lawyer's friend. When none was forthcoming, Michael continued. "Norris was with Garcia when I found Jon's truck."

"And Norris was the one who said he found drugs in the truck," The Lawyer finished for Michael. He sat back in his chair and made a tent with his fingers. "Well, isn't that something."

"Also, I met with Paula for lunch..."

The Lawyer winced.

"...she talked to the guy from the liquor store." Heat blossomed on Michael's face. "He said he's seen Detective Norris and another big man around the nights before some of the murders."

"Davis is a pretty big guy."

"So is Chamberlin. He was the guy in the restaurant the other night, wasn't he?

The phone rang in the outer office, and Mrs. Jones' muffled voice came through the wall. A light flashed on The Lawyer's phone. He held up one finger and picked it up. "Lawson...Hi, Carol, he just got here. Let me put you on speaker." He pushed a button on the phone and hung up. "Michael found out some interesting facts about our local constabulary."

"I saw his notes. He did a great job," Carol's disembodied voice came from somewhere under the papers that littered The Lawyer's desk.

"Jim helped me do a cross check between the victim's names and the names you gave me. You saw the guys who were connected to all the victims." Michael felt strange talking to the box on the table. For him, reading a person's body language was as important as hearing their words.

"What do you think of Norris and Davis?" The Lawyer injected. "Mike has an informant who saw Norris and another big guy near some of the crime scenes before the murders. As an investigator, Mike's not too bad for a kid who's only been in town a week."

Hearing pride in The Lawyer's voice, Michael's hackles rose a little.

"Who's the informant? Will they go on record or testify?" Carol asked.

The Lawyer raised his eyebrows.

"I'm not sure he wants anyone to know who he is. He's worried for his safety," Michael said.

The Lawyer looked up and frowned at the tension in his voice. "He doesn't want to get set up as a target." Even though Paula said he was concerned, Michael couldn't imagine anything scaring Cletus.

"Do you think he would change his mind if I talked to him?" Carol asked. "I'm pretty persuasive."

The Lawyer raised his eyebrows, again. Michael shook his head.

"Why don't you use your feminine wiles on someone on the police beat and see if there is any gossip about Norris and Davis. I know Ray Chamberlin, we're in the same bowling league. He's a complicated guy. I can ask around about him." The Lawyer sat up and leaned his elbows on the desk. "All we have is conjecture. Nobody is going to convict police for being seen in a high crime area, or for dealing with criminals."

"I'll see what I can do," Carol said. "Give me a day or two. I can't be too direct, or they'll close ranks. You know the thin blue line..." Michael tilted his head at The Lawyer who held up a hand and shook his head. "...if it is bad cops doing these murders, I'll have the story of the century."

Carol's voice reminded Michael of a coyote yipping that she caught her prey. "Do you have anything more for me to research?" he asked.

"I can't think of anything right now. Why don't we meet for dinner tomorrow?" Carol's voice had softened. The tone made his stomach churn.

"I...uh, I'm not sure what my aunts might have planned for tomorrow. Why don't I call you if I can make it?" Sweat started out on his forehead. He really didn't want to be alone at a restaurant with Carol Kowalski.

"OK, lover boy, call me." She actually giggled. "David, I'll let you know if anything breaks." The dial tone indicated she'd hung up.

Michael took a breath he didn't know he'd been holding.

"She's a real piece of work, isn't she?" The Lawyer asked.

"She makes me feel as if I were a steak dinner."

The Lawyer leaned back in his chair and laughed until

he was gasping for air. Michael couldn't help but smile. He leaned forward wiping his eyes. "She *is* a cougar."

Michael nodded. Carol sure wouldn't lose her prey. Like the mountain lion, Náshdóítsoh, she would wait for her chance to pounce. He just had to be moving fast enough that she didn't land on him when she jumped. "I'm skittish, that cougar isn't going to get me."

The Lawyer started laughing, again. He rubbed tears from his eyes.

Michael scratched his ear and looked down at his feet, figuring it would be best to change the topic. "What's the thin blue line she was talking about?"

Still chuckling, The Lawyer said, "The police are the blue line. It means they'll stick together and protect each other."

That made sense to Michael. The police were a tribe. Of course, they would protect each other. It was a relief to recognize somebody's motivation here in the city. He just wished the knowledge was something that would help Jon. "Do you think the blue line is why Norris planted drugs in Jon's truck?"

"It could be. Unfortunately, there's no way to prove it." Lawson sighed. "I don't want to upset your aunts with this until we know more. I'm going to call Chamberlin and see if he wants to go bowling. Do you bowl?"

Michael nodded his affirmative. He'd done it once on a school trip, so he knew how. He thought it was kind of a waste of time, but it would be a good way to get information.

The Lawyer tapped a pencil on the desktop. "I have a little more work before I can leave. Why don't you get a cup of coffee and we can ride back to the house together and talk? You can get your truck in the morning."

"Is there a computer here I can use?" Michael pushed

away from the file cabinet. "I want to look up information about people who've done a lot of murders."

"You mean serial killers? I suppose, if Carol's right, that's what we're dealing with." The Lawyer scratched his head and absently patted the long hairs back over his bald spot.

"I think she is," Michael said.

"Ask Mrs. Jones to give you a login."

Out in the front office, Mrs. Jones was packing her briefcase sized purse to leave. "You boys seemed to be having fun in there."

"Yes, ma'am. I guess we were. I was wondering if I could borrow a computer for a little bit." He poured the last of the coffee from the pot.

She set him up on a computer at her desk and punched in the codes that would let him use the internet. "Could you rinse out the coffee pot and put the trash in the bin outside before you go?" she asked. She picked up her purse, again. Before she got to the hall door, she turned. "Don't let him stay too late. I don't want to find him sleeping at his desk again."

"I'll get him home at a decent hour."

Her pinched face brightened with a smile. "Don't worry, Michael. If anyone can get your cousin out of trouble, it will be him." She tilted her head toward his office door.

"I hope so, ma'am." He resisted the urge to give this woman his troubles, to tell her that Jon wouldn't survive in jail, and how helpless he felt being unable to save him. But tradition was in his way. Don't burden strangers, especially elders, with your troubles. The mere fact that Michael wanted to tell her made him a little sick to his stomach. It was bad enough he'd already vented to Paula. *Who am I becoming?*

MICHAEL SPENT A COUPLE HOURS LOOKING AT THE DARK world of serial killers. He was raised with Navajo stories of people who chose an evil path to their life. They called them witches. He didn't know much about witches, but thought he'd met some nasty folks in his twenty years. Until he started reading, Michael never would have believed the huge volume of people who preyed on others. There were so many serial killers, they were given categories—a lot of categories. The article he read had a debate about whether these people were psychotic or just had antisocial personalities. As a good man of the Diné, he didn't understand the debate. To him, anybody who wanted to kill lots of people was definitely a psycho.

The murders in Phoenix fell under the category of a mission-oriented serial killer who was intelligent and had what one doctor called a "mask of sanity." Michael found a couple of examples of this type of killer. One was an ex-soldier turned civil servant named Dennis Nilsen who was trying to rid the world of people who didn't meet his religious expectations. Another example, Vlado Taneski, was especially disturbing because he was a journalist and crime reporter who killed bad guys. It made him think about his reaction to Carol Kowalski. Was his unease around her because an older woman was making sexual innuendoes to someone his age, or was it because he was reacting to her as a predator? He had a lot to discuss with The Lawyer on the ride home.

The setting sun lent the walls of the shabby building a golden glow when they finally left the office. The Lawyer was walking with slow, careful steps as he headed to his car. The older man's shoulders were slumped. Michael turned the opposite way to carry the bag of trash to the dumpster for Mrs. Jones. He was throwing the bag into the open bin when the metal gave a loud bong, and a chip of something flew off and clipped his forehead. It took him a second to realize what happened. *Someone's shooting at me*, he thought. His legs, more sensible than his brain, were already propelling him behind the mass of the dumpster when the second shot careened off the side of the container. "Take cover!" Michael shouted, hoping The Lawyer realized what was happening. More shots rang out.

Dropping to the ground, Michael looked around the corner of the bin. The Lawyer's car door slammed. Michael could just see the shape of a man in the space between the buildings across the street. He had time to register a large hulking figure when another shot cracked out, echoing between the walls of the buildings. The asphalt a few inches from his hand erupted. He scooted to the center of his shield and leaned back against the metal. Warm blood dripped from the cut on his forehead. Michael wiped it from his eyes. Sweat from the heat of the asphalt and metal soaked through his clothes. The smell of garbage increased the bitter taste of adrenaline in his mouth. The sound of a couple more shots echoed against the buildings, but he didn't see evidence of their path.

There was no place to run. The shooter had a clear line of sight around the sides of the dumpster. He had a clear line on the car as well. Michael heard the engine sputter to life. He hoped The Lawyer would get away and call the police. He debated making a run for it while the shooter's attention was on the car, but there was a ten-foot-high fence blocking the end of the alley between the buildings. He might make it to the fence, but would be a perfect target trying to get over the top.

Michael couldn't just sit here as though he were a rabbit hiding under a bush. It wouldn't be long before the shooter would walk down on him and put a bullet in his head. He looked around, hoping he might be able to break a window and get into the office. Another shot echoed along the walls. He'd missed his chance.

The Lawyer's car turned around the edge of the building and slammed to a stop in front of Michael, partially shielded behind the dumpster. Two shots careened off the roof of the car. The back door flew open, without hesitation Michael threw himself prone on the seat, landing awkwardly on The Lawyer's briefcase. Another shot spanged through the back window, hitting the passenger seat a foot from his head.

The Lawyer stomped on the gas, and they swerved to roar down the space between the buildings. Michael pulled in his legs as the open door hit the dumpster and slammed shut. "What about the fence?" he yelled.

"Hold on," The Lawyer said through clenched teeth. He braced his arms on the wheel, and they smashed through the fence. The windshield shattered into a million crazed lines. A right turn behind the office building took them out of the shooter's sight. They slammed to a stop. Michael was thrown to the floor in the back. The Lawyer was breathing heavily. "Get up here and knock out this glass, I can't see."

Michael pulled himself over the seat and used his feet to punch out the windshield. As it flew onto the hood, the car started moving. It bounced over the curb and into the busy road. The shattered windshield fell to the pavement. Horns blared, and brakes screeched, but they didn't slow down. The Lawyer made a hard left between two frantically swerving cars, and tore off down the street. Michael got his feet off the dash and turned in the seat. The Lawyer's side window was broken out and blood, leaking from his chest, ran down the front of his pale blue suit.

"You're shot."

"You're going to have to drive." His breath made a bubbling sound. He made a random turn and pulled into the parking area in front of an abandoned barber shop. Michael got out and ran around to help him. The Lawyer's wound was steadily oozing.

Michael used his forearm to wipe the blood out of his own eyes. With The Lawyer's arm under his shoulder, they staggered around to the passenger side and he levered the older man into the seat. Michael took off his shirt and wadded it into a ball to press into the chest wound. The Lawyer groaned, and his head lolled back on the seat.

"My phone," he said, patting his jacket awkwardly with his right hand.

Michael took his father's hand and pressed it to his shirt covered wound. Fishing around in the inner pocket of the suit coat he found the cell phone. "Who can I call?"

"Hit two, two, seven to unlock it, and call 911," The Lawyer said in a hoarse whisper.

"What if it was the police who shot at us? If Norris and Davis are part of the murders, aren't we a target?"

He nodded and winced. "Call the police, and call Carol to meet us at the hospital. Her number's in the phone."

Realizing the shooter could be coming up the road, Michael ran around and got into the driver's seat. Once they were in traffic, he punched 911 and explained what happened. The lady on the other end of the line had a high pitched whiny voice. She wanted him to stay on the phone. He told her they were headed to County Hospital and hung up on her. The Lawyer was getting very pale. Michael drove as fast as he could, weaving in and out between the other cars. He used his bare arm to rub the blood from his eyes as he drove.

At a stop light, he called Carol, trusting she wasn't a Vlado Taneski type serial killer.

"Get to the hospital as fast as you can," Carol said. "I'm going to talk to someone at the police department that I trust. Stay with your father, if possible. You might not be right about who shot at you, but whoever they are, they don't want any witnesses."

"I'm not sure what I saw." Michael turned to The Lawyer. "Did you..." Lawson was unconscious; his hand had slipped from the compress. "Carol, I have to go, I'll see you at the hospital." He snapped the phone shut and reached over to put pressure on the old man's wound.

He wondered why The Lawyer hadn't driven away when the shooting started.

Chapter 38

ANOTHER ALL-NIGHTER

THE CAR HORN ECHOED OFF THE BRICK WALLS AS MICHAEL drove into the ambulance bay. People wearing baggy green clothes boiled out of the sliding doors. They hesitated when he jumped out of the car covered in blood with no shirt.

"He's been shot!" Michael yelled waving at The Lawyer. The people in green maneuvered the wounded man out of the car and onto a rolling bed.

"Sir, you're bleeding, we need to check you out." A redheaded nurse put her hand on Michael's arm.

He was shivering from the evening's chill, but shook her off and followed the medical crowd through the spasming doors into a small brightly lit room. "I can't leave him. I'm all right. Just check me here." Michael sat in a chair away from the commotion around the bed.

The nurse sighed, and started searching drawers. She cleaned his face with gauze pads. She smelled of Ivory soap. He tried not to flinch when she put stinging antiseptic on his wound. He could tell the cut tracked across the middle of his forehead just above the eyebrows. It was longer and deeper than he thought.

"You're going to need stitches," she said. "You're lucky it wasn't an inch lower. You could have lost an eye." She taped a pad to Michael's head.

He shrugged. "Is he going to be all right?" Michael tipped his chin toward The Lawyer. The doctors had cut away the unconscious man's shirt, stuck needles in his arm and hung bags of blood. A blond doctor was listening to his chest with one of those little medallion things that had tubes to his ears. Michael was too flustered to remember its name.

The doctor stuck another needle in The Lawyer's chest. There was a hissing noise and blood spurted out. "Get me a chest tube. He has a pneumothorax."

The others started scrambling around.

Ivory-soap nurse stepped in front of Michael. He lost sight of The Lawyer. "Are you related?" The nurse said.

"He's my father." Michael couldn't look around her to see what they were doing.

"They're taking good care of him. Let me get you a scrub shirt and a doctor to stitch you up. They should know more about your father soon."

She left, to be replaced by a plump woman with short black hair that hugged her head like a helmet. The new woman was carrying a clipboard.

"Sir, can I ask you some questions?" Helmet-head tapped her pen against the clipboard.

"I guess."

Writing on her board, she took down their names and the details Michael knew about his father. He tried to explain that he was part of the Navajo Nation, but she stiffened her shoulders and made a clucking sound. He didn't think she believed him. He didn't know about The Lawyer's insurance, so she said when they bagged his possessions, Michael could go through his wallet. The commotion around The Lawyer had slowed. He took that as a good sign.

As the helmet-head woman disappeared, two police detectives came to ask about the shooting. Michael sat up straighter. The cops looked at him as if he'd been the one doing the shooting. They introduced themselves as Sam Burton and Jefferson Reed. Reed was very tall, like a skinny giant. He reminded Michael of one of the Yei people he'd seen in sand paintings. The other, Burton, was short and muscular, a bear. His skin was as dark as Cletus'. Michael considered forgetting English for a while but realized it would just get them mad. Michael wished Carol or even Paula were here. They knew how to talk to police.

"Mr. Lawson, are you up to talking about what happened?" The bear man asked.

The two men loomed over him sitting in the chair. His breathing rate increased. Michael didn't think it was safe to correct them about his name.

"Where did the shooting happen?"

"At my father's law office." He couldn't remember the building number, so just gave him the street and described the building.

The doctor who had been giving orders to the people around The Lawyer came over. "Mr. Lawson..."

Michael bit his lip and nodded.

"...we're taking your father down to surgery. He's lost a lot of blood. We'll know more when we get the bullet out."

"Can I go with him? I don't know who was shooting at us." He moved his eyes to indicate the police. "I'm worried they might try to get to him. I need to be there."

"Don't worry, he'll be safe." The doctor had a shiny bald head, his skin was very pale.

"The Yei cop glanced at Michael and nodded. "I'll go with your father to surgery."

"I'd rather stay with him." Michael started to get up.

"You get yourself stitched up. We can come and get you when he comes out." The

Yei cop put a hand on Michael's shoulder. "I promise, no one will get to him." He started out the door, following the rolling bed, but turned back. "Is there any chance you know what caliber the bullet was?"

"It was from a rifle, I couldn't tell what caliber. It sounded bigger than a twenty-two but other than that I can't say." Michael could see the shorter of the policemen writing in a little book. He could feel sweat starting out on his bare skin as he watched the tall cop follow his father down the hallway.

"Mr. Lawson?" Michael couldn't help but think of the man talking to him as "the bear." "What can you tell me about the shooting?"

"I...I don't know what to say."

"You just answer my questions."

"Do you know Detective Davis or Norris?" he blurted. He stood to watch down the hall.

"I've heard of them, but can't say I ever worked with them. Do you want me to call them?"

"No. No. I just..."

The redheaded nurse came in with a thin green shirt and a needle full of clear liquid. She turned to the Bear. "You need to wait outside a minute so I can numb his head. Doctor Ashaad will be sewing him up in a few minutes."

Michael watched the cop leave, wishing Carol would come soon. She could keep an eye on The Lawyer while they fixed him up. A new worry sprang to mind. *How much is this going to cost?* He didn't think the medical coverage he had from the Navajo Nation would work in the city. He'd heard hospitals were expensive.

"You need to get stitched up."

The adrenaline that got him to the hospital had washed out of his system like water swirling down a drain. He didn't have the energy to argue; he nodded.

He could feel the Bear watching as he pulled on the green shirt. Redheaded Nurse's badge stated her name was Becky. She changed the sheet and had him lie on the table where The Lawyer had been a few minutes before. Other people bustled around the room removing bloody bandages and medical tools. He didn't want to lie on the table where people had died. He was spending much too much time in unwholesome places like this hospital. If he could afford it after paying the hospital bill, he'd need to have a Hatali sing a Night Way Ceremony to help find his balance again.

"I won't lie to you," Nurse Becky said. "This is going to sting a little." She pulled the pad off Michael's forehead and began inserting the needle along the line of the wound. She didn't lie. "We'll give that about ten minutes to take effect, just stay there. The doctor will be in soon."

While he waited, Michael felt his skin twitching as disembodied spirits tried to creep inside him. He tried to think strong thoughts to drive them away. He hoped the doctor would get there soon, so he could get out of this place.

Instead of the doctor, the Bear cop came in after Nurse Becky left. "I need to take your statement while it's fresh. Describe what happened tonight, to the best of your knowledge."

Michael told him what he remembered, and drew a picture of the area, marking where he thought the shooter was located. He didn't have much luck describing the figure he saw across the street.

"Do you know why someone was shooting at you and Mr. Lawson?"

Michael thought for a minute. If the police were involved in the murders, he didn't want to let them know how far along they were in their investigation. "I just got into town a few days ago, but I understand a lot of people don't care for lawyers."

Bear cop rolled his eyes. "We'll check out your story and get back to you. Where are you staying?" He wrote the address of The Lawyer's house and continued writing for a few minutes. Michael started to worry when Bear cop finally stalked out the door.

A policeman in uniform came in carrying The Lawyer's briefcase. "The window of your car was missing. This was on the seat. I thought you'd want to keep it safe." He sat it by the chair. "We'll do everything we can to find out who did this. I hope your father will be OK." He followed the detective down the hall. At least he sounded sincere.

Michael was left alone with his jumbled thoughts. He told them the truth, but did the police want the truth? His forehead was numb, and he couldn't resist poking at it. He pulled Becky's loose bandage off so he could see it in the mirror over the sink. The cut was jagged, deeper than he thought. It glistened with fresh ooze. He could see the white of bone.

Doctor Ashaad and Nurse Becky came in and directed Michael back to the table. He'd sewn up cuts on his cattle and seen a lot of wounds, but his stomach still churned when he thought of the needle going into his skin. Nurse Becky put a blue cloth with a hole in it over his face.

"Have you heard how The L... my father is doing in surgery?" Michael asked from beneath the cover.

"I'm sure they're taking good care of him. You can go to the family waiting room when we're done here," the doctor said.

Michael's mind was rambling, trying to find something that made sense. He centered on Doctor Ashaad, who was currently poking a needle in his head. He looked to be a Mexican with a square face, dark complexion, and thick black hair that had gray scattered randomly throughout. He had an accent Michael couldn't place, so the doctor couldn't be Mexican.

A loud voice broke Michael's reverie. "He's my nephew. I need to see him."

"Ms. Kowalski, you can't go in there."

Obviously the plea didn't work. He smelled Carol's perfume through the blue towel.

"There you are, Mike, I recognize those boots."

"Hi, Carol." Michael shifted a bit.

Somebody put a hand on his chest. "Don't move. Just a couple more stitches."

"Who the hell was shooting at you?" Carol asked.

"I didn't see who." Michael waved his hand indicating the doctor and nurse. "I think we need to talk."

ONCE THE DOCTOR WAS FINISHED, MICHAEL CALLED HIS father's house. Aunt Lila answered. She dropped the phone when he told her what happened. Aunt Jean picked it up. "Michael, what happened, a fright got Lila!"

He repeated the story.

"Oh, Oho, Oh," Jean wailed. "This city will kill my whole

family, first my little sister, then it got my boy, now you, Oh Oho"

He could hear Lila comforting her in the background.

"Auntie...Auntie!"

"What?"

"I'm taking care of things here. Could you bring me and David some clothes when you come? Ours got...dirty. I'll wait for you at the hospital where we were for Jon's operation."

There was a sniff at the other end and the dial tone beeped. Carol watched him through the whole conversation. When he closed the phone, she pounced. "What the hell happened?"

Michael gave her the whole story while they walked to the waiting room.

"Who's guarding your father now?"

It surprised him she knew someone would be guarding him. At his quizzical look, she stopped. "Somebody better be guarding him. You told them he was a lawyer, didn't you?"

Michael nodded.

"They usually will protect victims, but in cases where an officer of the court is attacked, they need to guard him."

"The Yei..." Michael had to think for a second. "... Officer Reed said he was guarding my father at the surgery. He said he didn't know Davis or Norris, but if police are behind the shooting, I'm afraid he might try to finish The...my father. Should I go down there and watch the cops?" Michael's head pounded even though the stitched area was still numb. He could smell the antiseptic scent of his forehead, and it was making him sick to his stomach.

"Even if it was cops who tried to shoot you, I can't

imagine any police assassination squad being more than one or two guys." Carol gave him a wicked grin.

"What if you're wrong? What about the blue line?" The idea of police as a tribe was disturbing Michael more and more. He decided to pace.

Carol frowned. Then he saw the realization in her eyes.

"Murder of someone who isn't a criminal is a line most police wouldn't cross." She sat on one of the padded couches. She continued, "Of course, it might not be the police at all. He might have some pissed off clients who wanted to take a shot at him." She tapped a perfect red fingernail against the arm of the couch and stared out the window. "I've been calling Garcia to get a comment, either he's really busy with the task force or he's dodging me." She licked her lips. "I'd vote for dodging me. The task force is a sham. They are just going through the motions."

Michael stopped pacing and flopped into a chair opposite Carol. She questioned him about the shooting. The antiseptic smell emanating from his forehead was making him nauseated. He excused himself and hurried to the bathroom. He felt better after his stomach was empty. A handful of water rinsed his mouth. The mirror showed him a stranger's face, haggard and bruised, with haunted eyes. The green shirt they'd given him accentuated his pallor. He took a deep breath. He didn't have time to be weak right now. After shaking himself like a dog he squared his shoulders and went back to Carol.

"It's a big coincidence that someone would decide to shoot at us right after I did research on the police being connected to the murders in your article," he said deciding to stand, because the chair looked too inviting.

Carol nodded. "It *is* a coincidence, since only you, me, and David knew about your research."

"I left my notes by the computer when I went to lunch. Anybody going down there could have seen them. They were on your desk, too." He started to pace again. "It's probably nothing, but I had a bad feeling about Jim."

Carol didn't seem surprised by his statement. "I'll check it out." She got up.

"Let me know what you find. No matter what time, you can call me on The Lawyer's phone."

The first shot was at him, not The Lawyer. Michael said as much to Carol. "I think he only got shot when he came to get me with the car. I don't know why he didn't just drive away."

Michael didn't see Aunt Lila walk up. "Your father wouldn't leave you."

"He did leave me." He spoke to her in Navajo.

"That was a long time ago. His life was different then. He'd lost himself," she replied in kind.

"It's been over twenty years," Michael started and stopped. The waiting room wasn't the place to have this conversation. He turned to Carol. "Sorry, family stuff. This is my aunt."

"You speak Navajo well."

"It's my first language. I was raised on the Navajo Nation," he said.

Aunt Lila's tight lips told him their other conversation wasn't over. "I'm going to see if I can find out how David's doing." Michael scuttled out of the room. Turning the corner into the hall, he nearly ran over Aunt Jean.

She grabbed his arm with a grip like a badger. She wasn't letting go. "Boy, what you running around for?" She looked up at his bandage. "You got shot in the head. Did it make you crazy?"

"I just got a cut, Auntie. I'm going to check on The Lawyer."

"Why don't you call him your father?"

She must've sensed weakness for her to be after him about The Lawyer at a time like this. "I don't know. I need to go check on him." She released his arm, and he fled to the nurse's desk.

Chapter 39

SNAKE IN THE GRASS

CAROL KOWALSKI TAPPED A FINGERNAIL AGAINST THE EDGE OF her computer keyboard. The office was a lot quieter after midnight, but there were still people in a few of the other cubicles. An elderly Asian man wearing gray coveralls was emptying trash cans. She'd posted her story about the shooting at Lawson's office only because she had to make the deadline.

She wasn't proud of the account. It was bare facts, the police standard supposition that a disgruntled client had done the shooting. She was sure there was more to the story. It nagged at her. She ran her hands through her hair and stretched her arms up before reaching for her coffee. She never believed in coincidences. It sure wasn't one of Lawson's clients who shot at Michael on the very the day he connected two cops to a series of murders.

The face she made when she sipped the cold coffee would have scared small children. Her nail tapped again. Helpless wasn't one of her better states of being. She had to find a connection. The leads were slim, but she was going to do something tonight, no matter how futile. The first step was to get fresh coffee. It was going to be a long night.

Back at her desk, properly caffeinated, her journalist instincts started to kick in. The primary question was who tipped off the shooter? It had to be someone in this building or Lawson's office. She decided to go on the assumption that the shooter was either Norris or Davis. Looking up their phone numbers took seconds. She jotted the numbers on a pad and set up a search program to call up the phone records out of this building for today. She hoped whoever ratted out Michael didn't use a cell phone.

The *bing* of the computer snapped her head off her arms. Carol looked at the clock looming over the cubicles like the wrath of God. It was 3:00 A.M. Her neck ached from her awkward sleeping position. "I'm getting too old for this shit." She yawned widely, automatically reaching for the coffee mug. As she scanned the computer screen, a smile broke out on her face. "Got ya, you stupid son-of-a-bitch." She picked up the phone and called Michael.

Chapter 40
BETRAYAL

"Jesus, Carol, it's four in the morning." Jim tightened the tie on his maroon and tan striped bathrobe.

Carol pushed past him, striding into his tiny apartment. Michael followed her in.

"Come on in, I guess," Jim said as he followed her, four steps into his living room. The apartment walls were dirty gray. A pizza box lay on the glass-top coffee table. A pile of cans overflowed the trash can sitting next to the faded plush lounge chair. Jim shifted newspapers off the couch.

Carol shoved him. He fell, face down. He scrambled around to a sitting position. "What the fuck, Carol?"

"Stay down you piece of shit. You're lucky I don't put my foot up your ass." Carol loomed over the small round man.

"Are you batshit?" Jim was trapped on the sofa between the coffee table and the irate woman.

"What did Norris pay you, you slimy little worm?" Carol leaned over and put her hand on Jim's chest. "Don't deny it. I've got the phone records."

"Look, Carol, everybody does it. I just passed on some trivial information to a couple of guys. They were cops, for

Pete's sake." Jim tried to work up some righteous indignation.

"What—did—you—tell—him?" She poked a crimson fingernail into his chest with each word.

Michael leaned against the wall and watched. The Lawyer was right, she was a cougar, with all the big cat's ferocity.

"Ow, Carol. Back off." Jim tried to disappear into the couch.

Carol slowly made a fist with her perfectly manicured hand. She made a point of tucking her thumb, so the sharp nail extended between her fingers. She did this while pointedly looking at Jim. "What did you tell Norris?"

Jim's eyes were showing white all the way around. "I just let them know the kid was doing research." He tipped his chin toward Michael.

"Jim?" Carol ran a finger over the sharp edge of her protruding nail. "When I get done I'll let Michael have you. He was raised Indian. He has better interrogation skills than me."

"All right, all right, I told him the kid connected him, Davis, and Chamberlin to the murdered prostitutes and junkies." Jim watched the ripple of muscle as Carol's jaw clenched.

"Who else did you talk to?" She glanced at Michael.

"It wasn't anything you wouldn't have printed in a few days anyway. I was just doing my civic duty." Jim's voice had taken on a whine more suitable to a five-year-old.

Carol tapped her protruding fingernail and pursed her lips.

"OK, OK, I talked to Ray Chamberlin, too. He's off on sick leave and was checking some information for his partner. Come on, Ray's a good guy."

"You incredible asshole, you don't have a clue what you've done. You'd better find a deep hole to hide in." Carol turned and stalked out of the room. Michael followed her, wondering what Indian interrogation skills he was supposed to have. They didn't bother to close the door.

TWO HOURS LATER CAROL LEANED AGAINST THE DOOR labeled "Chief Internal Affairs - Bill Jacobson." She didn't dare sit or she'd fall asleep. It was a long time since she'd pulled an all-nighter. Michael'd gone back to the hospital. The kid was looking rough. She sure hoped Lawson survived.

When the balding, fifty-something head of the department arrived, he stared at his guest. "Good morning, Carol. To what do I owe this visit from the fifth estate?"

"Bill, you have a big problem." She pushed herself upright.

"I'm doing great. Thanks for asking." His smile faltered then sagged, the crevasses on his face matching his rumpled suit. "You're serious?"

The look Carol gave him answered his question. "Come into my office. I'll make some coffee."

Chapter 41
CIRCLING

FOR THE SECOND TIME IN AS MANY DAYS, MICHAEL STOOD AT the window engrossed in the dawn breaking on the nameless mountain south of the hospital. This was the tenth hour of his father's surgery. The rising sun glinted golden flashes off buzzards' wings as the birds circled over an arroyo that gouged the mountainside. His mind was circling, too. Scenes from the past eight days flashed behind his eyes. Fierce Carol dealing with round Jim. Jon in the clown mechanic suit in the court. Salina's anger at her brother. Paula describing the big cop at the murder scenes. The glimpse of the figure with the gun between the buildings.

He kept coming back to The Lawyer driving between the buildings to rescue him. The man could have gotten away easily. Why did he come back? Aunt Lila said it was because The Lawyer loved him as his son. That was nonsense, of course. The man barely knew him. Jean had a more likely reason. She thought he didn't leave Michael because he felt guilty. That, Michael understood.

His head was pounding and he just wanted to get Jon, go

home, and look after his cattle. He didn't want emotional complications with The Lawyer on top of trying to help his cousin. When he'd said as much last night, Lila told him "You don't get to choose what happens, only how you deal with it."

He watched Aunt Lila's steady breathing. She slept on the couch alone this morning. Aunt Jean had convinced the guard to let her stay in Jon's room. She was safe. There was small consolation that these women he loved were resting and safe.

Michael leaned his temple against the cool glass and closed his eyes. When he opened them again, more time than he realized had past. The sun was well up; the whole mountain lit with bright dawn. The buzzards lost their golden shine. They were just black birds now, following their instincts. There must be something wounded or dead in that arroyo on the side of the mountain. The stockman in him felt the need to go there and check to see if there might be a cow in need of rescuing. Taking care of livestock was what he knew. Something he could do that was right and good. He sure wasn't any good at taking care of people. So far he'd failed everyone.

The buzzards continued to circle. They would make short work of whatever was up on that mountain. *Nothing goes to waste in the desert*, he thought. He wished he was out walking the country smelling the sage and mesquite instead of the plastic, cleanser, and sickness odors of this hospital. Clean light would be so much better than the stark shadeless corridors of the hospital redolent with the unseen gibbering spirits of the dead.

Shoes click-clacking down the hallway behind drew his attention. He didn't turn. Nurses didn't clatter when they walked. They had soft shoes; they snuck up with news, good or bad. He heard someone clear their throat. I took a deep breath and turned. Mrs. Jones stood there. Her eyes were bloodshot. A few hairs had escaped the tight knot at the back of her head.

"How is he?" She dabbed her nose with a pink tissue.

"The last report was a couple hours ago. He's still in surgery. They said he was holding his own. I think that's good."

She sat on one of the couches. Her back was very straight. "You're hurt."

"It's just a scratch."

"The police said someone was shooting at you." She stood back up.

"Yes, ma'am."

"They wanted a list of our clients. I didn't know what to do." She plopped down on a chair next to The Lawyer's briefcase.

"I don't know what to tell you." Michael was suddenly weary. He found a chair near Aunt Lila. She stirred and sat up. Her eyes were red, wisps of her hair escaped from her folded braid.

"Have you rested, boy?"

He shook his head. She gave him one of those looks that said she was worried but wasn't going to berate him in front of strangers. He introduced Mrs. Jones, who perched on the edge of her chair. He left them chatting and went to get coffee. His skin itched and his lungs felt like raw meat from all the hospital chemical smells. The walls of the hallway seemed to be getting closer together. He needed to get away from this damaged place.

A doctor was talking to the ladies when he walked up with the coffee. At least this doctor didn't have dancing cats on his hat.

"Your father is going to be OK," Aunt Lila said. "We can go see him in a few minutes."

A policeman with white hair and an equally white mustache sat outside the door to intensive care. The man's belly filled his lap. He was resting a book on its bulge. The man stood as they approached with the doctor. Michael looked him over carefully. He had a big gun on his hip, but he seemed harmless in a big friendly dog sort of way. Michael rubbed a hand over his eyes, wincing when the gesture tugged at his stitches. He wanted to tear the bandage off and scratch until he bled.

The Lawyer, his father, looked awful lying in the bed with tubes in his arms and down his throat. His skin was almost paper white. Blue skin sagged under his eyes. Aunt Lila and Mrs. Jones went to either side of the bed. Michael stood by the door. His father's eyes never left his son.

He made a writing gesture with his hand. Michael nodded and went out to ask the nurse for a pad and pencil. When he returned, the women were talking to his father, whose eyes were closed.

"Is he asleep?" Michael asked.

The Lawyer's eyes popped open. He made the scribbling gesture again. Michael handed him the pad and pencil. "You OK -- head?'" he wrote.

"I'm fine. Just a few stitches. They think it was a ricochet, a part of a bullet."

His eyes widened.

"It's just a scratch. Do you have any idea who was shooting at us?"

The Lawyer shook his head. He wrote on the pad "seemed tall."

Michael frowned and nodded while meeting the older man's eyes. He remembered the image of the shooter between the buildings. "The cop Norris is tall." Michael started to pace in the small room. "But he's not as big in the shoulders as the shape I saw."

He wrote, "Trick of the light?"

Michael shook his head, trying to reconcile the images in his mind, remembering Norris as he'd seen him in the diner. "I don't know."

He wrote "Need to tell someone."

"I wouldn't know who to trust."

He waved a hand toward Mrs. Jones.

The woman in question was following the odd conversation. She patted Michael's father's hand and said, "Don't worry, David. We'll take care of everything. You rest now. I'll help Michael."

Chapter 42

PROTECTION

"Boy, you need to sleep." Aunt Jean stood in front of Michael.

He was leaning against the wall, listening to the beep of the heart monitor counting the moments of his father's life. He hadn't seen or heard her come in, so she was probably right. He thought, *some guard I am, an old lady snuck up on me.*

"You were shot in the head, boy. Did it make you stupid? You need to rest."

"I was just scratched, Auntie. But, you're right, I need sleep." The thumping of his head made what he said a lie, but he didn't want to worry her.

"You must be hurt bad if you're listening to old women now." She reached up and patted his cheek.

Michael smiled, took hold of her hand, and held it to his heart for a moment. Letting her go, he settled into the orange lounge chair in the corner. Every muscle in his body sang a happy song. The tune went sour when Carol came in. A green-eyed, balding man in a wrinkled gray suit followed her. He had the face of a sad bulldog, all sags and creases. This was the first time Michael'd seen Carol look less than business-like. Bits of her hair had come out of its perfect hood. Most of her makeup looked as if it had been rubbed off. When she smiled, lipstick glazed her teeth.

Carol introduced the bulldog man as Chief Bill Jacobson, the head of Police Internal Affairs. Michael sat up, but kept his face blank.

"He's one of the police who investigate bad cops," she said.

Michael raised a weary eyebrow, and felt a twinge from the stitches.

"You can trust him, Michael. He's here to help us."

"Is he going to let Jon out of jail?" Aunt Jean asked.

"We're hoping our investigation will help your son's case, Mrs. Pete. Mainly, we're trying to catch the person who shot Mr. Lawson and Mr. Yazzie." The bulldog man's voice was deep and raspy, like someone who smoked for many years.

Lawson stirred on the bed. Aunt Jean moved to a guard position and crossed her arms.

"Maybe we should talk in the hall." Carol motioned to the door.

Michael pushed up from the comfortable chair. Every joint protested. He was creaking as if he were an old man. In the hall, he turned to Carol, rudely ignoring Chief Jacobson. He spoke in his calmest voice, not wanting Jean to come out and make a fuss. He also didn't want to disturb his father, lying there with tubes coming out of him. "The police are the ones trying to kill us. They put drugs in Jon's truck. They probably tried to kill him in the jail. They shot at me, nearly killed my father, and you want me to trust this police."

"Yes, I do." Carol was Michael's height without her high shoes. She looked him right in the eye. "I trust this man. He is the one who protects people from the bad police. The information you found gave him a reason to open an investigation. You can trust him. He'll catch the bad guys." She put her hand on Michael's arm. "You have to trust someone."

He took a shuddering breath, closed his eyes, and nodded. The sound of the machines around his father seemed louder than the other hospital noises, the *swish* of breath and the *bip* of his pulse.

Michael didn't open his eyes when the raspy voice started. "We have some evidence related to the people who may have shot at you. We have undercover police stationed around the hospital. They're guarding your cousin, as well as your father and aunts. It's just a matter of time before we make an arrest."

Michael opened his eyes and tilted his head so he could look at his father through the door and see the Chief of Police Internal Affairs as well. "Is it Detective Norris who is doing these murders?"

"I can't discuss an ongoing investigation." He rubbed his bulldog jowls, pushing the skin smooth before it fell back to saggy wrinkles. "You don't have to worry. No one can get to your family. We're doing everything we can to protect you."

Michael looked at Carol. She gave him a weak smile. He had his answer. He didn't have confidence in the police, but the man's intentions were good. Time would show him if the wrinkled man knew what he was talking about. Michael didn't know when he quit trusting what people told him. It probably wasn't long after he drove into Phoenix.

"Michael," Carol said. "You're dead on your feet. Don't worry. Bill will take care of everything." She patted the rumpled man on the shoulder. He just stood there with his jowls drooping.

Michael took a deep breath. "I'm going to sleep." He closed the door behind him. The Lawyer's eyes were closed.

He hoped the old man was sleeping. Aunt Jean was sitting in a straight chair next to the bed. The orange chair in the corner beckoned. For the second time in his adult life, he slept after the sun was up.

Michael dreamed his yellow cow was stuck in the waterhole. Every time he got her to her feet, she sunk even deeper with her next step.

Chapter 43

A WALK IN FRESH AIR

MICHAEL WOKE WITH EVERY NERVE IN HIS BODY TINGLING. He wondered if the lost souls in the hospital had made him sick. The machines connected to The Lawyer were still clicking and beeping. The old man's eyes were open, watching his son.

Michael stood and stretched. "Do you need anything?"

He waved his hand in negative. There was a wire clipped to his pointing finger.

"Did Aunt Jean or Lila tell you about the police protection?"

He nodded.

"Do you think it is good enough? Are they just using you for bait?"

He held his arm out and wiggled his open hand from side to side. He reached for the pad on the rolling table next to the bed. "How long since I was shot?"

Michael had to think about it. "You were shot the day before yesterday in the evening, so it's been a full day and two nights. It's morning now."

Writing some more, his breathing rate increased. "You here the whole time?"

Michael nodded.

"Your aunts?"

"They'll be here soon. The doctor told us you will be okay. Jon's doing better, so they went to your house to clean up and sleep."

He raised an eyebrow.

"I don't trust the police to protect you."

A tear rolled down the old man's cheek. He wiped it away quickly.

"I'll go let the nurse know you're awake. Maybe they'll take that tube out. It must hurt." Michael hurried out...to give his father some privacy.

As he left the nurse's desk, Aunt Lila came out of the elevator. She gave him a maternal look. "You slept?"

"Most of the night." He didn't tell her his head still pounded like a ceremonial drum.

"You need to get outside and feel the earth. To find hozoh." She tilted her head at the door. Find some balance. Go outside and walk. I'll look after your father."

———

MICHAEL STOPPED IN FRONT OF THE WINDOW LOOKING TO THE mountain. Buzzards still circled. He knew he wouldn't find hozoh, but he needed to breathe some clean air. The nurse, whose badge read "Tanya," walked up. "This is my favorite view. That's South Mountain Park." She gestured at the mountain framed by the window. Leaning on the window sill, she turned and looked up at him from her diminutive height.

Michael was glad the mountain had a name. "Do you know a place nearby where I can take a walk?" he asked.

"South Mountain Park is about a half-hour drive from here. There are nice trails. I hike up there a lot."

"I don't want to get too far from the hospital." He didn't want to mention that it was in case the killer came back.

"I understand," she said. "The hospital grounds are nice." She smiled up at him. "There's a little garden you might like." Tanya gave him directions to thread the maze of the hospital corridors and find the garden.

The area around the hospital was supposed to be guarded by police. Michael thought it would be a good idea to see if they were doing their job.

THE AIR OF THE CITY WASN'T EXACTLY FRESH, BUT IT WAS better than the inside of the hospital. The garden was very green. It smelled juicy. The huge brightly colored flowers growing in pots seemed vaguely obscene to Michael's sensibilities. Maybe it was their cloying odor in the hot sunlight. Traffic noises and disembodied voices floated in the air echoing off the cement walls.

He left the garden and found his way out to the walkway around the building. The hospital covered almost two city blocks. Light flashed off the bronzed windows, sending crazed reflections along the sidewalk and the grass planted beside the road. While he walked, Michael scanned for people who might be undercover police, but didn't see anyone who looked the part.

He wracked his brain trying to piece together why someone would try to kill The Lawyer. They had to be getting close to something? He wished he knew exactly what.

After his first circuit of the hospital, his head was pounding, so Michael sat down on a bench in the shade of the overhang by the loading docks. He watched people coming and going in the nearby emergency room entrance, still trying to spot the police who were supposedly guarding the place. After a half-hour he had lost faith in Carol's friend's ability to protect The Lawyer. All sorts of strange-looking people were going into the hospital. Any one of them could be a crazy killer.

An ambulance without flashing lights pulled up to the loading dock near him. Less than a minute later a plain tan car pulled up next to the ambulance and the angular form of Detective Reed got out, followed by his bear-shaped partner. Michael couldn't remember his name. The men didn't notice Michael in the shadows under the overhang.

"Where the hell is the coroner? The press is going to figure out something's going on," the partner said.

"They'll be here," Reed replied.

A slender man in the uniform of an EMT pulled out two canvas duffles that rattled like bone wind chimes. He sat then on the ground beside the ambulance.

"Wait until the coroner gets here," Reed told him.

"This is bullshit. Why didn't the coroner do the pickup?" the slender man said. He took out a kerchief and wiped his face.

"We don't want the press making this a circus until we inform next of kin," Reed said.

A black van backed in near the ambulance. A sign on the door said 'Maricopa County Coroner'. EMTs pulled a stretcher with a covered body from the ambulance. The attendants were having trouble with the gurney. One of the wheels stuck out at an odd angle and squeaked like a trapped rat as they pushed it toward the coroner's van. A gust of hot wind blew the blanket back from the top of the corpse on the stretcher. Michael's eyes widened in disbelief. It was Detective Garcia. He stood up to see better.

Reed and his partner observed Michael with calculating looks.

"What you doing out here?" Reed asked. He walked over to where Michael stood.

"I've been inside too much and needed to get out and walk around. I couldn't breathe in there anymore," Michael said gesturing at the building. "What happened to the Detective?" Michael tipped his chin at the gurney disappearing into the coroner's van.

"We can't talk about that right now. How's your father?" Reed asked.

"The doctors think he'll live."

"Glad to hear it. You need to move along now." He tilted his head toward the front of the hospital. "We'd rather you didn't talk about this. His family doesn't know yet. It would be harder on them if they found out from the news." Reed made a vague gesture with his hand toward the van.

"Don't worry," Michael said. "I won't say anything." He stepped back, instinctively uncomfortable at being so close to the corpse and wondering what rattled in those bags.

The attendants finished loading the bags and the gurney with detective Garcia's body.

Two more cars pulled up, disgorging several more people.

"Jeese, are we having a convention?" The bear detective asked.

"Let it go. Everyone liked Rudy." Reed rubbed his eyes with a weary hand.

Michael thought he remembered a few of the faces gathering around the coroner's van from the police station. The police tribe was gathering to mourn the death of one of its own, he thought. The last guy out of the car was the fat desk sergeant with the wormlike fingers. His face was tense, molded into a stricken frown. Michael wanted to console the man who had been kind to him that first night when he was looking for Jon. He didn't have a clue about how White people dealt with tragedy. Saying nothing was probably better than saying the wrong thing. Reed nodded to Michael and walked over to the men who'd gotten out of the cars. The bear gave Michael a last lingering look and followed his partner. Michael had no place in the police tribe's grief. He had his own problems, hopefully the death of Garcia wasn't connected to what happened at the Lawyer's office. But what if it was? He walked around to the front door of the hospital, making a mental list of questions that needed answers. Who killed Garcia? Was it the same guy that shot The Lawyer? What did Garcia's death mean for Jon? Too many questions, with no answers in sight. His head thumped and his stomach twisted uncomfortably. He needed to stay away from dead bodies.

On his way through the spinning doors at the front of the hospital he saw the man who'd been with Garcia and Norris in the diner entering the elevator. The man looked up and their eyes met. His blue eyes were as cold as a lizard's. The man smiled. Michael hurried through the crowded entry, but the elevator was gone before he got there.

Chapter 44

THERE ARE SICK PEOPLE IN HOSPITALS

Visions of the blue-eyed man killing his aunts flashed across Michael's brain. He stabbed at the call button and looked around for a stairway. None was close. Michael was sure his skin was going to peel off in strips if he didn't get to them. He pounded the wall.

Finally, the ding and a light showed him which car was next. He jumped in as the elevator doors were opening and crashed into a young woman with brown hair. A short bald man wearing a white coat and an older woman with curly blue-gray hair made startled noises.

The woman shoved Michael away, saying, "Hey, buddy, take it easy."

"I'm sorry," he said, stabbing the fourth-floor button four times in quick succession. "My father's in the ICU." Michael knew he looked out of place with his bandaged head, sweaty shirt, dusty jeans, and boots. The tidy people in the elevator moved as far from him as the small space allowed. The doors opened on the second floor. Michael was jittering, shifting his weight from foot to foot.

"Excuse me," the blue-haired lady said.

He realized he was in front of the doors. Stepping back to the wall, Michael repeated, "I'm sorry."

"I hope your father is OK," the old woman said as she and the brown-haired woman left.

He stabbed the close-door button. A deep breath gave him the antiseptic smell of the hospital mingled with the soap smell of the bald man. Michael's hands clenched into fists as he realized he should have run up the stairs. The bald man moved as far from him as the elevator allowed.

The hairs on his neck told Michael the cold-eyed man was here. He hoped his aunts had gone back to The Lawyer's house or were visiting Jon. Carol's police friend lied about protecting Michael's family. The old, fat man guarding The Lawyer stood no chance against Cold Eyes.

On the third floor, the bald man scurried out. Michael could see white all the way around the brown irises of the man's eyes. Michael hit the close-door button four more times. "Come on." He bounced on the balls of his feet.

The doors opened. Detective Norris stood there.

Past him, Michael saw no one in the chair in front of his father's door. "What are you doing here?" he shouted.

"My job. What's it to you?" Norris shouldered past into the elevator.

Michael stood in the door. Felt it bump against his back. Listening down the hall in the direction of his father's room, he heard no commotion. His intense gaze met Norris' expressionless eyes.

"You should go home, kid. You're in way over your head here." Norris' voice was as dead as his eyes.

Michael turned and ran down the hall past the nurse's station to his father's room. Machines rhythmically beeped and clicked behind the door. Holding his breath, he pushed it open. Aunt Lila looked up from her magazine. The

Lawyer was sleeping. Fewer tubes sprouted from him than had been there when he left that morning.

Air rushed from Michael's lungs. "Is everything good? The police aren't by the door." His voice had a squeaky quality he'd never heard before.

Lila stood up. The magazine dropped from her lap. "What happened?"

"There was a man, a policeman we saw at the diner. I was worried he was coming here." Michael stumbled over to a chair and folded into it. He closed his eyes and pinched the bridge of his nose. His head was thumping. "The Flat Head police stopped by to check on your father. Jean is over with Jon." She sat back down. "What is happening that you worry about police coming here?"

"The detective who arrested Jon is dead. They just brought his body to the hospital. Something is going on with the police." He pressed his fingertips to his temples. His head was thumping along with the beat of his heart. Michael explained about his research pointing to police. "If you see any of those men we saw in the diner, call somebody. Don't let them near The Lawyer."

"You mean your father," Lila said, looking at her nephew steadily.

"Yes." Michael leaned forward, elbows on his knees, and let his face fall into his hands. "My father." He didn't have the energy to resist her.

A younger police woman with a cap of curly dark hair stuck her head in the door. "Hi, I'm going to be on the door this shift. I'm Karen. If you need anything let me know."

She didn't seem very strong, but she had a big gun and a bunch of tools on her belt. Michael said, "You need to watch out for big bulky men. Let me or my aunts look at anyone before you let them in, okay?"

The young woman nodded and backed out, closing the door. Michael heard the chair creak as she sat down.

Lila wasn't distracted by the officer's intrusion. She thrust a small plastic tub of Jello at her nephew. "Eat this. Then you go wash up, and get in that ugly chair to sleep some more."

"It's only one in the afternoon. It's too early to sleep." Michael's thumping head chided him for protesting.

You been shot in the head. You need more rest. Jean and me will be here."

Michael obeyed the tone of authority without arguing that his wound was only a scratch. He didn't think that line would fool her anyway. She knew him so well.

While he was drifting to sleep, he wondered if he was wise letting the women look after him. He fell asleep smiling. It was the most natural thing in the world...they had always looked after him.

IT WAS FULL DARK OUTSIDE WHEN CAROL CAME IN. SHE WAS wearing black pants and a pale gold shiny shirt. Michael usually had a sense of what time it was, but he had to look at the clock. It was half past ten. His mouth tasted like it was full of cotton. He rubbed the crusty grit from his eyes.

The Lawyer wiggled his fingers at Carol, and she gave him a smile. Michael could smell the sweet musky odor of her perfume.

"I want to let you know what's going on. I wasn't able to talk in front of Bill, but I think it's Detective Tom Norris who committed the murders and shot you."

"He was here earlier." Michael closed his eyes and thought of Norris and of the shape between the buildings.

Were they the same? Norris didn't seem bulky enough. "I can't be sure."

"When he was here. I talked to him," Lila said. "He wasn't mean."

Carol sat in one of the straight back chairs next to Lila. "He wouldn't be confrontational with a civilian. The department doesn't have enough to indict him yet, but Judge Burton signed a bunch of warrants. Bill, the man you met this morning, will find something to bust him. It was Michael's research that convinced them. You did good, kid." Carol leaned forward and patted Michael's hand. "That weasel Jim was getting paid to pass information. I'm so mad at that little fucker, I could kick his ass through his ears."

Michael looked at Aunt Lila, who looked down quickly. Her cheeks tinged with heat. She wasn't used to people reveling in their violent tendencies. To change the subject he asked, "Did you hear anything about the bodies they brought in?"

"There were two skeletons that will take a while to identify, but the fresh body was Detective Garcia."

"Where did they find them?" Michael closed his eyes and swallowed, remembering the glazed eyes of the detective's corpse.

Carol nodded. "Some hiker found him and the skeletons up in South Mountain Park. They were dumped in an arroyo."

Michael thought of the buzzards circling over the mountain. He stood up and rubbed his arms. "We just saw the Detective the other day at the diner. He was there with Norris and another guy with cold eyes."

The noise from his father's breathing machine became louder. He was furiously scribbling on his pad. 'Saw him at the diner?'

"Yes," Michael said. "He was sitting with Garcia and Norris."

'Phil Davis,' he wrote, turning the pad for Carol to see.

Carol jumped up. "Oh, shit. I have to call Bill." She hurried out.

Noticing Aunt Lila's inquiring look, Michael explained the research he'd done, how Jim had helped, and how Davis, Norris, and a guy named Ray Chamberlin were connected to all the murders in Carol's story.

"The Lawyer scribbled a note. 'Ray is who you met at the courthouse. The big guy.'

"You know him. Do you think he could have killed all those people?" Michael asked.

The Lawyer shrugged. 'Just bowl with him,' he wrote on the pad.

"When I get the chance I'll do more research about him."

The Lawyer nodded.

Lila pushed herself out of her chair. "I'm going to talk to Jean. If those men are trying to hide what they've done, they may want to hurt Jon." She dusted off her skirt as though she were at home instead of the sterile room. "David, you go back to sleep. You heal when you're sleeping." The Lawyer gave her thumbs up. She looked at Michael. "Stay here. I'll bring some food for you." She went to the doorway, looking each direction before hurrying down the hall.

"She's right, you need to sleep. I'll keep watch," Michael said. He went to the bed and pulled the blanket up a little higher. "The doctor says if you're stronger in the morning, he'll take the breathing tube out."

David Lawson patted his son's hand and made an ugly face that must have been a smile distorted by the tube in his mouth. Michael turned off the lights, shut the door, and moved the orange chair to the corner behind the bathroom. With the lights off, facing the window, he could see the outline of South Mountain in the moonlight. Artificial lights glowed half way up the dark mountain, pinpointing the spot where the police were still searching for clues.

South, shádi ááh, was the direction for comprehension and planning. He was facing the right way. Michael's mind ran around and around with Carol's information, like a puppy chasing its tail. He thought of the sad people he'd seen since he came to this city. He could almost understand a cop wanting to punish people he knew had done horrible things, especially if the people were freed because of a stupid legal rule. But why would they kill Garcia, who was just doing his job?

What Michael couldn't understand was how a person dedicated to helping people could let an innocent man like Jon go to jail or shoot someone who was just trying to help. Among the Navajo, people who had lost themselves to evil, witches, were hard to spot and dangerous to be around. When a person was determined to be a witch, people avoided him or her. Their family would no longer say their name, as if they were dead. The elders would decide what to do with the witch. If the police were a tribe, the man Carol brought to see them, Chief Jacobson, must be the elder in charge of dealing with the evil police. The man Norris was a witch, maybe Davis was, too. Michael felt better having worked out the situation. He'd explain it to his aunts when they came back.

Chapter 45

SECURE PARKING

THE BRIGHT LIGHTING IN COUNTY HOSPITAL'S PARKING garage lit Phil Davis' brown Stetson and cast his face in shadow. Boots and denim were sufficiently different from the suit he usually wore; he wouldn't be identified as a cop. With a basket full of flowers he looked like any one of a dozen visitors. None of the people heading to their cars would remember him. Odds were the Yazzie kid wouldn't notice him either. Internal Affairs had already pulled in Norris. Tonight might be his only chance to sort out this mess.

He left the garage by one of the side doors and walked across the lawn to the building's west entrance. No one was in sight as he slipped inside. This late at night, the information desk was closed. The air-conditioned chill gave him goose bumps, and the antiseptic smell of the hospital made him cough as it burned his lungs. At least it was better than the stink of Garcia's rotting corpse. He felt bad about the kid. He'd had potential.

Moving down the hall toward the stairs, Davis couldn't believe what a fiasco this week had become. He just wanted to clean up the streets, fight the good fight, and all the other clichés. Now IA was investigating him. Stopping in front of the stairwell door, he took a deep breath. Sweat beaded his brow despite the building's climate control. How the hell did he get here?

"Screw it," he said through clenched teeth and pushed the door open.

Bill Jacobson, Chief of Internal Affairs, was standing on the second-floor landing. Phil, we need to talk."

Davis stepped back, letting the door swing closed. "Fuck!" A uniformed officer stood behind the information desk with his gun drawn.

"Stay where you are, Detective. Put down the basket. Show me your hands."

Tom closed his eyes and calculated his chances. The sound of hard-soled shoes, cop shoes, in the hall behind him, made the decision for him. He slowly put the basket down and raised his hands.

Chapter 46

DOWN FOR THE COUNT

THE HOSPITAL HAD GONE RELATIVELY QUIET, SETTLING DOWN for the night. His head had gone from pounding like a pow-wow drum to the beat of a one-man ceremonial drum. Having slept all afternoon, he was wide awake. The policewoman, Karen, who was watching the door, came and said they'd captured the suspects and she was leaving. Michael asked if the suspects were Norris and Davis. Karen said she couldn't talk about a pending case. It seemed a common police excuse. The shape between the buildings with the gun still nagged at him. Neither man seemed big enough to fill the shape in his mind.

The rhythmic sounds of the machines keeping his father alive were hypnotic. Michael tried to think of all the things he needed to do when he got back home. The list was a long one. He watched the stars outside the window and wondered how long it would be before they could get Jon out of jail. He needed to ask Mrs. Jones if she knew the papers to make it happen. Everything in the legal world seemed to need special papers.

The click of the door opening drew Michael's attention.

Dim light from the hall lit the curtain surrounding his father's bed. It must be Aunt Lila coming with food, or one of the nurses. He couldn't see the door from his corner. Then he realized there was no smell of food, so it wasn't his aunt. The nurses usually came directly to the bed. Michael silently put his feet under himself and stood up. A tall bulky shadow fell on the curtain. The image from between the buildings! A man's large hand started to push it back.

Michael leaped forward, grabbed the arm, and lunged for the door shouting, "Who are you?"

The man was taller than Michael, bulkier, too. A *pfft* sound came through the curtain. Something crashed into his ribs. Michael hung onto the man's wrist, spinning them both into the wall. They dragged the curtain with them. Slamming his shoulder into the man, Michael pinned the gun arm against the bathroom door frame.

He tried to hook a leg through the bigger man's to trip him, but Michael couldn't seem to organize his feet. There was a wheezing sound. He realized it was the air trying to get into his lungs. Spots and sparkles glittered through his sight. The strength was leaving his arms. Michael focused on keeping the gun pinned by the wall.

Light from the hall revealed The Lawyer's friend. Ray Chamberlin shook his other hand free of the curtain and smashed Michael in the face. He went down as if the man were holding a brick. Michael slid down the wall and dragged the big man to the floor with him, trying to hang onto the hand with the gun. The man turned, twisting the weapon. Michael tried to roll away, but his body wasn't working properly.

Falling on his side, Michael saw Aunt Lila. She didn't hesitate. Throwing her tray of food at the big man's head, she kept coming, and jumped on the big man's back, shouting for help. The force of her landing knocked the wind out of him and caused the gun to skitter away under the bed.

Distracted, the killer turned to push Lila away. Michael saw the knife from the dinner tray inches away. He grabbed it and shoved the knife upward under Chamberlin's ribs. A lifetime of hard work was behind his thrust.

Chamberlin's eyes widened, even in the dim light showing white all the way around. He made a clumsy swing at Michael. He ducked under the blow, twisting the knife. Chamberlin gasped, tried another grab, but it was obvious he was fading. Michael shoved the body away.

The big man's muscles were taut as he tried to push himself up. "Riley's medal," he gasped. He reached toward Michael.

Michael's leaden arm pulled his aunt away from the killer. A shadow darkened the doorway. Michael surged up, pushing his aunt behind him through the bathroom doorway with the last of his strength.

The lights came on.

"Police! What's going on here?" A uniformed policeman stood with his gun out. He stepped to the left out of the doorway. Blue eyes flickered, taking in the scene. With his gun still at the ready, the officer reached up with one hand to push a button on the box at his shoulder. "We have two people down on the fourth floor. I need some help up here."

The big man on the floor made a gurgling sigh, all his muscles relaxed, and he collapsed. The cop knelt and put a hand to the man's neck. His gun pointed at the ceiling. "Don't worry, ma'am, you're safe now," he said to Lila.

Aunt Jean appeared in the doorway. The cop held up a hand. "Ma'am, you can't come in here."

"Of course I can. My nephew is hurt." She strode past

him, stepping over the body without a look. She said in the direction of the bed, "David, are you all right?" A noise must have been a yes, because she helped Lila get Michael on his back. Someone pressed on his side with a towel from the bathroom. He looked down his body, then up at Lila's calm face. *It's funny*, he thought, *the hospital towels were white, not red.*

Tears were coursing down Aunt Lila's face and dripping on the red towel.

"Little mother, don't be sad," Michael wheezed. Trying to reach up to her, his hand didn't move. Michael wondered why his body wouldn't do what he was asking. He didn't feel much of anything. As Michael spiraled into darkness, he registered the sound of many feet, and Aunt Lila's familiar hand on his forehead. *This room is getting crowded*, was his last thought.

Chapter 47

PUBLIC OPINION

The interrogation room cameras were recording Phil Davis as he sprawled snoring in the room's uncomfortable chair. Another camera showed a similar room with Tom Norris, his fingers laced behind his head, lips pursed. He seemed to be whistling.

"They don't seem to mind being on the other side of the table," Captain Jacobson said, looking at the monitor.

Detective Reed's shoulders slumped. He had circles under his eyes. The faint, sickly sweet smell of formaldehyde floated around him. "Do you believe the story they are telling about using Rudy to investigate Ray Chamberlin and his old partner?"

"Unofficially, I sure hope that's what they were doing. Their stories are holding up, so far. We've only had one go round, though." The older man swatted an empty cup off the table. "They should have brought it to IA. If we'd been alerted we could have..."

Reed looked down at the Chief, tilted his head, and raised his eyebrows.

The Chief sighed. "Yeah, yeah, I know nobody trusts IA,

but this back street shit doesn't fly." The chief shrugged. "It looks like Gelender and Chamberlin went off the reservation when Ray's son, Riley, died of an overdose ten years ago." The Chief supplied.

Our sleeping beauty in there says they got suspicious three years ago when they suspected Chamberlin's old partner, Jamie Gelender, of framing someone for the murder of a prostitute. Three goddamned years!"

"I didn't know Gelender. I just heard the stories about him and Chamberlin. They made some big busts."

The old man rubbed a hand across his face, stretching his wrinkles flat. "I'm sorry this mess got dumped on you, but you're the lead on Garcia's murder since you're the only detective not related to any of the mid-town murders." The Internal Affairs chief patted the slender man on his shoulder.

"You couldn't have kept me away." Reed took a shuddering breath and consciously relaxed his clenched fingers. "Garcia was a good kid. He would have been a great detective. I can't believe Chamberlin would go that far off the rails." He leaned his back against the window. "We're sure it was him? I was at the morgue watching Rudy's autopsy. I haven't had time to look at the details."

"The ballistics from the bullets found with the two skeletons were conclusive. Ray was carrying the same gun at the hospital. The one he shot Lawson's kid with." The Chief sighed.

"I just sent down the bullet from Rudy." Reed shook his head. "How could anyone kill their partner?" It was Reed's turn to rub his face as though he were wiping away a bad memory. "Any idea why he went after Lawson?"

"Lawson and his kid were starting to put the pieces together. Garcia's wife said he'd talked about the case with

Chamberlin last week. We found a rifle in Ray's trunk. We're waiting to compare the bullets to the one they pulled out of Lawson." The Chief rubbed his sagging jowls. "When we picked up Norris and Davis, we pulled the protection detail off the lawyer. Chamberlin saw his chance to do some cleanup and tried for the counselor again." Jacobson pulled the bottom of his suit coat to straighten it. "Lawson's son surprised him. Our former detective shot the kid and was about to finish him, but the kid got him with a butter knife first."

"A butter knife?"

"The Yazzie kid was hurt when his aunt came in, so he was motivated and improvised."

There was a sharp, gritty sound of teeth grinding. "What put you on to Davis and Norris?" Reed asked. "Do we still think they're implicated?"

"Michael Yazzie's research put them in all the right places." Kowalski's voice came from the doorway. "Here's the file." She strode into the room holding up a manila folder.

"Aww, Carol, you know you can't be here." Jacobson scratched behind his ear and looked at the floor. "Who gave you that file?"

"It's the same research I gave you." She patted the Chief of Internal Affairs on his shoulder. "You owe me, Bill."

"How's the Yazzie kid?" Reed asked. He took the file from the reporter and leafed through the papers inside.

"He's out of surgery, holding his own." Carol pulled the corner of her eye with her index finger and drew a deep breath. "He's a good kid. I hope he makes it."

Reed turned to the rumpled Chief and gestured with the file. "You're sure all this is verified."

"Sorry to say it is. I've had a couple guys going over it for the past day and a half. It's all circumstantial, but it adds up enough to stink to high heaven."

Reed pinched the bridge of his nose squeezing his eyes shut. "The military has a term for this situation, and it begins with cluster."

"Don't I know it!" Chief Jacobson shook his head.

"Give me an hour to go over these notes and I'll re-interview Norris and Davis." Reed was already frowning in concentration. "I'll need the tapes of their first interrogations."

"I don't suppose you'll let me watch the interviews," Carol said.

The Chief shrugged holding out his hands palm up. "Come on, Carol. You know better. You'll get the exclusive."

"Yeah, yeah, but you can't compromise an ongoing investigation. I know the drill. It'll be months before I can write this, and I brought the story to you." Carol pushed her mane of hair back. "Life definitely isn't fair, speaking of which, what about Yazzie's cousin, Jon Pete? Did you get him released, yet? "

"We're working on it. It's been less than a day," the Chief said.

"Any idea who knifed Jon when he was in jail? You think maybe Chamberlin called in a favor?" Carol's eyes narrowed.

"Who knows? No con is going to admit to attempted murder just to jam up a dead cop."

Carol made a disgusted noise.

"Look, Carol, an exclusive when the DA says it's time is the best I can do. What more do you want?" The Chief's face sagged into a multitude of wrinkles.

"Can you at least buy me dinner? I always make men

buy me dinner if I'm getting screwed." Kowalski held the back of her hand to her forehead with false drama.

The older man gave her a long-suffering look. "Do I at least get to pick the restaurant?"

"Not on your life."

Chapter 48

LONG-LOST FATHER

CONSCIOUSNESS CAME BACK SLOWLY. MICHAEL'S SENSES returned one at a time, starting with smell. Antiseptic vied with the cottony odor of clean sheets for his attention. Cotton also seemed to be filling his mouth, along with a taste reminiscent of peppermint. Something laid on his upper lip was tickling his nose. Next, light illuminated his closed eyelids. When he opened his muck filled eyes, the worried face of Aunt Lila peered down at him. Finally, sound filtered in from a distance, with equipment beeps and clicks as background Lila's said, "David, he's awake."

Lila drew back the curtain and he saw his father and bright daylight outside the window. He wondered how long he'd been out of it. Jean sat in the ugly orange chair. Mrs. Jones, her hair crisp in its tight bun, was in a straight-backed chair nearby.

The Lawyer wiggled his fingers in greeting. "You gave us quite a scare."

Michael told his arm to move to return the gesture, but it seemed coated in lead. Michael met his aunt's worried eyes.

"Don't be sad Little Mother, we're all safe now." His voice was as raspy as an unoiled windmill.

Lila patted his hand. "You were shot through your chest, but they were able to fix it. You did well. Don't try to move. Rest now."

———

THE NEXT DAYS WERE PAINFUL FOR MORE THAN MICHAEL'S body. After intensive care, they'd moved him and The Lawyer into the same room. He convinced his aunts he didn't need their constant attention and they started going back to The Lawyer's house to rest.

He was a captive audience, so his father talked. Michael couldn't help but listen. At first he talked about random things: life in Phoenix, what the military or college was like. Michael was bored enough to ask questions about those mundane topics. But when the conversation turned to Michael's mother and how life was when he was a child, Michael's questions stopped.

"Your mother was the love of my life."

Michael wouldn't look at the man. He wished it didn't hurt so much to roll onto his side. All he could do was stare at the ceiling.

"I was emotionally drained when she died." The Lawyer waited for a response and received none. "You were better off with Lila and Jean. You have to understand, I was a shell with nothing in it."

The pleading tone in The Lawyer's voice set Michael's jaw.

"I just locked the doors of our house and joined the army to fill my days and forget." He droned on about how the army paid for him to become a lawyer.

"When I came back to the States, I checked on you. You seemed so happy. I was still a mess. I didn't want to ruin your life."

Michael said two words, "Twenty years." Then he clicked on the television. On the screen, a man with a flat haircut like Norris was getting people in crazy costumes to guess the prices of various products. The Lawyer quit talking.

Michael pretended interest in the show. He wondered if he could request being put in a room with Jon instead of The Lawyer. His aunts wouldn't approve, but if they came back and it was done, he'd be free from unwanted excuses.

A few hours and multiple useless TV shows later, the nurse caught Michael trying to figure out how to manage the tubes running into him so he could go to the bathroom. He was embarrassed at his weakness and had to let the nurse help him. He was breathing hard when he came back. The Lawyer was hanging up the phone. To Michael's relief, he didn't say anything.

THE NEXT MORNING, LILA CAME IN WITH THE LAWYER'S scrapbook and a box. After greetings, she sat next to Michael and started going through the pictures. "Oh, look, this is when you graduated first grade."

Michael remembered all his friends lining up for that picture. He, with his blond hair, stood out among his swarthier classmates. His hair was obviously still wet from Aunt Jean trying to tame his curls.

"Look at this one when you were at your first rodeo in Raton," she said, holding up the book. "David, that is a great picture, you caught it at exactly the right moment.

He was on his old pinto horse roping a steer. The lariat was fully extended, the loop just dropping around the angus calf's neck. It was a good shot.

Another picture showed him playing basketball in Kayenta. Lawson had dozens of pictures of him. Michael didn't ask how he'd taken them without being seen.

Michael didn't know what to think when Aunt Lila handed him a worn shoe box full of faded letters, each dated on his birthday, one for every year of his life. She pulled the curtain around his bed and left him to read on his own. He could hear her murmuring to The Lawyer. He opened the yellowed envelope. Bit his lip and began to read.

Dear Michael,

I want you to know that I love you. It broke my heart leaving you with your aunts. I'm not strong enough to go on without your mother. She was a shining light that kept the shadows of the world from overwhelming me. Since she is gone, I've been existing in the shadows. You are so little and sweet, and deserve to live in the light. When you started trying to take care of me, bringing me your toys to make me happy, I realized I couldn't force you to live in the shadow of my grief. With my last strength I took you to your aunts, to a better life.

I love you, son. I hope someday you will understand.

Daddy

By the second letter, tears ran down Michael's face. Subsequent letters told of his father's personal struggle, and his dream that Michael's life wouldn't be tainted by his father's depression. The letters made more of an impact than anything his father could have said.

Michael understood then. He was right about his father all along. He was a ghost man walking in flesh. He just didn't want to haunt his son.

Chapter 49
HOME ON THE RANGE

MICHAEL'S BAY MARE KEPT TENSION ON THE ROPE, BACKING steadily away as he guided the fool yellow cow out of the mud by the spring. The cow's twin calves stood outside the mucky area, smarter than their mother. Every year he swore this cow was going to be winter jerky, but every year she had twins. She was one of his best producers, so he had to put up with her nonsense.

He was glad the mare was steady enough to be doing most of the work. It had been two months since he was shot, and he still got dizzy when using his full strength. He was always tired and woke up a couple times a night, all over sweat, with Ortega and Detective Garcia's ghosts gibbering at him. He'd have to get up to wash the imagined blood off his hands.

After fifteen minutes of pushing and shouting, Michael watched the yellow cow, dripping mud, waddle off toward the rest of the herd.

They said it was lucky he was shot point blank. The bullet went straight through his lung and out his back. It didn't tumble and tear him up too much. Michael didn't feel so lucky as he leaned over holding onto the stirrup with one hand and his side with the other. It was time to take a break.

He was sitting on a rock, waiting for the energy to climb back onto his horse, when Jon rode up on his mother's pinto. The little horse ambled to a stop. Jon slouched comfortably in the saddle and rested one wrist over the other on the saddle horn.

"You're timing's perfect, as usual." Michael got up and hooked the coiled rope to his saddle with a loop of leather. "The work's all done."

Jon grinned. "You need to come home. There's company."

"Who is it?"

"It's a surprise."

Michael dragged himself into the saddle and they headed home. No amount of cajoling could get Jon to tell him who was waiting. Jon's adventures in the city hadn't changed him. Michael wished he could say the same. He took a deep breath of the dust and juniper-scented air to dispel the lingering stench of the city that haunted his mind.

The cousins rode in companionable silence for a couple of miles. When the ground leveled out in the wash near the hogán, they looked at each other, and let the horses run like they did as kids. Roaring around the end of the sheep pens, they slid to a stop not far from a big rusty Cadillac and his father's car.

"What's wrong with you boys? You're going to break your necks." Jean stood next to the cars, hands on her hips. "You might enjoy eating the dust, but I don't. Go take care of them horses and get cleaned up."

As they rode by, Michael waved at Paula and Cletus sitting in the shade of the arbor next to the hogán. Paula was wearing such a bright pink dress, he was surprised the horses didn't spook. The couple had glasses in front of them, so the courtesies were being observed.

Michael stepped off his bay. Staggering a little, he grabbed the saddle to steady himself. He resisted pressing against the deep ache in his chest. "Hey cousin, can you put her up?" He threw the reins to Jon.

"Pump the water. Go get Michael. Put the horses up. All I do is take orders." Jon's grumble was softened by his grin.

Michael squared his stance. He didn't think anyone noticed his weakness. Jon led the mare off. The shade where the guests were sitting looked real good. Michael ambled over to settle into an old plastic chair next to Paula. He nodded to Cletus, who grunted a greeting. The big man was leaning back in a wooden chair with his long legs stretched out. He was studiously balancing one heel on the toe of his other foot

"Hey, baby boy, how's the world treating you?" Paula had pink lipstick and nails to match her dress.

"Better than the last time I saw you," Michael replied. She'd visited him in the hospital not long after he was shot. Paula cried so much her makeup ran down her face and one of her eyelashes fell off. Michael remembered thinking she had a spider on her cheek. The drugs had him thinking strange, fuzzy things for weeks. It would be rude to ask why they'd come to visit, but Michael was curious. "So what's happening in the big city?"

"Things are just crazy. The police been all over the neighborhood asking questions about that cop Chamberlin. Somehow, Cletus' name came up while the cops was investigating—"

"That little fucker at the liquor store pointed them at me." Cletus rumbled.

"—so we decided to take a drive to avoid unfortunate questions about our lifestyle."

"We never had a vacation, so here we are."

"I'm glad you could come." Michael's stomach churned as he tried to be polite. The sight of the man lying on the floor, the gun, flashed behind his eyes. He realized no one had mentioned the man's name since it happened. The smell of blood filled Michael's nose, his heart started to race.

Jean had walked up behind her nephew. "That man shot Michael. He needed killing." She laid her hand on his shoulder.

He'd stiffened. Once he relaxed, she took a couple steps over to sit on a bench next to Cletus. Jean looked like a child next to his bulk. "Did they hang them other ones yet?"

Paula sat up a little straighter. "No, ma'am, they don't hang folks no more. Those boys gave a big long story to that Kowalski woman. We brought the paper for you."

Cletus' deep voice continued, "They said they was helping Phoenix by investigating the bad police. They didn't have nothing to do with the murders."

"I knew some of those folks that got killed, and the cop who killed them wasn't too wrong." Paula poked her finger into Cletus' thigh.

"They still didn't need to let my boy be in jail." Jean chimed in.

"Norris planted drugs in Jon's truck," Michael said. "He may not be as bad as the one who killed those people, but he's still a bad man. I think you were wise to get out of town. It would be a shame if he tried to get you, too."

"You're sure right." Paula turned to Michael. "Anyway, they investigated and found two other people who got framed, like they was trying to do to Jon."

"They just let them out of the prison this week." Cletus finished for her. "Your daddy was the one who did that."

"What did he do?" Jon slouched up, carrying bridles. He hung them on the corner post and washed his hands at the water barrel spigot.

"Dave went to the courthouse and demanded they let those fellas go He had his picture in the paper and everything." Paula threw her arms up as if she was watching a basketball game. "That Kowalski woman wrote a big article about him."

"We brought you the news." Cletus handed Michael the paper.

He unfolded it to the center page. The article had a little picture of Carol at the top and was titled "To Protect and Serve? Vigilantism in the Police Department."

After reading the headline, Michael looked up from the paper. The sun was still high in the sky. Shadows hid the interior of the hogán. Aunt Lila appeared in the doorway carrying sweet fry cakes. His father was behind her. He still looked worse than Michael, but a contented smile spread to his eyes. His son's acceptance had healed some of his inner wounds.

The fry cakes smelled wonderful. Lila put some of her hoarded cinnamon on them. Michael heaved himself up and went over to the water barrel to wash his hands and arms under the tap. Once he was clean, with a fry cake in one hand, he pulled his plastic chair aside to read Carol's article.

IN THE PAST EIGHT YEARS, SIXTEEN PEOPLE IN THE GREATER Phoenix area were killed by two police officers. Not killed during the commission of any crime. They were executed by vigilantes.

Detective Tom Norris, who was part of the task force investigating the multiple homicides, summed up the police findings. "Two decorated police officers felt the court system had failed, so they decided, on their own initiative, to clean up the streets. When a person was released by the court system due to a technicality, the officers, Raymond Chamberlin or his partner Jamie Gelender, took it upon themselves to remove that person, permanently.

"The murdered people were not stellar citizens. Every one of them had multiple convictions for crimes ranging from drug dealing and prostitution to murder."

A LIST OF THE VICTIM'S NAMES, THE CRIMES THEY WERE accused of, and the technicality they were released on followed. Michael skipped past that part since it was his research Carol used to write this part of the story. At least, that's what he told himself. Maybe he didn't want to read a second time about the horrible things those people had done

A RECENT POLL SHOWS THIRTY-TWO PERCENT OF GREATER Phoenix residents who were questioned think the officers were justified in the killings. "They [the murder victims] were scum. The city is better off without them. These were public service killings. They should have given those cops medals," said Wilton Roberts of Sun City.

There were several paragraphs about the psychology of vigilantism and post-traumatic stress among police officers. Michael figured he'd read that in more detail later. It might give him better insight into understanding city people. His father kept hinting that Michael should come help him in his investigations in the summers when he was not too busy with the cattle. Michael didn't want to go back to the city, but a cash-paying job would be useful. It might do him good to go back and face the city again. Maybe he'd be able to sleep through the night after facing those demons.

A picture of detective Garcia wearing a uniform was beside the next few paragraphs.

"I just don't know when the two good cops started to go bad. I think it was post-traumatic stress," said an officer who chooses to remain anonymous. Evidence shows Detective Raymond Chamberlin and his partner were responsible for at least thirteen murders. Since his partner's death by heart attack two years ago, Detective Chamberlin murdered at least four more people, including fellow officer Detective Rudolpho Garcia, a devoted husband and father of two young children.

The rogue detective also attempted to murder local attorney David Lawson and his son Michael Yazzie after they found evidence to exonerate a client represented by Mr. Lawson. Currently, no evidence from any of the murders or attempted murders incriminates anyone else in the police department. A review of additional unsolved murder cases is ongoing.

In addition to the murders, in the past three years, two men were falsely convicted for murders perpetrated by Chamberlin and Gelender. Amerigo Velasques was sentenced to life in prison in the death of Tiffany Castain, and Mario Kootenai was serving twenty years for the murder of Bradford Allen Thomas. More recently, Jon Pete was indicted for the murder of Simon Ortega. During their appeal trials, court records indicated all three men were framed, either by Chamberlin or his deceased partner. They have since been released, thanks to the efforts of local attorney David Lawson.

"They [Chamberlin and Gelender] should have left well enough alone and relied on the system," said Homicide Detective Tom Norris. "They just kept getting deeper and deeper. When Rudy [Detective Garcia] was killed, I realized one of my fellow officers was totally out of control."

MICHAEL WOULD HAVE THOUGHT NORRIS COULD FIGURE someone was out of control after the first person was killed. He knew Flat Head Norris was a bad cop. How far would he have gone to get Jon put in jail? Michael could only hope they were still investigating the detective. How different was Norris from the man Michael killed to save his father?

ACCORDING TO SOURCES IN THE DEPARTMENT, DETECTIVE Raymond Chamberlin was stopped just as his fellow detectives were about to arrest him. Using his status as a police officer, he'd entered Mr. Lawson's hospital room in an attempt to murder him. Detective Chamberlin was killed during a struggle with Mr. Lawson's son Michael Yazzie. Mr. Yazzie was critically wounded while protecting his father.

Michael guessed Carol didn't want to upset people by telling them the details of how the Indian kid stuck the big policeman with a butter knife. Personally, he thought it would have added a little excitement to the story. The sweet fry cake he just ate, with its slightly bitter taste of cinnamon was perfect complement to his emotions while reading.

Carol continued the story, explaining how Michael became involved while investigating Jon's case. He was glad she kept his part of the story just bare facts.

Over the past eight years, the deaths of so many were lost in the bustle of the city and discounted by an overworked system of justice. In the future, perhaps the lives of the marginalized poor will be considered as important as those of the more affluent. If it were not for the dedication of a young man trying to keep his cousin from being unfairly prosecuted, the disenfranchised citizens of Phoenix might still be in danger. We can only hope incidents such as these will not be repeated either through negligence or intent.

Michael put the paper down and looked around. Surrounded by his friends and family the events of the city faded from his mind. The aunts were bustling industriously as always.

"Boy, you need more food. Grown man like you needs to eat more," Auntie Jean said, her gruff tone showing her affection in her own special way.

"Yes, ma'am," her son agreed and accepted more stew into his bowl.

Paula passed his father a plate and sat next to him, smoothing her skirt, and balancing her own bowl on her knees. Cletus was telling a story, and everyone was laughing. Stretched out on a hammock strung between the posts, Jon held his stomach to contain his mirth tried not spill his food. He failed, but didn't move not wanting to disturb Cletus' tale. The air was redolent with kindness.

Aunt Lila handed Michael his meal, the container brimming with squash, beans, and mutton. Love in a plastic bowl. He took a savory mouthful, stretched back in his chair, and listened. Wind rattled through the guardian cottonwood by the spring. Horses stomped in the corral. A jay landed below Jon's hammock squawking as it grabbed at bits of food. Jon's spill not going to waste.

This place was the center of the world. All things were true and good, hozoh. Laughter and comfort from his family and friends echoed through Michael's heart. Their conversations were aimless, talking for the joy of the company just being sociable...just being human.

t'áá ákódí

ABOUT THE AUTHOR

Lee Gull is the pen name of a collector of experiences, and writer of fact and fiction. Under her own name, she has over twenty published creative nonfiction articles. Writing as Skeeter Enright, she has an urban fantasy novel, *Carnival Charlatan.*

Check out her website: leegull.weebly.com

She currently lives on a farm in Ohio with the world's cutest donkey and a disgruntled guard pig.

ISBN: 978-1-937979-55-3

Enigma House Press

Goshen, Kentucky 40026

EnigmaHousePress.com